Michelle Moore

SARAH JIO is the *New York Times* and *USA Today* bestselling author of *The Violets of March*, a *Library Journal* Best Book of 2011; *The Bungalow*; *Blackberry Winter*; *The Last Camellia*; and *Morning Glory*. She is also a journalist who has written for *Glamour*; *O, The Oprah Magazine*; *Redbook*; *Real Simple*; and many other publications. Jio's novels have become book club favorites and have been translated into more than twenty languages. She lives in Seattle with her three young boys and a geriatric golden retriever. Learn more about her at sarahjio.com or facebook.com/sarahjioauthor.

Praise for *The Last Camellia*

"This tale has it all: an English garden, a brooding lord of the manor, and a story that bestselling author Jio deftly unveils as fast as you can turn the pages."
—*Coastal Living*

"Jio infuses her haunting story of love and loss with an engrossing mystery that will linger long after the final page."
—*Romantic Times*

"The images of the flowers, the landscape, and the manor house are vivid and make for a tantalizing read."
—*Kirkus Reviews*

"An engaging story of two generations trying to move forward despite the powerful pull of the past. A thoughtful examination of history's ability to haunt the present and the power of forgiveness to set things right." —*Booklist*

Praise for *Blackberry Winter*

"Terrific . . . compelling . . . an intoxicating blend of mystery, history, and romance, this book is hard to put down." —*Real Simple*

"Ingenious . . . imaginative." —*The Seattle Times*

"*Blackberry Winter* never loses momentum. . . . Jio's writing is engaging and fluid." —*Mystery Scene*

"A fascinating exploration of love, loss, scandal, and redemption." —*Publishers Weekly*

"This novel will enchant Jio's fans and make them clamor for her next offering." —*Kirkus Reviews*, "A Most Anticipated Book of Fall 2012"

"There's no doubt that anyone who picks up this book will instantly fall in love with it and the author." —Brodart

"Sarah Jio's writing is exquisite and engrossing." —Elin Hilderbrand, bestselling author of *Silver Girl*

Praise for *The Bungalow*

Pulpwood Queens Book Club, Official Selection 2012

"*The Bungalow* is my favorite book of the year." —Jen Lancaster

"Jio's first-person, Hemingway-ish writing style, like her *The Violets of March* (judged by *Library Journal* as one of the Best Books of 2011), is a pleasure to read. . . . Jio has done a superb job of pulling together the themes of friendship, betrayal, and endearing love. These keep us engrossed in the novel to an unpredictable conclusion." —*The Historical Novels Review*

"Unabashedly romantic . . . thanks to Jio's deft handling of her plot and characters. Fans of Nicholas Sparks will enjoy this gentle historical love story." —*Library Journal*

"A captivating tale." —*Booklist*

"A heartfelt, engaging love story set against the fascinating backdrop of the War in the Pacific."   —Kristin Hannah, author of *Home Front*

Praise for *The Violets of March*

A *Library Journal* Best Book of 2011

"Feed the kids *before* you settle in with journalist Sarah Jio's engrossing first novel, *The Violets of March*. This mystery-slash-love story will have you racing to the end—cries of 'Mom, I'm hungry!' be damned."   —*Redbook*

"A gem . . . True escape fiction that can take you away."   —WGBH-TV

"Masterfully written."   —*The New Jersey Star-Ledger*

"In a sweet debut novel, a divorcee visiting her aunt on gorgeous Bainbridge Island, Washington, finds a diary dating to 1943 that reveals potentially life-changing secrets."   —*Coastal Living*

"The right book finds you at the right time. *The Violets of March* will become a source of healing and comfort for its readers."   —*The Costco Connection*

"In *The Violets of March*, debut author Sarah Jio beautifully blends the stories of two women—one of the past, one of the present—together to create a captivating and enthralling novel of romance, heartbreak, and redemption."   —*Times Record News* (Wichita Falls, Kansas)

"Jio's debut is a rich blend of history, mystery, and romance. Fans of Sarah Blake's *The Postmistress* should enjoy this story."   —*Library Journal*

"[An] endearing tale of past heartbreaks and new beginnings. The story's setting and sentiment are sure to entice readers and keep them captivated page after page."   —*Romantic Times*

"A perfect summer read for an escape into a fictional character's challenges with the charm of a local Northwest setting."   —*425* magazine

"Refreshing . . . lovable."   —*First for Women* magazine

"Mix a love story, history, and a mystery and what takes root? *The Violets of March*, a novel that reminds us how the past comes back to haunt us, and packs a few great surprises for the reader along the way. "

          —Jodi Picoult, author of *Sing You Home* and *House Rules*

Goodnight June

A NOVEL

Sarah Jio

A PLUME BOOK

PLUME
Published by the Penguin Group
Penguin Group (USA) LLC
375 Hudson Street
New York, New York 10014

USA | Canada | UK | Ireland | Australia | New Zealand | India | South Africa | China
penguin.com
A Penguin Random House Company

First published by Plume, a member of Penguin Group (USA) LLC, 2014

P REGISTERED TRADEMARK—MARCA REGISTRADA

LIBRARY OF CONGRESS CATALOGING-IN-PUBLICATION DATA
Jio, Sarah.
    Goodnight June : a novel / Sarah Jio.
        pages cm
    ISBN 978-0-14-218021-1 (pbk.)
    1. Aunts—Death—Fiction.   2. Estates (Law)—Fiction.   3. Letters—Fiction.
4. Brown, Margaret Wise, 1910-1952.—Fiction.   5. Domestic fiction.
gsafd   I. Title.
    PS3610.I6G66 2014
    813'.6—dc23
    2013039109

Printed in the United States of America
10 9 8 7 6 5 4 3 2 1

Set in Granjon LT Std
Designed by Eve L. Kirch

For my sister and dearest friend, Jessica Campbell

Everything that anyone would ever look
for is usually where they find it.

—Margaret Wise Brown

Author's Note

Do you remember the first time you read *Goodnight Moon*? While many discover the book as a child (with more than fourteen million copies sold, it's delighted countless children around the world since its first printing in 1947), I was only vaguely familiar with the story until I received a copy as a baby shower gift. I remember the first time I read it to my eldest son, Carson, when he was a baby. We both became instantly fascinated with the tale—a lullaby, really—about a little bunny going to sleep. At the end of each day, I found it so calming to read those pages (which I soon memorized). Night after night, it was a comfort to return to the "great green room."

My two younger sons soon joined in our nightly read. All three have a favorite page, and each adores looking for the mouse. Over the years we've come to affectionately call the story Moon Book. (My littlest, Colby, can't pronounce the word *book*, so he calls it Moon Cook.) And it's fair to say that *Goodnight Moon* has become as irreplaceable in our home as it has in our hearts.

I once wrote a humorous parody of *Goodnight Moon* for *Parenting*, which went on to be one of the most popular pages on the magazine's website. Clearly, more than a half century after its publication, *Goodnight Moon* continues to speak to us.

When I come to love a book, I tend to want to learn about its author. So, I set out to research the life of Margaret Wise Brown. I wanted to know more about the vivacious, beautiful children's book author who penned more than one hundred stories before her untimely death in 1952, when she was just forty-two years old.

I read everything I could get my hands on about Margaret, and in my research, I found that we have a lot in common. She was restless and goal oriented, just as I am (two traits that make for a productive yet sometimes tortured writer). She was also, like me, a dreamer. A rabbit-shaped cloud in the sky might inspire a new book, just as a canoe ride to a little island near her home in Maine could provide the muse for a brand-new series.

Margaret was fiercely creative. And in reading about her life, I know that she must have felt, as I do, creativity can be a force of (human) nature. Margaret wrote of stories coming from every direction. Some mornings, upon waking, she'd jot down ideas for new books she had dreamed about overnight.

When your brain works in this way, it can be both exciting and crazy-making. (Imagine being halfway through a first draft of a novel, when characters from a new book begin whispering in your ear relentlessly—this is my life.) My novelist friend Carol Cassella, who also happens to be a doctor (overachiever, no?), calls this state, half jokingly, a "chronic illness." Good or bad, it seems that Margaret and I have this in common.

While vulnerable as a kitten in matters of love, Margaret was also a smart and often shrewd businesswoman who looked after her interests in publishing, along with the interests of her illustrator friends, never settling for second best.

I love this about her. She was both spirited and determined, yet she was also a gentle soul and a loyal friend. She was impulsive, too. One of my favorite stories about Margaret involves her spending the entire sum of a royalty check on flowers, hundreds of them. She's believed to have bought the whole cart on a New York City street; she then decorated her home with flowers and threw a party for her friends.

It's no wonder Margaret Wise Brown left such an impression on the world, but because of her sudden death, she left secrets, too. Nobody really knows, exactly, the true inspiration for *Goodnight Moon*. Margaret is believed to have written the story in the period of a single morning at Cobble Court, her New York City cottage. So I began to imagine what *could* have been the glimmer of the idea for the iconic children's book, and, like Margaret, I let my imagination take me away.

Soon, my characters were whispering. There was June Andersen, a thirty-five-year-old New York City banker whose high-stakes job is taking a toll on her health; and her great-aunt Ruby, who has left her life's work, the legendary Seattle children's bookstore, Bluebird Books, to her beloved niece. The bookstore is full of secrets, and in it June discovers letters between her aunt Ruby and the late Margaret Wise Brown—letters that detail a beautiful friendship that may have had a profound impact on the author.

But while I wanted this to be a story inspired by Margaret's life and her artistic genius, I also wanted my character June to take center stage. This is, after all, *her* journey. It takes courage to be vulnerable, to face a rocky past, and to attempt to start over again, to love again. June will have to figure out if she can do that, and when the bookstore falls into financial peril, the fate of Ruby's precious Bluebird Books is in June's hands. Will she save the place and its secrets? Will she save herself?

Margaret Wise Brown left this world twenty-six years before I was born. And while our paths never crossed, I often think about what it would have been like to meet her, to sit down over a cup of coffee (or maybe a lunchtime cocktail, as Margaret may have liked) and discuss the writing life, cottontail bunnies, the three little bears sitting on chairs. All of it. I'd tell her about this novel I've written, and hope she'd be pleased. We'd laugh and tell stories, and I'd share how my four-year-old, Russell, is enamored with her book *The Sailor Dog*. We'd talk about the plight of brick-and-mortar bookstores in the digital age, and the challenge of keeping children loving literature when television and video games and other shiny new things have such allure. I'd compliment her on the flower cart stunt (if only I had the guts to pull off something like that), and I'd thank her for being such an inspiration.

Simply put, just to be in her presence, I'd be over the moon.

—SJ

Goodnight June

Chapter 1

New York City
May 3, 2005

Everyone has a happy place, the scene that comes into view when you close your eyes and let your mind transport you to the dot on the globe where life is cozy, safe, warm. For me, that place is the bookstore, with its emerald green walls and the big picture windows that, at night, frame the stars twinkling above. The embers in the fireplace burn the color of a setting orange sun, and I'm wrapped in a quilt, seated in a big wingback chair reading a book.

"June?"

I open my eyes quickly, and the stark white walls beyond my hospital bed reset my frame of mind to reality. The thin sheet draped over my body is stiff and scratchy, bleached one too many times, and I shiver as a nurse places her icy hands on my wrist.

"Didn't mean to wake you, honey," she says, fastening a blood pressure cuff around my arm.

I stare at the tattoo on her forearm, a butterfly with a lot of pink and purple detailing, as she squeezes the black pump between her fingers. I immediately thank my seventeen-year-old self (profusely) for not actually going through with that wraparound dolphin ankle tattoo I was once *this close* to getting. A moment later she rips open the Velcro and frowns. "High," she says. "Too high for a woman your age. Dr. Cater is going to want to talk to you about this."

I see the disapproving look in her eyes and I want to blurt out, "I'm a vegetarian! I run marathons! I haven't even had dessert in two years!" But my cell phone chimes, and I pick it up quickly. It's a text from my boss, Arthur.

"Where are you? Thought you were working on second-quarter reports tonight?"

I feel my heart beat faster and I take a deep breath. He doesn't know I'm in the hospital, of course. No one does. And no one will. The nurse begins to speak, and I hold up my hand for silence, then sit up to compose myself before hitting Reply. "Got sidetracked with another project," I type. "Will be in asap." The project, of course, is this pesky health condition of mine. If my body would just *cooperate.*

I look up at the clock on the wall: It's after eight. I was admitted at noon with high blood pressure—dangerously high, the ER doctor said. "Am I having a heart attack?" I asked. I've been having symptoms for at least a month, but at a business lunch today—me, and eleven men in suits—I had to excuse myself. I felt dizzy, nauseated. My hands tingled. I couldn't let them see me like that, so I lied and said I had to go back to the office and put out a fire. Except I didn't go back to the office. I got into a cab, and I went to the emergency room.

I fidget with the IV in my arm that's slowly administering blood pressure medication. This isn't supposed to happen when you're thirty-five. I eye my bag on the chair across the room anxiously. *I need to get out of here.*

As I stand up, the door opens and an older man in a white coat appears. He's frowning. "And where do you think you're going, Ms. Andersen?" Although in place of my name I imagine him saying "missy."

I don't like his tone, even if he is a doctor, even if his ultimate goal is to save my life. "I'm feeling better," I say, still fiddling with the wire attached to my arm. "I have an important project at work that I have to get to."

The doctor walks closer and sets my chart down on the table beside my bed. He's obviously in no hurry to have me discharged. "What's it going to take?"

I look at him, perplexed. "What do you mean?"

"What's it going to take to get you to slow down?"

"Slow down?" I shake my head. "I don't know what you're talking about."

He points to the folder on the table. "I read your chart."

I gave the ER doctor a rundown of my typical day: up at five, to the office by seven (and that's after running six or seven miles), then work, work, work until eight, maybe nine p.m. (and, actually, sometimes later).

So what? I'm a *vice president* at a major bank, the youngest VP in the history of Chase & Hanson Bank International, and with eight thousand employees worldwide, that's saying something. I have to prove myself. Besides, I'm good at what I do. It's maybe the only thing I'm good at.

"Listen, Dr. . . ."

"Dr. Cater."

"Dr. Cater," I say in the slow, confident voice I use to negotiate with debtors. "I appreciate your concern, but really, I'm going to be OK. Just give me the prescription, and I'll take the pills. Problem solved."

"It's not that simple," he says. "You're a complex case."

I let out a little laugh. "Thank you, I think."

"Ms. Andersen, I see that you're experiencing numbness in your hands on occasion."

"Yes," I say. "I run a lot. New York is cold before sunrise."

"I don't think it's that kind of numbness," he says. "I believe you have a panic disorder."

"Excuse me—a *what* disorder?"

"Panic," he says. "I think your body is under a tremendous amount of stress and that it's compensating by shutting down, in a sense."

"No," I say, unwrapping the tape that's holding the IV in place. "I know what you're implying. You think I'm crazy. I'm *not* crazy. Others in my family, well, they may be. But I'm not." I shake my head. "Listen, are you going to take this thing out of my arm, or am I going to have to yank it out myself?"

Dr. Cater looks at me for a long moment and then sighs. "If you insist on leaving, we can't keep you here," he says. "But please, promise me that you'll at least consider slowing down. You're going to run yourself into the grave."

My cell phone buzzes again. What does this guy know about me? Absolutely nothing. I shrug. "Whatever I have to say to get out of here."

Dr. Cater reluctantly takes the IV out of my arm, and tucks a slip of paper into my hand. "This is a prescription for beta-blockers; they work by blocking certain nerve and hormone signals that cause anxiety," he says. "I'd like you to take the pills, at least for the next few months, and I strongly encourage you to lighten the load. Maybe exercise a little less; cut back on your workload. Take a vacation."

I stifle a laugh. No one at my level takes time off. Lisa Melton, the new VP on the ninth floor, took a week off after her wedding and even *that* was frowned upon. There's a certain expectation in finance that when you hit the big time, you pretty much live and breathe work. Vacation days just accrue into a lake of time off that you can never think of dipping into, unless you want to drown. It's just the way it works. "I appreciate your concern," I repeat, reaching for my coat and bag. "But I have to go."

"There you are," Arthur says, smirking a little. "I thought we'd lost you." My boss is shrewd, cunning. But I know that deep down he has a heart, or at least some semblance of one, which is why I once told him that he's the nicest asshole I've ever met. For his twentieth anniversary with the company, I had a gold plaque engraved with those very words.

"Sorry I had to leave the lunch today," I say. "I . . . I . . . listen, I had a *thing* come up."

"A *female* thing?"

"No, no," I say, making an annoyed face. *Men.* "Nothing like that." I snap back into work mode—all business. "Listen, I'm sorry. I'm here now. It won't happen again."

Arthur's eyes narrow. "What in the world are you wearing?"

For the first time, I realize what I must look like after spending the past eight hours at the hospital. Disheveled hair. Smeared eye makeup. I quickly pull my wool peacoat tighter around my neck when I realize I'm still wearing the light blue hospital gown. "I came from home, didn't have time to, er, change," I say.

Arthur shrugs. "OK. Anyway, let's get to work."

We sit down at the conference room table, and he lays out a stack of file folders. "Every single one of them in default," he says. "Who are we going after first?"

I lean in and pick up the folder on top labeled SAMANTHA'S

KNITTING ROOM. I've long stopped feeling sorry for small business owners who can't make ends meet. At first it was hard, cracking down on mom-and-pop shops. And I'll never forget my first assignment. I cried when I delivered foreclosure papers to a café in New Orleans that had been in business since the turn of the century. It was one of those old venues with intricate wrought-iron railings and a green-and-white-striped awning. Beloved by everyone in the city, of course. When I walked in the door, I was greeted by the owner, an old woman. The café had been her father's. It was a New Orleans tradition. John F. Kennedy had eaten lunch there in 1959. On the wall were signed photographs of Ella Fitzgerald, Judy Garland, Louis Armstrong. She brought me coffee and a plate of sugar-dusted beignets. My hands trembled when I handed her the envelope that would shutter her family's pride and joy forever.

It got easier after that. In time, I learned to handle each case with the precision of a surgeon. In and out. No emotion. My guiding tenet: It's business, not personal. I don't care how cute, quaint, or beloved your business is. I don't care if the Pope was born there or if your father got down on one knee and proposed to your mother in the storefront window. The fact of the matter is, if you can't pay your bills, the bank—well, *I* will repossess and sell off your assets. It's that simple.

I like to think that Arthur chose me to mentor because he saw a certain spark, a skill that I had that no other junior banker did. But no, I know that when Arthur saw me, he simply saw clay. I didn't have a life outside of work. I was devoted to my job. I was malleable.

He helped me hone my skills in banking. Everyone called him "the ax man," because he had no qualms about closing an underperforming business and auctioning off prized possessions. He didn't even bat an eye in the face of distressed clients. He only saw the bottom line. And he trained me to see that too. He shaped me into his ax woman, and together we became the bank's highest-performing department. We cut the fat. We got results.

Of course, not all cases require a personal visit. Usually we can get the papers signed from afar. Usually people cooperate. But some don't. Some let the letters stack up on their desks and ignore our phone calls simply because they want to delay the inevitable. It's hard facing your failure. I get that. But that's life.

I hold up the folder for Samantha's Knitting Room and thumb through the papers inside. Samantha, who, I see from the original loan application, was born the same year I was, 1970, is seven months behind on her payments. I review the contact log, and see that she's ignored our department's calls and letters.

"Looks like someone needs to pay Miss Samantha a visit," Arthur says. His eyes light up the way a detective's might when he has someone in his sights and knows he'll be cuffing them soon.

"Yeah," I say vacantly. My fingers are tingling again, and my head feels heavy, like a bowling ball attached to my neck, which strains under the weight. What's wrong with me? My scalp begins to tingle next. The heavy feeling dissipates and my head begins to feel like a balloon, one that's floating above my body. I should be invested in this discussion with Arthur. I should be approaching each case with my usual zeal. *Why can't I?* My heart beats faster, and I clutch the edge of my seat. The numbness in my fingers has spread to my hand, and I can barely feel my palm. *It's happening again.*

I eye the door. "Arthur," I say quickly, "I think I ate something funny." I clutch my stomach for believability. "I'd better excuse myself."

He shrugs, collecting the folders into a neat pile and then handing them to me. "OK, well, it is getting late. You can go over the files this weekend. I flagged the ones that need the special June Andersen touch."

I force a smile. "Right. Of course."

By the time the cab drops me in front of my building, I've gotten control of myself, sort of. The numbness, except for a slight tingling sensation in my left pinky, is gone. I check my mail in the lobby and take the elevator to the seventh floor, then slip my key into No. 703.

I think back to that horrible biology teacher I had in my junior year of high school. I got good grades, mostly, but I'd always struggled with science. After I'd failed an exam, he called me to his desk and told me, "You know, your mother was a student of mine. She wasn't good at science either. If you don't study harder, you're going to turn out just like her. Do you want to spend your life working at the checkout counter of a grocery store?" I hated the look on his face: condescending, cavalier. My eyes stung, but I didn't give him the satisfaction of seeing me cry. I saved that for later. If Mr. Clark could only see me now. If he could see the career I have, the apartment I own (mortgaged to the hilt, but so what—my name is on the title).

Sure, I don't have a husband, kids, a dog. But how many thirty-five-year-olds can say they purchased their own two-bedroom Manhattan apartment with parquet floors, a chef's kitchen, and windows with peekaboo views of Central Park?

I throw my coat on the upholstered bench in the entryway— *take that, Mr. Clark*—and set my keys on the glass table against the wall (the decorator insisted on it, and yet every time I hear my keys click onto its surface, I hate it all the more), then sort through the mail. I recognize the handwriting on the letter atop the stack and inwardly wince. Why is *she* contacting me again? I have nothing to say to her. I walk to the kitchen, where I toss the envelope, unopened, into the recycle bin. It's too late for I'm-sorrys.

I slump down onto the couch and sort through the rest of

the mail: bills, a few magazines, a postcard from my old friend Claire, in Seattle. She and her husband, Ethan, and their baby son, Daniel, are in Disneyland. "Greetings from Cinderella's castle," she writes. "Sending you lots of sunshine! xoxo"

It's sweet, of course, but if I'm being completely honest, sentiments from blissfully happy friends only feel like daggers in my heart. I stopped going to weddings, and now I only send presents to baby showers. My assistant wraps them beautifully with lots of ribbons and bows. It's easier this way, managing friendships from afar. No one gets hurt, especially not me. The only person outside of work I keep in touch with anymore is my accountant friend, Peter (smart, kind, handsome, and, I might add, very gay). And I can't even take credit for our continued friendship; Peter does all the calling.

I sigh. Beneath a Victoria's Secret catalog is a manila envelope from the Law Offices of Sherman and Wills. It looks official. I tear open the edge cautiously, the way I always do when inspecting legal papers, and pull out a small stack of pages with a cover letter paper-clipped to the top:

The Law Offices of Sherman and Wills
567 Madison
Seattle, WA 98101

TO: June Andersen
RE: The Estate of Ruby Crain

Dear Ms. Andersen,

By now, I'm sure you have heard that your great-aunt Ruby Crain has passed away. Let me express my deepest condolences for your loss.

I pause and place my hand over my heart. Ruby? Gone?

We were retained to handle the distribution of her estate, and I am pleased to tell you that your aunt has left her entire estate, including the children's bookstore, Bluebird Books in Seattle, to you. Enclosed you will find the attendant paperwork. Please sign the flagged pages and return all to my assistant. You might consider coming out to Seattle to get things in order. As I'm sure you know, Ms. Crain was quite ill for the months before her death. In any case, I trust you will find it a great pleasure, as Ruby did, to own the store. If I can be of help to you in any way, please don't hesitate to be in touch.

Best regards,
Jim Sherman, attorney

I set the letter down on the coffee table and shake my head. *Ruby died? How did I not know?* Tears sting my eyes, and then I feel a surge of anger. Why didn't Mom tell me? Probably too busy with her new boyfriend to even think to mention it. And yet, I realize the person I'm really angry at is myself. I could have written Ruby. I could have visited her, but I was always too busy. And now it's too late. Now she's gone.

I stare at the paperwork in disbelief. Of course, we were close, at least when I was a child, but I had no idea that Ruby would choose me as her heir, bypassing my mother and sister, Amy, even. *Amy.* How will she feel about this? It still feels strange not to be able to pick up the phone and call her. We shared everything growing up (everything except a father, though neither Amy's nor mine was ever in the picture). I think of her face, that blond hair, just like our mom's, her plump, pouty lips that always drove boys crazy, her cerulean blue eyes. It's been five years since the incident, and yet the memory of it still smarts, so I turn to the past instead, when Amy and I were rosy-cheeked girls, skipping hand in hand to Green Lake.

I catch my reflection in the window and I do a double take. What happened to me? That curious little girl with blond braids and her nose always in a book has grown into, I hate to admit, a woman who has little time for family, much less books. I rack my brain and try to remember the last time I even spoke to Ruby, and then I hear her voice in my ear. She called on Christmas Day last year. She'd attempted to organize a Christmas dinner at the store. There'd be a burnt turkey in the oven and a platter full of sugar-dusted cookies. Just like old times. I couldn't make it, but she called on Christmas Day just the same. Mom and Amy were there. I could hear them laughing in the background, and it made me tense up. Ruby sensed that.

"Is everything all right, June?" she asked.

"Yes," I lied, "everything's fine."

"I know you're so busy in New York, June," she said. I could hear the hurt in her voice. I still hear it. "But I really hoped you could visit."

"I just couldn't break away this year; I'm sorry." I said, staring at my lonely apartment, bare of holiday decorations. A Christmas tree for one seemed like such a waste.

"Are you ever going to come home, June?" she asked. Her voice sounded older than it ever had. It was airier and it crackled a bit around the edges. That frightened me. The passage of time has always frightened me, but it especially did in that moment.

"I don't know, Ruby," I said honestly, wiping a tear from my eye. The truth is, I didn't know if I could ever go home to Seattle. I hadn't thought about my home in a long time. When I left, I left for good. Laura Ingalls Wilder said, "Home is the nicest word there is," but as the years passed, I began to feel that those sentiments didn't apply to me.

Though we always lived in Seattle, our little family of three moved from apartment to apartment when I was a child. Mom, Amy, and me. To her credit, Mom was good at finding jobs, just not very good at keeping them. She waited tables, worked the night shift at a 76 station, and punched tickets at the movie theater, but all were short-lived. She'd call in sick too many times, or forget her shift, or arrive late, or *something*. Eventually Mom found work at a little grocery store down the street, and I'm not sure if her boss was just really nice or maybe she'd learned from her mistakes, but she wasn't unemployed anymore after that. On summer days, Amy and I used to sit on the curb outside the store and munch on sunflower seeds. We'd crack the shells open with our teeth and then toss them in the storm drain beneath us. Every few minutes the automatic sliding doors would open and close, sending a blast of icy, scrubbed air-conditioned air onto our skin. I still remember the way that air smelled: slightly sweet, like the skin of ripe bananas, with a tinge of cleaning solvent.

Mom worked hard at the grocery store, and on her days off, she played hard. There was a never-ending stream of boyfriends with names like Marc, or Rick, or Mac. Many of them played the guitar, and Mom would always go out to watch them in bars around town. My sister and I would stand in the doorway of the bathroom and watch her style her long blond hair. She was an expert with a curling iron, setting her bangs in thick rolls before feathering and teasing them back with her teal green pick. She'd finish the look with a thick layer of hair spray, then apply green eye shadow to her lids and pink blush to the tops of her cheeks. She was beautiful, and she knew it. A spritz of Jean Naté, and she'd be out the door.

The lemony, musky scent of her perfume would linger for hours after she went. The familiar smell comforted me when it was stormy out, or when the back door creaked in the wind. I knew I couldn't cry, even at eight years old. It was my job to take care of my little sister. Amy was only four.

Standing on the step stool to reach the stove, I'd manage to open a can of SpaghettiOs or a box of Kraft mac and cheese. I didn't know how to make the latter, so I guessed and boiled the noodles with the powdered cheese sauce. I remember the time I found a hunk of old cheddar in the fridge and threw that in too. The result was a soupy, gooey mess that Amy and I ate anyway. I'd usually dish our dinner up in mugs (because the bowls were always dirty and piled high in the sink), and together we'd watch TV until Amy got sleepy. I'd help her into her pajamas and tuck her into bed, then read her a story. We didn't have much, but we always had books, thanks to Aunt Ruby, who brought over boxes of them. And because of her, we learned of entire worlds that existed beyond the walls of our drab apartment. We followed Madeline through the streets of Paris and made pumpkin pie with Laura and Ma in *Little House in the Big Woods*. And every night, I read Amy her favorite book, *Goodnight Moon*.

It was my favorite too. I came to love the nursery with its green walls and striped curtains, the sense of love and warmth. The old woman (the mother? grandmother? a great-aunt like Ruby?) hovering near as the child nestles into his bed. She doesn't leave her child like Mom left us. She stays and knits, rocking in her chair as he sleeps, as the nursery darkens ever so slowly and the stars sparkle out the window. To me, it seemed the epitome of love.

Ruby hated the way Mom raised us. And for years, she didn't even know how we lived. Mom told her a different story. And she squandered the money Ruby gave her to help pay for our school clothes and necessities (Ruby, though not wealthy by today's standards, was very generous, and we were her only family). For a time, Mom spent it on booze and tube tops in every color of the rainbow. One evening Ruby showed up on our front steps and saw the house in its state of disarray. Mom was passed out in the bedroom. Amy and I were watching TV. Ruby had tears in her eyes when she took my hand and then lifted Amy into her arms. "Come on, girls," she said. "You're coming with me. I won't let you live like this. Not anymore."

She gave us a warm bath that night in her little apartment above the bookstore. Mom showed up two days later, sober and apologetic. They went downstairs together, and Amy and I heard a lot of shouting. After that, things were different. Sort of. When Mom was home, she paid more attention to us. She even took us to the zoo one day. We came to spend more time with Ruby at the bookstore, too. We'd stay for entire weekends and sleep in her apartment a couple of nights a week. It was an open, loft-style space, with exposed brick walls and high ceilings. Ruby hated being confined by walls, she said, so she kept her little bed in the living space and set up the bedroom for Amy and me. I loved it there. Amy and I each had our own twin bed with fresh sheets and big comfy quilts. I hated going home. I wished we could live with Ruby.

She'd read to us for hours, feed us picnic dinners by the fire. I feel a funny flutter in my stomach when I think about Bluebird Books. In the mid-1940s, Ruby was a pioneer of sorts, opening the area's first children's bookstore on Sunnyside Avenue, just a few blocks up from Green Lake, and building it into a Seattle institution.

I stand up, and without knowing why at first, I walk to my

bedroom and open the closet. Far in the back is a box containing the few remaining relics of my childhood: a diary I kept from the age of ten to twelve; the dried wrist corsage Jake Hadley gave me on the night of the homecoming dance; my baby book, in which Mom only bothered to fill out two pages; and a stack of children's books from Aunt Ruby. When I left Seattle at age eighteen for college on the East Coast, I had just one suitcase. I'd wanted to pack all of my books, every one of them. But Mom wasn't willing to pay for shipping—even book rate—nor did I have the money to do it myself. So I picked the books that I loved most, and on top of the stack was *Goodnight Moon*.

I pull the book out of the box and hold it in my hands. It's a full-size hardback, not the tiny board books bookstores sell these days. I flip through the pages, and my heart contracts when I think of Amy's tiny fingers pointing to the mouse hiding on each page. It was our little game to find him, and we never tired of it.

I sit down on the floor and lean back against the side of my bed. It's dark, and I can see an almost-full moon outside my window, outshining the city lights all around. I don't think of work or the stack of folders on the dining room table requiring my attention. Instead I think of Seattle, Ruby, and the life I left behind so many years ago.

I think of Bluebird Books.

Chapter 2

"You're going *where?*" Arthur demands on the phone the next night. The moon is out, and I'm in a cab destined for JFK. In a few hours, I'll be on the red-eye to Washington state.

"Seattle," I say nervously to my boss. "It's a . . . sort of a family emergency."

This confession stops his tirade, momentarily.

"*Sort of?* Sort of a family emergency? Did someone die? Because if someone didn't die, then it's not—"

"Someone died," I say.

"Oh."

"Listen," I add, feeling my heart beat faster. I riffle through my bag and find the prescription pill bottle I filled at the pharmacy before I left. I pop a blue pill into my mouth, swallowing it with a swig from the water bottle in my hand. "I won't be long. Just a week, tops. There's, well, some things I have to sort out."

The taxi zooms along, weaving through lanes of traffic. Horns honk. City lights blink from the skyscrapers above. I'll miss the energy of New York. But in that moment, I wonder if it's leeching mine.

"I left the files with Janice," I say.

"All right," Arthur replies. In my eleven years with the bank, I've never behaved this way. And I suppose it surprises him as much as it does me.

"I'll be in touch," I say.

He's too stunned to respond before I end the call.

The plane touches down with a bump and a skid at Sea-Tac airport. I peer out the window at the city I left behind so many years ago. The sun is just peeking over the horizon, illuminating the familiar gray clouds, soggy with rain, that hover overhead.

The passenger next to me, a middle-aged man wearing a blue fleece vest and Tevas with socks, lets out a contented sigh. "Good to be home," he says.

"Yes," I manage to say, biting my lip nervously. The truth is, I've spent the entire six-hour flight regretting the trip, turning the decision over and over in my mind. On one side, I hear Arthur's voice, telling me I'm losing my edge. On the other, doctor what's-his-name at the hospital, saying, "Slow down. Take a vacation." And then there's Ruby. Without thinking, I place my hand on my chest, attempting to quiet my rapid heartbeat.

"Live in Seattle?" the man asks, extracting me from my inner dialogue.

"No," I say. "I mean, I used to. A long time ago."

He nods, reaching for his bag under the seat in front of us. "Best city on earth." He takes a deep breath. "Feel that?"

"What?" I ask, confused.

"There isn't the pressure there is in other cities," he says. "You can feel the calm."

I nod politely and almost forget his words entirely, until my cab drops me off in front of Bluebird Books. I take a deep breath, and just as the stranger predicted, I feel suffused with the very sense of calm he described. Or maybe it's just my blood pressure medication finally kicking in.

The store is just as I remember it, though, like me, I suppose, it's showing signs of age. The brick facade, always a bit rustic, is shedding its mortar. The big white picture windows in front look like they could use a good scrub. Above the old green paneled door is the sign, still hanging proudly. I eye the familiar lettering:

Bluebird Books
A Place for Children
Established 1946

I reach into my bag and pull out the envelope with the key. The attorney was kind enough to overnight it to me. When we spoke on the phone, he explained that Ruby had been ill for many months leading up to her death. The bookstore had been closed for at least six months, maybe more. "Ruby just couldn't keep it up," he said. "But she tried, until the very end."

Thinking about his words makes my heart sink. The tingling sensation returns in my fingertips.

"Ms. Andersen," he said. "Are you all right?"

"Yes," I said quickly, taking a seat and reaching into my bag for another blood pressure pill.

I insert the key into the old brass lock now, and the door creaks and jingles as I pull it open. And then I remember Aunt Ruby's bells tied to the door handle. Jingle bells, she called them. Ruby had a way of making ordinary things seem extraordinary, and I smile as

I close the door behind me and venture inside the old store, breathing in the air of my past.

My heels click on the plank wood flooring, and the room before me blurs as my eyes well with tears. There is Aunt Ruby's desk, covered with files and papers. Books are stacked precariously high, anchored by the old black rotary telephone she refused to replace. Beside the desk rests the store's Victorian dollhouse. I kneel down and pick up a pint-size sofa that has fallen to the floor. My sister and I sat here for hours playing, imagining a dream world where we had our own bedrooms, nice clothes, and a mother who didn't leave us all the time. I blow a layer of dust off the roof and rearrange the furniture in the library the way I always liked it: sofa on the right, table on the left, with room for the Christmas tree. Ruby made tiny ornaments for it by painting peppercorns red and gluing them on to the boughs.

I stand and run my hands along the emerald-green walls of the bookstore. The color of pine trees, Ruby always said. The paint is peeling in places, but it's hard to tell, as the walls are covered with framed artwork. A painting of a cow jumping over a moon hangs beside a signed black-and-white photo of Roald Dahl. He wrote, "To all the children of Bluebird Books, never stop imagining."

I pull back the faded old green-and-yellow-striped drapes. Once billowy and grand, they are dusty and sun bleached now, tattered at the hem. I smile to myself remembering the time Aunt Ruby showed me a photograph of a circus tent as her inspiration for the drapes. I flip the light switch and the crystal chandelier overhead strains to light the room. It's missing a lightbulb, or twelve. I make a mental note to replace them.

I walk to the back staircase and climb the steps to Ruby's apartment above the shop. It's small, but the high ceilings and exposed brick walls make it feel bigger, grander somehow. And even though

I know it's been several months since Ruby passed, the place has a lived-in feel, as if she might have made eggs and toast this very morning before leaving for a walk around Green Lake. The toaster's still plugged into the wall, a teakettle sits at attention on the little stove, and the faucet drips quietly into the sink.

I peer through the doorway of the little room off the kitchen where Amy and I used to stay. The two twin beds are still there, as well as the little nightstand. The porcelain lamp with its vintage tassel-trimmed shade holds court on the mahogany side table. I weave my way to Ruby's bed, through a path lined with boxes of assorted memorabilia and stacks of books, some piled as high as me. The familiar crimson velvet coverlet is pulled taut, perhaps painstakingly so, as if the last time Ruby made the bed she was expecting company. I run my hand along the soft fabric, threadbare at the center, where she sat for so many years, propped up reading a book like she always did after she closed the store at five each evening. She'd wait until eight to eat dinner, "fashionably late," she'd say.

I study a familiar throw pillow and my eyes well up with tears. I cross-stitched a pink rose on it when I was ten and gave it to Aunt Ruby for her birthday. She kept it all these years. She looked at it every day when she woke up and when she laid her head down each night. Did she think about me? I didn't mean to, but I forsook Ruby along with the rest of my past when I left Seattle. My heart beats faster. I can no longer suppress the emotion I feel. "Oh, Ruby," I cry. I feel my chest constrict as a draft of cool air seeps in from the old double-hung windows. I shiver as I glance down at the nightstand, where there's a small mahogany jewelry box, a framed photo of me and my sister, and Ruby's old oval locket on its gold chain. I remember it dangling from her neck so long ago. My sister and I would ask her what she kept inside it, but she'd always give us a secret smile and tuck it back beneath her sweater set. "When you're older," she'd say. But we never did get the chance to look inside.

I pick up the necklace and fasten it around my neck, but I won't open the locket. No, I don't deserve to see what's hidden within. I'll wear the necklace, and it will be my reminder of Ruby from this point forward. I'll never forget her. And I'll keep her secret hidden away. I'll guard it.

In the style of Ruby, I tuck the necklace beneath my sweater, and then beside the jewelry box I notice a white envelope inscribed "June" in script that is unmistakably Ruby's. I sink to the bed and tear open the flap.

My dear June,

If you're reading this, I have passed. I knew the end was growing near. So I prepared this place for you. They're taking me to the convalescent home. My God, me in a convalescent home. Can you imagine?

I stop reading, and wipe away a fresh tear, hearing Ruby's playful voice in my head as I do.

But it is time, they tell me. So, I've put fresh sheets on the bed and tidied the kitchen. I'm sorry the floor is in such disarray. These days, it's hard for me to part with anything, so I tend to keep it all. It would be an honor to me if you'd stay here. Make yourself at home. I truly hope you will. Because it is your home now, June.

Bluebird Books was always to be your legacy. You see, my dear, we share the same sensibilities about life. I knew that even when you were a wee child. Your sister would spend hours with her dolls, but you'd sit in the window seat with a book in your

Sarah Jio

lap, wide-eyed. You loved books as I do. I hope you've never lost the love of literature, the sense of discovery and wonder.

It hasn't been easy for me since you left Seattle. But I understood why you had to go. You needed to spread your wings and fly. And you did. I only wish you'd have flown home every once in a while. I have missed you so.

I trust that you will love Bluebird Books and care for it as much as I have. It won't be easy. Children aren't reading the way they did in my day. And I will confess, I worry that the love of books is dying. Children's literature today is facing a state of emergency. My most loyal customers are straying for the glitz of media, the lure of this thing called the Internet. Two years ago, a little boy named Stuart and his mother Genie used to come into the store often. He would listen to me read at story time with wide eyes, eyes of an active imagination. But he stopped coming as frequently, and when his mother brought him in last summer, I could see that the spark had died out. His mother lamented that all he's interested in these days is movies and video games. As a result, literature doesn't speak to him in the way it once did.

I've done all I can, all I know to do. And now I leave it to you. It is the problem of the next generation to solve. What is childhood without stories? And how will children fall in love with stories without bookstores? You can't get that from a computer.

I know that keeping Bluebird Books afloat will be a challenge. But I have faith in you, June. If anyone can save this store, it's you.

So I leave this beloved place to you, and with it, all of its secrets. And there are many, all here for you to discover.

As Beatrix Potter once said, "What heaven can be more real than to retain the spirit-world of childhood, tempered and balanced by knowledge and common sense."

And this is what you will find here, my dear child.

With love, always,
Your devoted Aunt Ruby

I place the letter to my chest and sigh. *She wants me to save the store.* I shake my head. *How can I? I live in New York. I have a job. I can't stay in Seattle. I can't do this.*

I hear Ruby's voice then: *Yes, you can, dear.*

And for a moment, I believe her.

Chapter 3

The next morning, I wake up in Ruby's bed at five a.m., which would be eight a.m. New York time, and I chastise myself for sleeping in. Under normal circumstances, I would have been up hours ago. I'd have already run six miles, showered, and would be sitting at my desk with a phone in one hand and the other scrolling through e-mails on my computer.

I stand up quickly, remembering the way my mom used to sleep late. And when I say late, I mean past noon. My sister and I could hardly rouse her. We'd lie beside her and watch her chest rise and fall, just to make sure she was still breathing. Her hair would always be frizzy and wild from a night of partying, and she'd smell of cigarettes and alcohol. Often there'd be a man in her bed. Amy and I never liked that. Once we took a permanent marker and drew a mustache on one guy's upper lip. He was too hungover to notice when he woke up two hours later and staggered out the door. We never saw him again, but I often imagined him catching a glimpse of his reflection in a window somewhere and trying to rub it off. It still makes me laugh.

It's hard to blame Mom for her behavior. Her own mother,

Aunt Ruby's estranged older sister, died when Mom was just thirteen. At the time, Ruby hadn't even met her nieces and nephews, as her sister, Lucille, had forbidden it. Evidently a longtime rift between the two sisters began when their parents had only enough funds to send one daughter to school back east, and they chose Ruby.

In her sudden death, Lucille left Mom to care for her younger siblings while her emotionally distant father worked long hours. I remember overhearing Aunt Ruby and Mom talking, when they thought I wasn't listening. "Janet," Ruby said to Mom, "it's understandable that you don't want to be a mother because you were forced to be one at a young age. But you have two girls who depend on you, and love you dearly. Can't you try a little harder for them?"

I wondered a lot about Ruby's relationship with her sister, Lucille. It seemed heartbreaking to me that a wall of icy silence could grow between two sisters, and yet . . . it happened to me. I shudder, forcing my mind to change the subject.

The clock ticks loudly on the wall, and I dress quickly. I pull on a pair of running leggings and a long-sleeved T-shirt. The sun is just coming up, and through the window, I can see the foggy mist rising over Green Lake. There'll be time for a jog before I begin sorting through the store.

I lace up my running shoes and walk down to the shop, where I hear the hiss and spurt of the old radiator. I smile, remembering the way I used to warm my hands over it on wintry afternoons.

The door jingles as I open it and make my way out to the street. Seagulls squawk overhead, as steam rises off the rooftops of the nearby buildings. The owner of the toy store across the street is just arriving. I see her holding a large bag in one hand and a box in the other. I smile politely, but she frowns and turns away from me, disappearing into the darkened store. *That's strange. Maybe she doesn't remember me.* Ruby used to let us cross the street to visit the toy store now and then. Amy was always more enamored with toys than I was, but I loved seeing how happy it made her to stare at the Barbie aisle, even if I had no interest in playing with the dolls.

I try not to give much thought to the encounter as I bend my right leg into a stretch. The street looks the same, mostly, untouched by time. There's the hardware store and a café, where the first customers are already sipping espresso. The toy store, of course. The stationery shop on the corner, where my sister and I would buy stickers with the coins Aunt Ruby gave us. But the Italian restaurant next door to Bluebird Books, that's new.

I eye the green awning painted with the name "Antonio's." I peer through the window at the little tables with checkered tablecloths and drippy wax candles in Chianti bottles inside, and I can almost detect the smell of garlic roasting in the kitchen.

The sun's taking its time rising, the way it always does in Seattle. It's as if the entire city, solar system included, presses the snooze button. I blow warm air into my hands, and begin running. I turn down a side street that leads to the lake. Where I remember the bustle of people, bikes, dogs, and kids, there is only quiet. Just a handful of runners and I, plus the occasional bicyclist, round the curves of the 2.8-mile path.

I finish one loop and stride into another. It feels good to breathe in the moist May air. Everywhere, flowers—daffodils, tulips, plants I don't recognize or haven't noticed before—are pushing up through the earth. A robin pecks at a twig on a park bench, and I smile, remembering the time my sister and I discovered a bird's nest by the lake. We watched over the little nest with its four Tiffany-blue eggs until Mom drove by in some guy's car and waved for us to get in the backseat. I tucked the nest into the crook of a tree branch and hoped for the best. We never did know if the birds survived; two weeks later, when Amy and I went to check on them, they were gone.

I finish my second loop around the lake, then sit down on a bench in front of a boat launch, and I think about Amy. We haven't talked in five years, not that I have anything to say to her. But I don't like the ache I feel, even now, when I think of her. I hate that my heart has reserved space for someone who hurt me so badly.

I look out at the lake ahead, where a man is stepping out of a kayak onto the dock. He secures it to a cleat, then pulls a black cover over the hull. He smiles in my direction, and I look away quickly. I stand and turn back to the path that leads to the street. I'm not in the mood for chitchat, but I hear his footsteps behind me, and when we're both stopped at the crosswalk, he smiles again.

"Nice day," he says. He's tall, with dark hair that looks a little wavy in the morning light. There's the glistening of sweat at his temples. He's wearing the uniform of Seattle guys—a wrinkled flannel shirt and a pair of khaki cargo shorts ruggedly frayed at the edges.

"Yes," I say curtly, trying to remember if men in Seattle are forward or just really friendly.

We both cross the street toward Sunnyside Avenue, and he grins. "We must be going to the same place," he says, pointing to Joe's Café on the corner.

"Guess so," I say a bit guardedly.

He holds the door open for me and I walk inside, inhaling the scent of coffee grounds and steamed milk.

I order a double Americano and he asks for the same.

"So," he says, as I pour a generous amount of half-and-half into my cup. "I haven't seen you around the lake before."

I shake my head. "I don't live here. I'm just . . . visiting."

"Oh," he says, extending his hand. "Then welcome. I'm Gavin."

"June," I say, taking his hand. It's warm and strong, steadying, somehow, and I catch myself holding it a moment longer than I should.

"Well," I say, looking at the door. "Nice to meet you."

"Wait," he says, walking ahead with me. "Let me walk you . . . to where you're going."

I smile and shrug. "I'm not going far." I point to the bookstore. "My aunt passed away recently and she left it to me."

Gavin's eyes widen in astonishment. "Bluebird Books?"

I nod.

"It's just that . . . well, I didn't realize Ruby had passed. Last I heard she was in a convalescent home. I'm . . . so sorry."

"Thank you," I say.

"Well," he continues, "she must have really thought a lot of you to leave you her store. It's been open for something like fifty years, right?"

"More," I say. "The sixtieth anniversary is this fall, actually." I'm conscious of the fact that if all goes as planned, I'll have the place gutted and sold by then. I hate to think of it, but the only thing that makes financial sense these days is selling to a developer. They could turn the building into an eight-plex. I won't tell him that now, of course. I won't tell anyone right away. But I'm a realist, and I know I can't keep the store. I need to stay focused. I can't think of Aunt Ruby's letter. I'll approach this like any of the small businesses at work. In and out.

"I own the Italian restaurant next door," Gavin says. "Antonio's."

"Oh wow," I say.

"We could cater an anniversary party for the store. I mean, if you're interested."

I smile politely. I can't tell if he's fishing for business or just being nice. "I do love Italian food," I say nervously. "But I'm not sure that . . . listen, there's a lot of work to be done before . . ."

"Well," he says, taking a sip of his coffee, "you know where to find me if you need anything."

"Thanks," I say, turning back to the bookstore.

I close the door behind me, and sink into one of the gray upholstered chairs by the windows, tucking my knees up to my chest the way I did as a girl. I look out into the store with its rows of bookshelves, and I see a page from my childhood.

Aunt Ruby is there, her gray hair cut blunt at her shoulders, dark-rimmed glasses on her nose—beautiful in a literary sort of way. She's trying to interest Amy in a book, with little luck. Amy is four, maybe five. She still has chubby cheeks and pigtails. She wears a dress with white cable-knit tights, with a hole in the right knee, and holds a Cabbage Patch doll with yellow yarn hair, grubby hands, and a smear of dirt on her cheek. Ruby opens a copy of *Where the Wild Things Are*, which I think is funny; Amy is a wild thing. She's moody and throws tantrums. Mom's afraid of her, I think. Because whenever Amy cries, Mom looks as if her world might end.

Amy pushes the book away, and Ruby makes one more attempt to interest her in the opening pages, in which the little boy is a beast to his mother and he's sent to bed without supper, which Amy should understand because we didn't have supper last night. We were half-starved when Mom dropped us off at the bookstore this morning on her way to work. Ruby immediately fed us peanut butter and jelly sandwiches, and nothing ever tasted so good.

"I'll read it with you," I say to Ruby after Amy runs off to the dollhouse. I nestle into the spot beside her and smile apologetically. "Amy doesn't like books very much."

Ruby's face is solemn as she opens the book again. "She will in time," she says. "She must. For what is a life without stories?"

I didn't know what she meant then, not really. But I do now, and my heart sinks when I realize that I can't remember the last book I read, the last time I sank into an imaginary world and got lost the way I used to love to do. Ruby would be horrified.

I think about the letter she left me. She'd written of secrets. *So I leave this beloved place to you, and with it, all of its secrets. And there are many, all here for you to discover.*

What secrets did Ruby want me to discover? And why?

She revealed very little about her life and her personal thoughts. As far as I know, she never loved. And though she was beloved by many, she kept most at arm's length. I look out at the store just as another lightbulb flickers and pops in the chandelier overhead.

"Ruby, what do you want me to find?" I say into the dimly lit air.

And then I remember her reference to Beatrix Potter. I wind down through the bookshelves, until I come to a shelf that contains several volumes of Potter. I pull out an old copy of *The Tale of Peter Rabbit*, and a yellowed envelope falls into my lap. It's addressed to Ruby, and the return address reads simply, "MWB; 69 Bank Street, New York, NY."

Chapter 4

I lift the flap of the envelope and pull out the pages inside, squinting at the handwriting:

February 1, 1946

My dearest Ruby,

I miss you. Spring is coming, I can almost taste it. Seattle must be lovely now, with the crocuses just starting to push up from the cold earth. I saw a patch of them in the East Village yesterday, and though a bit trampled, I picked a bunch and found them a nice vase on my windowsill. They wilted by evening. It's a shame they don't keep, though the best things in life never do.

I'm so glad we've stayed friends all these years. I suppose it was quite a coincidence that we ever became friends, really, you being my pupil in the creative writing class and all. My, were those old teachers at Dana Hall School stuffy or what? I never fit in. I don't know what possessed me to think I'd try my hand at teaching. Probably Mother. Every practical thing I do is a result of something my mother said to me. But, my, if

I hadn't become acquainted with you, I think I might have died of boredom that year.

Remember how we vowed that if we ever survived that year at Dana Hall (each of us in our own private torment: you with your studies and missing home; and me in my quest to establish myself as an adult and a professional) we'd take a steamship somewhere exotic like Madagascar (can one get to Madagascar via ship?)? Well, I think that is what I need. I think I need a change of scenery, something to spark my muse. New York is becoming quite the same to me, I'm afraid. Everybody's so serious.

Yes, I need a trip. If not Madagascar, maybe Seattle? Heavens, I've been talking about making a visit for years now. Maybe this summer?

You're more of a sister to me than mine will ever be. Roberta and I were always close as children, but in adulthood, the gap has widened between us. She chose a different life, of marriage and children and homemaking. And while I wouldn't say she's flaunting that life in my face, I do believe she's disappointed that I didn't choose the same path. Our interactions are strained. We don't laugh together anymore. May I confess my deepest fear? I worry that she's turning into my mother.

Remind me, do you and your sister get along well? You haven't mentioned her much in previous letters. Well, in the interest of sisterhood, I've invited Roberta to lunch next week. I'll let you know how it goes. (She disapproves of spirits, so I'll have to hide my liquor bottles in the cabinet before she arrives.)

Now, to another subject. I shall be honest, and confess the dire condition that all writers loathe: I am stuck. Stuck in the worst way possible. Everywhere I turn, I'm looking for my next idea. Just when I think I've seen it as plain as day, it's a naughty bunny that skips off around the next bend. And when I try to chase it, it can't be caught. It's sneaky and sly, and keeps me wanting.

I seem to be at an odd place in my career. I have made a name for myself (or so one might say). I've published dozens of children's books, with more in the pipeline, so you'd expect I'd feel fulfilled, wouldn't you? Well, I don't. I want to believe that my best work is ahead, and yet (here's the problem), I don't know if it is. What if it isn't?

I don't mean to bore you with my writerly problems. I just appreciate being able to tell someone.

I received a letter from my mother last week inquiring about my financial state. I expect she heard how I spent my most recent royalty check. I'll admit, purchasing an entire flower cart in the East Village might not have been my wisest decision, by a long shot, but my, did the blooms make a grand scene for the party in my apartment that Saturday night. Oh, Ruby, you should have seen it: I lined the carpets with petals of white lilies and pink roses, then scattered orchids around every surface. At one point the sink was filled high with roses. Just imagine it!

You only live once, I say.

I have a new beau. He's fine. Rich, and he looks nice in a tux, but I'll be honest: I don't think much of him. I look good on his arm, and he looks good on mine, but that's the extent of it, I suppose.

How is Anthony? If I ever write a novel, which I do hope to do someday, it shall be a story inspired by the two of you. So tragic, and so beautiful at the same time. Please tell me the latest, and I want every detail. I will devour them with my dinner and savor each word.

Yours,
Brownie

I feel a swirling sensation in my stomach as I read the last words. Brownie. MWB. I run upstairs to the apartment and pull my laptop out of its case. I check the wireless connection, see a weak signal coming from "Antonio's Restaurant Wireless," and I decide that the guy I met this morning, Gavin, wouldn't mind if I used it. It's unsecured, and I'm able to pull up Google quickly. With the letter in my hand, I type in "MWB" and then "Brownie," and then the address, "69 Bank Street," and I gasp when I see the search results on the screen. It seems my Aunt Ruby was a personal friend of the late legendary children's book author Margaret Wise Brown, who penned *Goodnight Moon*, *The Runaway Bunny*, and at least a hundred other titles. Ruby never mentioned her—but why? And why did she underline Beatrix Potter in her letter? To prime me for a literary scavenger hunt?

I think fast, remembering the Easter egg hunts Ruby used to plan each year for my sister and me inside the store, with eggs hidden behind books and under shelves, each with a clue leading us to the next destination.

Yes, she's left me this letter, and perhaps more, for an important reason. I walk downstairs and begin to tuck the copy of *Peter Rabbit* back on the shelf, when I notice a gap in the pages. I pick up the book again, and see that I've missed a second letter tucked inside. This one, from Ruby to Margaret:

February 8, 1946

Dear Margaret,

I can't tell you how your letter cheered me. To know that I'm not the only one who sometimes feels like a square peg in a round hole, to know that you struggle, as I do, with the business of going about life, well, it made me love you all the more. If we cannot be our true selves among friends, how can we even know our own selves?

Ah, yes, sisters. We have more in common than we even knew. My relationship with my sister, Lucille, is icy, at best. My parents only had enough funds to give one of us a college education, and they chose me. I'd always been a bookworm, and Lucille spent hours presiding over her dollhouse. In their mind, the choice was obvious: Send Ruby to school; keep Lucille home. She forgave my parents, of course, rest their souls, but she never forgave me. I can see the jilted look in her eye every time we see each other.

Like your sister, mine has opted for the domestic life. She is married and keeps a perfect household. She takes joy in that life, and I am happy for her. I just wish she could be happy for me, for the life I have chosen. I feel I can never please her. She visited my apartment last week, and practically fainted when she found out I had no coffee or tea or anything to eat (I usually pick up a sandwich for dinner on my way home from work and eat it on the streetcar). She actually said my living situation was "primitive." Primitive!

Lucille gets under my skin, yes. But I try to remember that we once shared a bond, and I pray that bond returns. Why must it be so hard with sisters? And why couldn't you and I have been sisters? I'm confident we'd be free of all of this nonsense. Be sure to write and tell me how your luncheon with Roberta went, all right?

You asked about Anthony, and I will tell you. He is well—divine, actually. It hardly seems possible that two months have passed since we met that day at Elliott Avenue Books. I know I wrote of our meeting briefly in my last letter, but I'll tell you more now. Besides, it gives me quite a thrill to write about it.

I was working in the children's section, where I spend most of my time tending to the collection, which I always feel could be more expansive (but that's for another letter), when Anthony and his daughter, May, walked in. I saw her first—wearing a smart pink wool coat and patent leather flats, hair styled in soft dark curls—and then my eyes lifted and met Anthony's.

I cannot explain it except to say, Brownie, it was as if the world stopped spinning the moment our eyes locked. And then his daughter spoke, and the world resumed motion.

"Do you have <u>The Poky Little Puppy</u>?" she asked. I could tell by the way she spoke that she was used to being waited on, tended to.

"Yes," I said, taking her to the section where I'd just shelved a stack of new copies. I put one in her gloved hands. "Here you are."

"Father," she said, turning to the man, "I'll just go over and read it while you finish shopping."

"Yes, May," he said, turning back to me.

There we were, two strangers, surrounded by children's books, unsure of where to begin.

We both spoke at the same time.

"I'm Anthony Magnuson," he said.

"I'm Ruby Crain."

I recognized his name at once. Everyone knows the Magnuson family in Seattle. They're a wealthy clan of politicians, business owners, that sort. But he didn't fit the mold. I knew just by looking at him that we were kindred spirits. We talked about all sorts of things, mostly about books (he loves reading), until May returned.

And, that was that. We parted ways, and of course you know what was to come. I asked around, and learned that he's married, to the socialite Victoria Gerhardt Magnuson. According to my sources, she has more money than God himself and her fortune practically saved the Magnusons from financial ruin. I believe it's why he married her. From what I've heard, it seems their union was, more or less, a carefully constructed business deal.

A girl who works at the bookstore here once made a delivery to Victoria, at their home. She said she was cold as ice to her; didn't even say thank you. If you ask me, they're as well paired as a dog and a cat. She's firm and rigid, he's kind and soft. I fear that he's terribly unhappy with her, but who am I to interfere? He made a vow.

Still, when Anthony comes to the bookstore, I positively light up. In fact, it would be quite an embarrassment to admit how many times I look up when the door opens. I'm always hoping it's him, at every hour of the day. He visits as often as possible, with May, and even without her. Honestly, those are my favorite times, when he pops in during his workday (his office is two blocks from the shop; he owns a manufacturing company). The little girl has the temperament of her mother, clearly, and does nothing but boss him around. "Father, I'd like this," and "Father, I need that." And yet, I feel for her. She's obviously terribly unhappy, even with all that wealth. I can't help but think that if I could just get through to her, show her the type of interest, love, that her mother doesn't give her, maybe she'd turn around.

Oh, Margaret, how I wish the circumstances were different. For as long as I live, I don't think I'll meet anyone like Anthony. Even in our brief encounters at the store, I feel as if I know him, really know him.

But there's the unspoken, of course: his life with Victoria. I can't deny my curiosity, and I will confess that on Tuesday night, I put on my overcoat and followed him on the streetcar to his home on Queen Anne Hill. You wouldn't believe the opulence of this place. It was almost off-putting in its grandeur, with its gold detailing on the cornices, a Grecian statue in the driveway. But then I remembered that it wasn't Anthony's doing. It screamed Victoria. Anthony wouldn't live this way on his own.

The lights were on in the front room, and I saw her. It gave me quite a shock. She is beautiful in a severe sort of way: sharp features, ebony hair. Of course, she was exquisitely dressed, which made me doubt the plain skirts and sweater sets I wear.

And then I saw Anthony walk in the room. He placed his hand on her shoulder, and the moment his hand touched her, a part of me died inside. I couldn't bear it. That's when I knew I was in love with him. Am in love with him.

So, this is the place where you are allowed to judge me—abhor me, really. I love a married man. There, I said it.

I don't know what will become of us, if anything. But I know I am beginning to fall in love, and I feel that he is too.

Well, here I am, going on and on. I hope I haven't annoyed you terribly. You have always been able to temper your feelings about men. I wish I was more like you. I wish I could control my heart.

I should sign off for now. I have to open the bookstore tomorrow, and I'll need to be up early.

Oh, and yes to Madagascar, or better yet—Seattle!

With love,
Ruby

P.S. I adore that you spent your entire royalty check on flowers. There never was and never will be another like you, Brownie.

I look up from the letter with tears in my eyes. Ruby was in love with someone. All these years, I never knew. And like me, both she and Margaret struggled with sister relationships. I take a deep breath. I can identify with Lucille. I felt betrayed by my sister, and rightly so. But Ruby didn't make an intentional choice to hurt her sister. Amy did. For a moment I feel the familiar anger rising up in my chest, and the sadness of losing someone I loved. Past tense. Ruby and Margaret may have wanted to make amends with their sisters, but no, I would never. Sometimes you have to close the door, and lock it.

With burning curiosity to know more about this friendship between the two women, I quickly pull the next few books off the shelf and search for more letters—none—before scanning the upper and lower shelf for any signs of pages tucked inside, which is when I hear the sound of the jingle bells on the door. Did I forget to lock it?

"Hello?" I say quickly, standing up. "Is someone there?"

I see Gavin and instantly feel relieved.

"Sorry," he says. "I didn't mean to startle you." He's holding a couple of takeout boxes. The scent of garlic and basil wafts in the air. "I thought you might be hungry, so I brought over some lunch."

I look at the clock and realize that it's almost noon and I've had nothing but espresso today.

"Thank you," I say, walking toward him. The letters are still in my hands, and I quickly tuck them in my back pocket.

Gavin looks around for a place to set the food down, finally settling on the only available surface: a tiny children's table flanked by two pint-size blue chairs. He grins at me. "This OK?"

"Yeah," I say, smiling as I cram myself into one of the minuscule seats. He does the same, and we both can't help but laugh at ourselves.

He opens up the first box and hands me one of the plates under his arm, then pulls out a cloth napkin wrapped around a fork, spoon, and knife. "Hope you like pasta puttanesca," he says.

"My favorite, actually," I reply, grinning. "How did you know?"

He points to his head. "I'm kind of psychic when it comes to food pairings." He's wearing a crisp white shirt, unbuttoned at the collar, and a pair of dark straight-legged jeans. "Show me a person, and I can find the perfect meal for them. It's all in the face."

I grin. "Oh, is it?"

"Sure is. See, when I met you this morning on the lake, you looked a little sad. I would have served you spaghetti pomodoro then."

"Spaghetti pomodoro?"

"Yeah," he says. "Spaghetti works wonders for curing the blues." He nods. "But the puttanesca, that's for new beginnings."

I busy myself with my napkin as Gavin looks around the shop and smiles. "But if you had come to me and told me you had a bad day, that things had gotten stressful, then I'd make you Bolognese sauce."

I can't help but smile. "And what do you make for harder cases?" I consider Ruby and, according to the letter I just read, the prospect of her broken heart. I also can't help but think of the way my own heart shattered five years ago. "What about broken hearts?"

"Now," Gavin says, "those are harder. But I find that in most cases, eggplant does the job."

I let out a little laugh. "Eggplant?"

"Nothing better," he says.

I smile as he dishes a helping of pasta onto my plate, then dip my fork in to take a bite.

"Wow," I say. "It's very good." I dab the napkin to my mouth. "Do you cook, or run the business side?"

"I do a little of everything, my business partner and I. Cook, wait tables, bus tables." He grins. "It's what you have to do when you run a small business."

I nod, thinking of a little Italian restaurant in Queens that I had to close down. The owner was just like Gavin, a jack-of-all-trades. He was sprawled out on the floor, fixing a faulty oven door, when I came in armed with legal papers.

"Then I give my compliments to the chef," I say, shaking off the memory.

His face twists into a look of discomfort for a moment before his smile returns. "So what do you plan to do with the place?"

I grimace inwardly, thinking of how the locals will take the news. I can almost write the headline: NEW YORK BANKER INHERITS BELOVED BLUEBIRD BOOKS; CLOSES ITS DOORS FOREVER.

"I, uh—"

"I imagine you'll want to do a little remodeling," he says, standing up and running his hand along a nearby bookcase.

"Yeah, I—"

"I can help," he continues. "I have a ton of tools in the basement. We had to do a full renovation before we could open the restaurant. I got pretty handy with a table saw."

"Thanks," I say. "But, well, I'm not really sure how much heavy lifting I'll need to do."

Gavin seems undeterred, even excited, by the challenge of fixing up the store. "You could refinish the bookcases," he says. "Strip them down and sand down the tops. A bit of paint here and there, and some new moldings—oh, and maybe a new checkout counter—and this place will be grand again."

I can't tell him the truth: that Bluebird Books will *never* be grand again. I can't tell him that I plan to call a truck, tomorrow, maybe, and pay someone eight dollars an hour to load up all the books and boxes and most all of Aunt Ruby's worldly possessions and cart them off to a local library. What can't be donated will be taken to the dump.

The dump. It casts a sad, hopeless shadow on Aunt Ruby's legacy. What would she think of me now? If I look carefully, I can almost see her patting the locket around her neck, which is when I remember that it's now around my neck. I touch the gold chain nervously.

"I can tell this place means a lot to you," Gavin says, his words jarring me back to the moment. "You grew up here, didn't you?"

"Yes," I say, a little startled. "How did you know?"

"Just a guess. I assumed your aunt would have left the shop to someone who loved it as much as she did." He grins. "And also, you seem more Seattle than the New York type."

His comment surprises me at first. New York has made me tougher, smarter, more driven. Can he not see that? "And I take it you know both types very well, then?"

He smiles playfully. "You might say that."

I wonder, for a moment, if Ruby knew Gavin, and if so, what she might have thought of him. "Did you get to know my aunt much?" I ask.

"A little," he replies. "We've only been here a year. Ruby closed the store about six months after Adrianna and I opened the restaurant. We, all of the business owners on the street, felt so bad for her, because we knew the depths of her loss. But she just couldn't keep up. Lillian and Bill convinced her that it was time to move to a retirement home."

I feel a pang of guilt. I could have called. I didn't even call. My heart beats faster, and I place my hand on my chest and take a series of deep breaths. My medication is upstairs; I'll take a pill later. "Lillian and Bill, the owners of Geppetto's, right?" I remember the way Lillian regarded me on the street earlier.

He nods. "She had a fall."

I gasp and cover my mouth with my hand.

"I started checking on her in the afternoons, just to make sure she was doing all right," he says. "And one day, I went in to say hello and she wasn't sitting at her desk. I heard a faint cry from the back hallway, so I rushed over, and there she was, lying at the base of the stairs, where she'd been since she fell that morning. I called an ambulance, and they took her to the hospital. She came back a few months later after a stay at a rehabilitation facility, but she'd changed by then. I could see the look in her eye. She was more frail than ever. I helped her move a few things around the shop. She was very particular about where she wanted things to be." He pauses for a moment. His eyes are serious, and they stare ahead at Ruby's desk. "It sounds funny to say, but I just had this deep feeling that she knew she didn't have much time left."

I dab the corner of the cloth napkin to my eye.

"I'm sorry," Gavin says. "I didn't mean to upset you."

"No," I say quickly. "It's just that I loved her so, and I—I just hope she knew how much."

Gavin places his hand on my shoulder. "I'm sure she knew."

"I wish I'd come home to see her, before . . ." I look up at him and our eyes lock.

"But you're here now," he says, pointing up at the ceiling. "And I'm sure she's looking down in anticipation of all you'll do for the store."

"Yeah," I say nervously. "I . . ." I take a bite of breadstick.

"So you spent a lot of time here as a kid, then?"

I nod between bites. "Our mom was . . . well, she was kind of out of it in the early part of our childhood, so my sister and I were here a lot."

"Oh, you have a sister? Does she live in town?"

"Yeah, she does now, but I . . . but we"—I shake my head decisively—"we don't talk."

Gavin looks more saddened than I'd expect. "Oh," he says. "That must be so hard for you. What happened?"

"Listen," I say, smiling a little nervously, "it's a long story, and I have a lot to get done today. I—"

"Forgive me," he says, standing. "I didn't mean to pry."

"No, you weren't," I say. "It's just kind of a long story. Another time?"

"Yes, definitely," he says, collecting our empty plates and the silverware, before walking to the doorway. He turns back to me once more. "If you're ever up for a walk around the lake sometime, just come find me."

I smile, at first because I find the very idea of walking quaint, and quite frankly, sort of a waste of time. I've structured my life around making the best use of time. It's why my daily jogs are more akin to sprints. It's why I schedule my workday in fifteen-minute increments. But Gavin smiles at me expectantly, and I remember that people go about life at a slower pace in Seattle. I remember that *I* used to be one of those people. I take a deep breath. "A walk," I say. "Sure, maybe sometime."

He waves good-bye, and then closes the door behind him. Ruby's jingle bells reverberate in my ears for a long time after.

Chapter 5

I look up at the cuckoo clock on the wall and see that it's already four thirty. I've spent a fruitless afternoon sifting through Ruby's boxes for more letters, and now the sunlight is waning. I'll need to replace the lightbulbs in the chandelier if I'm going to be able to work past dusk.

In all of my sorting, I've accumulated fascinating artifacts from Ruby's life: a set of blue china, a Cartier watch that looks as if it stopped ticking decades ago, and a pristine red gingham swimsuit, wrapped in white tissue paper inside a tan Frederick & Nelson box with a burgundy lid. I think of Ruby wearing it and smile, then my practicality kicks in: The tiny one-piece would fetch a pretty penny in a vintage shop.

I haven't been able to stop thinking about the letters between Ruby and Margaret. Margaret Wise Brown. My aunt, the confidant of arguably one of the greatest children's book authors of all time? Ruby did have secretive tendencies. The prospect of discovery makes me think about holding off on closing the store for good, at least until I can determine the real story Ruby's letters tell. Still, I'll need to review the store's financial records and begin making plans. I make a mental note to research the developers in the area and set up a few meetings.

I feel a chill come over me, and I stare at the old fireplace. Ruby used to keep it roaring from October to April, and sometimes even through May. I remember the supply of chopped wood, and I venture out to the alley. And there, under the eaves, the logs are stacked high, as if in her waning days at home Ruby arranged for one last delivery. For me.

I smile to myself as I lift a log from the stack, but I turn around quickly when I hear movement behind me. The alley is dim now that the sun has set, but I have the distinct feeling that I am not alone. "Hello?" I say in a shaky voice. But my call is met with silence until a cat cries in the distance.

I scan the shadowy corners behind the Dumpster: no one. Quickly, I pick up another log and carry the wobbly stack inside the shop, pausing to lock the door before setting the wood on the hearth. On the mantel, I find matches. Atop a stack of old newspapers blares a headline from January 7, 1963: MAGNUSON FAMILY DONATES $1 MILLION FOR NEW ART MUSEUM. I save the front page, wad up the brittle newsprint, and tuck it beneath a log in the fireplace, then light a match and watch as the fire takes on a life of its own, spreading to the log. I listen as it hisses and crackles, and then I make the connection.

The Poky Little Puppy! Of course. Ruby mentioned the book in her last letter. If I can find it, will there be more letters tucked away inside its pages?

I rush to the bookshelves again and search for the book I remember reading as a girl. "Five little puppies dug a hole under the fence and went for a walk in the wide, wide, world." I smile to myself. I went for a walk in the wide, wide world, and got a bit lost along the way. After an hour, I've almost given up on the search, but then in the firelight, I see the glimmer of a Little Golden Book spine on a high shelf across the room. And somehow, I just know.

I wheel the ladder over to the shelf, thinking of how as a child I loved climbing on that ladder and pushing myself from one side of the wall to the other. When Ruby went upstairs for any reason, my sister and I would take turns pushing each other, and when our aunt returned she'd pretend to be oblivious to our antics, even though the wheels rattled loudly enough to make that impossible.

I reach for the spot on the shelf, and there it is, *The Poky Little Puppy*. One copy. And sure enough, there's a bulge inside its pages. I open the stiff spine and reach for the two envelopes inside.

By the fire again, I lift the flap of the first envelope, from Margaret to Ruby.

February 22, 1946

My dearest Ruby,

I can't tell you how cheering it was to receive your letter. It cast a ray of light on my week, which has been otherwise atrocious. Where to start?

While I had invited my sister, Roberta, over for lunch in good faith that we were trying to forge ahead with our relationship, she used the hour as a time to lecture me about my "lifestyle." Why don't I get married, she asked. Why don't I start a family? Why don't I stop associating with all these artists and bohemians? But what she was really getting at was, why don't I be more like her? Well, I don't want to be like her, and I told her so. As you can imagine, my words were not well received. She reached for her coat and bag and stormed out of the apartment. I feel bad, of course. I do not want our relationship to come to this, and yet I long for the day that we can accept one another for who we are, she in her world of pressed and proper domesticity, and I in my unconventional one. I suspect this is how you feel about Lucille. Perhaps one day we'll all be able to forgive, accept, and move forward with the kind of love we all shared as girls. This is my hope, anyway.

One of the illustrators we work with here at the publishing house had complained of being lonely, so what did I think to do? I bought him a puppy. A blue terrier. Apparently he had little experience with canines, because the nitwit left the pup in his apartment and the poor thing urinated all over the paintings for a new picture book. There are also paw prints, in all the primary colors, scattered about the room, and muddled on the paintings. He's going to have to scrap the canvases and start over, and of course, he blames me.

Well, at least that's all behind us. And I won't be bringing gifts to illustrators anytime soon.

If Roberta's visit wasn't enough, Mother also came by last week and the purpose of her visit was quite unsettling. Marriage. I ask you, dear friend, is there anything more unsettling than the subject of marriage? She says she's losing sleep having an unwed daughter "gallivanting around the city." I poured her a glass of sherry and told her to go lie down. It did not work. She continued the torrent. She says she can't stop worrying about me, and I told her that if and when I decide to get married (let's be clear, though, I have no plans), she'll be the first to know. That calmed her down, at least for now.

The truth is, Ruby, how can I marry after watching my parents' own dreadful union? I feel, at my core, that marriage only leads to unhappiness, at least when it comes to my own life. People come to us for seasons, and when the season is over, it is over. My love affairs have always been short and to the point. I like it that way (at least this is what I tell myself). Honestly, though, Ruby, I wish I could believe what you wrote about me. I wish I could believe that I am immune to love and all of its perils, but if I am absolutely honest, I know it not to be true.

Still, I think I'd rather throw myself in the Hudson River in the middle of winter than to ever betroth myself to someone. It would be so stifling, belonging to another! Like property! Let's make a pact to never get married, my dear friend. We will be two lone reeds in a bustling brook who stand tall, firm. We will make our own fun. Make our own lives while everyone else gets swept up in the river of life. What do you say?

The problem with people today is they take themselves too seriously. Nobody likes to have fun anymore. So, a few of my New York friends and I have started what we call the Bird Brain Society. It's such fun, Ruby. I wish you could come to our meetings. I'm president, and have the authority to declare any day Christmas, in which case, one of our members must cook a roast and make pudding. It's a gas! I have made you an honorary member, so you can play along.

On to a more serious subject: Be careful with this Anthony Magnuson. I fear that he already has a grip on your heart. But I implore you to hold tightly to it. I've learned that when a man takes your heart, it can be hell getting it back.

I still think I need to get out of the city. Lately, I feel out of place, like the ducks from Make Way for Ducklings. Yesterday a cab almost ran me over on Fifty-Seventh, and I dropped the pages of a manuscript into a mud puddle. Ruby, you should have seen me. I fell down on my knees and just cried. I might have sat there wailing my head off all day had a kind old gentleman not stopped to offer me his handkerchief and help me up. The manuscript, I'm afraid, was ruined. Fortunately, I had a copy filed away in my brain.

There is something else I must write you about, but I'm afraid I don't have the energy to tell you just now. I have pages to edit and quite a lot on my mind to sort through before I put these thoughts to pen.

> Until then, my dear friend,
> Merry Christmas,
> Brownie

I set the letter down and stoke the fire with a poker. The wind has picked up a bit and I hear it howling outside, pushing through the eaves of the door and windows. I think of Margaret's hesitance to share her secret as I pick up Ruby's letter.

March 7, 1946

Dear Brownie,

You have kept me in such suspense! I trust that you will reveal this secret of yours in due time, but until then, I shall remain on the edge of my seat. For now, let me attempt to speculate. Theory No. 1: Despite your rant about love and men, I suspect that you have fallen for someone at your publishing house. An illustrator, perhaps? I recall in previous correspondence a man named Gregory. Still, by the tone of your last letter, I believe this isn't likely (though, you've surprised me before). Theory No. 2: You are ill, in which case, I will be saddened that you waited to tell me. In any case, I pray that you are well and that you are not suffering from any maladies. No. 3: You have lost yourself in a new story. Please, let it be this!

It pains me to hear of the way your family has been regarding you of late. If my mother were still alive, I suspect she'd share the same disappointment about me that yours does about you. And yet, we expect more of our sisters. This is why it's so hard. They blazed the trail in this wild world with us; they should be on our side. And yet why do they feel like the enemy? Why can't we find common ground? Take heart, at least Roberta is still speaking to you. Lucille has taken to ignoring my phone calls. The moment she hears my voice, she hangs up. Last week, I wrote her a letter. I poured out my heart to her. I even apologized for my education, the one she believed was owed to her. Truly, Brownie, I set my pride aside in the name of preserving our sisterhood, because I cannot imagine a world where one can regard her sister as a stranger. And so I wait, and hope.

I've been thinking about what you wrote about marriage, and I hate to disappoint you, but if Anthony Magnuson walked in today and told me he was divorcing his wife, Victoria, I'd leap into his arms and count the seconds until I could be his bride. And that's the honest truth.

Yes, I love this man, Brownie. I have fallen head over heels. I fear that I love him too much. But I can tell by the way he looks at me that he loves me too. Perhaps not as much as I love him, for he is a busy man with a complicated life. A family. But I don't care, I'll take even the tiniest corner of his heart. He still comes to the bookstore quite often. I told him my dream of owning my own children's bookstore and he said, "Why don't you just open one, then!" I had to break the news to him that not everyone has fortunes lying around at their disposal like the Magnusons do.

Last week, he asked me if I'd meet him for dinner downtown. Of course I said yes, even though the idea of us taking our friendship outside the bookstore frightened me a great deal. He sent a car over after my shift ended at six. I felt so funny sitting all alone in the back of that town car. The driver kept looking back at me in the rearview mirror. I wonder what he must have thought of me! But I didn't care, Brownie! I was on top of the world thinking of Anthony! When the car dropped me off in front of the Olympic Hotel, there he stood in his suit and tie. I felt so plain in my simple work dress. But Anthony told me I looked beautiful. But it wasn't what he said; it was how he *looked* at me.

We had dinner, and talked for hours. He told me about the time he nearly drowned as a child in Lake Washington, which is why he oversees a charity that teaches poor children to swim. I told him about my dream to see Paris, and read a book to children at the top of the Eiffel Tower. He smiled mischievously, and said, "Our children?"

I know he was only being playful, certainly not serious, but I must admit, my heart swelled then. The night was absolutely magical. I did worry momentarily, however, when a couple approached our table. They regarded me curiously. At first I worried that they were friends of his wife, and that they'd divulge our secret meeting. But Anthony didn't seem to worry at all, so I didn't.

Brownie, have you ever met someone you just feel at home with? That's how I feel when I'm with Anthony. I could curl up in his smile and sleep peacefully and protected for a thousand years.

It breaks my heart to know how unhappy Anthony is. He couldn't care less about wealth the way his wife does. Did you know that she goes to Europe every year and comes home with dozens of trunks of Chanel that she immediately casts off the next season? She won't even donate them. Anthony says she insists they all be destroyed. Apparently she finds it vulgar to think of another's skin touching fabric that touched hers. Can you even imagine that way of thinking?

I wonder why he stays? Of course, he worries for his daughter, May, though I must say the child seems to have the same disposition as his wife, surly and temperamental. I suspect it ultimately has to do with money. Victoria's fortune saved Anthony's father's real estate venture, and it also funds the Magnuson family's charitable efforts. If he left her, it could mean the end of all that.

I don't know what will become of us. Our friendship (if you could call it that?) remains uncharted, mapless. All I know is that I have never met a man like him. So I will continue on this strange and wonderful journey, wherever it leads me, even if the ending is destined to be an unhappy one.

I'm writing to you on a dark night in Seattle. It's quite late, and I'm sitting on the sofa of my apartment looking out at the moon pushing its way through a cloud. I've been thinking that you ought to write a children's book of verses about the moon. Think of it: No matter the circumstances of our lives, no matter our joys or heartaches, the moon always appears each night to greet us. I find that comforting somehow.

Oh Brownie, you said yourself that you need to get out of the city. Why don't you come to Seattle? Come visit! You can stay with me. It will be a hoot! Please come and let's cheer each other up. I'll make you laugh, and you can tell me a story, to tell me this life of mine will have a happy ending.

Write soon, please.

> Your friend,
> Ruby

I pull the grate over the fireplace and walk up the staircase to the apartment. I sink into the window seat and look out at the big sky, thinking about the words I have just read. They swirl around in my mind like the fizzy bubbles in a champagne glass. *Sisters.* Ruby valued her sister above all else, even her pride. I think about what she said: *I set my pride aside in the name of preserving our sisterhood, because I cannot imagine a world where one can regard her sister as a stranger. And so I wait, and hope.*

As far as I'm aware, Ruby did just that: waited and hoped, only to be greatly disappointed in the end. According to my mom, Ruby was stunned by Lucille's sudden death. Mom said that they hadn't spoken in years before she passed. I think of Ruby, hovering over Lucille's coffin—the coffin of a stranger, for all intents and purposes. A final good-bye. I close my eyes, and I picture Amy in the coffin instead of Lucille. I imagine myself at her funeral, and without my permission, my eyes flood with tears.

I take a deep breath and come to my senses. No, Ruby and Lucille's situation was not the same as Amy's and mine. I can't compare the two. Instead, I think about another significant revelation in the letters. Did my aunt really encourage Margaret Wise Brown to write a book about the *moon*? Is this what I think it is? The hair on my arms stands on end as I realize what I've just found, a literary discovery hidden for years inside the bookstore, inside Ruby's secretive mind. A treasure Ruby left me to unearth.

It's a clear night, and the moon outside dangles overhead like a painting made just for me. I think about what Ruby wrote about the moon, and think of all the times I gazed up at the night sky, dreaming of a different life.

I look down to the street when I hear the sound of a car engine. I watch as a dark SUV pulls up in front of the bookstore. It slows to a stop and a tinted window rolls down slowly. I see the flash of a camera, and then the vehicle speeds away.

Chapter 6

My cell phone is buzzing as I wake the next morning. It must be shortly after sunrise; the sun is low on the horizon and it streams in the window with such intensity, it pierces my eyes and feels wonderful and painful at the same time.

"Hello?" I say groggily.

"June?"

"Mom?"

"Where are you?" she asks. I hear an airplane taking off in the background and wonder if Mom and her new boyfriend, what's-his-name, are off on a trip somewhere.

"Where are *you*?" I ask, a little annoyed.

"Oh," she says, "Rand and I are at the airport. We're going to Vegas for a few days."

Rand. I'm not sure if this is his actual name, or maybe it's short for Randy or Randolph, or something like that. But I don't ask.

"Oh," I say. Mom and I don't have the best relationship (if you can even call it a relationship), but we do talk, in fits and spurts. She calls every couple of months, sends a card on my birthday and at Christmas. And that's enough for me, though I suspect she's less than satisfied with the arrangement. Still, I find I can handle her best in small doses. "Mom, I'm in Seattle."

"Seattle?" she asks. But this time, her usual carefree voice sounds concerned.

"Yes," I say.

"Are you at Ruby's?"

"I am."

"Oh, June," she says. "So you know—"

"That she died, yes."

"I wanted to tell you, sweetie, I really did, but I—"

"Just didn't think to mention it?" I don't even attempt to mask my annoyance.

"June, don't snap," she says. "I was going to tell you, I—"

"But you wanted to wait and let the attorney notify me?"

"The attorney?"

"Yes," I say. "I received a certified letter. Ruby left me the bookstore, everything."

"Wow," Mom says. I can't tell if she's upset or just surprised.

"I'm here now, sorting through her belongings before I decide what to do."

"Will you sell it?" she says. "June, you couldn't possibly—"

"I don't know, Mom. I mean, yes, I probably will. I can't stay here. I have a job, a life in New York." It isn't much of a life, but I don't have to explain that to Mom, especially when I'm trying to prove my point.

"I could help," she says, sounding suddenly desperate. "I think it needs to stay in the family. Amy does too."

I'm momentarily stunned, then I feel a surge of anger. I made Mom promise she wouldn't bring up my sister's name to me again. My cheeks burn. "What does she care about the bookstore?" I say.

"What right does she have to tell me what to do with it? It's my problem to solve."

"Honey, she loved Bluebird Books too, don't forget." Mom lowers her voice. "And she misses you terribly. You really should call her. She said she's tried calling you. Isn't it time to end this nonsense between you two? You're sisters."

I think of Ruby and Lucille, Margaret and Roberta. I want to feel the way they did about their sisters. But the only way I know I can is if I could find a way to turn back the clock, to erase the hurt, the pain I endured.

"No," I finally say. "Mom, I have nothing more to say to Amy. You know that."

"People change, June. I wish you'd see that."

"No," I say. "They don't."

Mom's quiet for a moment. "You did."

I'm stunned into silence.

"Sometimes I think I don't even know you anymore, June," she continues. "New York has changed you. It's hardened you."

I bite my lip. She doesn't have the right to talk to me this way, to talk as if she knows me, or ever knew me.

I hear a voice on the airport loudspeaker. "That's our flight," she says. "We're boarding. I'll be back in a few days. I'll come by."

I want to say, *Don't, I can handle it*, but I hold my tongue.

"Good-bye, Mom," I say instead. "Hope you win the jackpot." And then I hit the End Call button with more intensity than usual.

I feel anxious, the way I did when I left New York. I find the prescription bottle in my purse, swallow a pill, then pull open my laptop. For someone who habitually checks her e-mail every four minutes, I'm shocked when I realize how little I've thought about work since arriving in Seattle. I open my in-box and see that the messages have stacked up. There are several flagged with red, high-priority exclamation points, and I open the one at the top first. It's from Arthur. I feel a pit in my stomach as I read the one-line e-mail:

WHEN ARE YOU COMING BACK TO WORK?—A

The truth is, I purchased a one-way ticket because I didn't know how long it would take to put Ruby's affairs in order. I hoped to wrap things up quickly, maybe in a week, but now, a few days into my stay, everything's becoming more complex—Ruby's secrets, the future of the bookstore, my memories. I hit the Reply button and write back:

Busy working out final details here. Will know more by the weekend. Will keep you updated.—June

I hit Send, and as I do, I feel my blood pressure rising.

I reach for a jacket and slip into my running shoes. I walk out to the street and jog past Antonio's. The restaurant is dark and the chairs are still turned over on the tables. I look away quickly when I see my reflection in the window. I hoped to see Gavin, and somehow admitting this to myself makes me feel silly. As I make my way down to the path around the lake, I reaffirm my plan to move forward with the liquidation of Ruby's estate. I'll make a spreadsheet and categorize everything, the way I do when selling off assets for the bank. I'll hire the movers to load everything into trucks. I'll find a good auctioneer. I'll get it done.

After I've logged five miles around the lake, according to my Garmin, I slow for a cooldown walk, then stop on a bench to watch a mother duck and her ducklings push through the reeds and cross the banks of the lake to a spot on the dock ahead. The mother waddles proudly with her six fuzzy ducklings behind her. The last one is smaller than the rest, and he's having trouble keeping up. The mother and the larger ducklings have already made their way back to the lake as I watch the littlest one lose his bearings. He looks right, then left, as if he's not sure where to turn. He's lost. In that moment, I want to run over to him, scoop him into my arms, and carry him back to his mother. I rise to my feet and take a step forward, but with lightning speed, a large rat scurries out of the thicket and lifts the duckling into his mouth, and the two disappear in one dreadful swarm into the grasses beside the bank.

"No!" I scream. "No, you can't have him! You can't do that!" I feel helpless and horrified. At once, I am nine years old, hovering over an abandoned robin's nest beside Amy, fretting over the fate of the baby birds. I stare out at the bank for a long while, and then I realize I'm not the only one watching. The mother duck is watching too. She knows.

I think about that scene for a long time as I walk the final quarter mile up to the crosswalk. I think about the nest and the eggs, and the mother duck and her babies. There will always be rats and ducklings. There will always be predators and prey. And banks and small businesses in default. And people like me who swoop in like rats and take what's owed to them, or what they're hungry for. It's the circle of life, but at this moment, I don't like my place in it.

I'm red faced and my mind is reeling when I walk past Antonio's on the way back to the bookstore. I smell garlic cooking now, and I breathe in the comforting scent. The door is propped open a bit, so I know Gavin must be inside. I poke my head in cautiously. "Hello?" I say, taking a step inside.

"Hello?" I say again, admiring the rich red of the dining room walls and the dozen or so attractively set tables. There's a wooden slab counter that might accommodate six more guests, but all in all, the room is small and intimate, and I love it instantly.

A wood-fired oven burns slowly behind the counter, and I can smell the warm, smoky scent of cherrywood smoldering. There's a clanging sound in the kitchen, as if a pot's fallen to the floor, before the door swings open and Gavin appears. He smiles when our eyes meet. There's a smudge of tomato sauce on the white towel that hangs from his waist. "Hi," he says. "Sorry, have you been waiting long?"

"No, no," I say. "I was just walking back from a jog around the lake, and I thought I'd stop in and say hi."

"Hi," he says, still smiling.

He turns back to the kitchen when a timer beeps. "Come with me," he says. "I'll show you around."

I nod and follow him through the swinging door to the immaculate kitchen. It's a little larger than the dining room. On either side of a big stove is a bank of stainless steel countertops. At the center is a large, sturdy table with strong legs. It looks like something salvaged from an old Italian villa.

"It's gnocchi day," he says, pointing to the flour-dusted cutting board, where an impressive mound of orange-tinged dough lies at the center. "Have you ever had sweet-potato gnocchi?"

I shake my head. "No, but it sounds like heaven."

"Good," he says. "You can help me, and earn your lunch."

I grin and head to the sink to wash my hands, then return to the table, where Gavin shows me how to roll out the dough in long, snakelike lines. Next, we cut them into one-inch sections. He hands me a wooden tool called a gnocchi paddle, which is basically a flattened piece of grooved wood affixed to a stick. We roll the segments over the paddle and it gives the dough a pressed and finished look.

We set them on a sheet pan dusted with cornmeal, talking as we press more dough. It feels good to work with my hands, mindlessly. I'm overcome with a relaxing calm.

"Have you always liked to cook?" I ask, piling a batch of pressed gnocchi on the sheet pan.

"Yeah," he says. "I used to play restaurant with my sister and brother. I liked being the chef."

I smile. "But the real question is did you have an Easy-Bake Oven?"

He laughs. "No, but my younger sister did, and she'd never let me play with it." He smiles to himself as if recalling a funny childhood memory. "I'll confess that one night I snuck out of bed and took it out of her room. I stayed up baking chocolate brownies. But I think I managed mostly to eat the dough."

"Good choice," I say.

He smiles. "The truth is, I could never do anything else but work in a restaurant. I love the energy of it. Every night it's like a theater production. I thrive on the pageantry." He looks up from the dough at me. "You know, I never asked you what you do for a living—I mean, besides owning the bookstore, of course."

"Oh," I say, suddenly self-conscious. "My work's not very exciting."

"I'm sure that's not true," he says, waiting expectantly for me to divulge more.

"I work at a bank in New York," I say. "Finance. See? *Boring.*" I'd rather keep it brief than go into detail about the specifics of my job in banking. I've had enough experience chatting with people at parties to know that nobody finds my division of the bank at all charming, the same way undertakers don't draw smiles over cocktail conversation.

"Just the same," he says, grinning, "I'd love to hear how you got into finance. Was banking always something you were interested in?"

I finish the line of gnocchi I'm working on and venture a response. "If you mean did I used to play bank teller with my sister as kids, well, no. It was a career I sort of fell into."

"Do you love it?"

"I'm good at it," I reply.

"There's a big difference," Gavin adds.

"What do you mean?"

"Well, take me, for instance," he says. "Right out of college, I went to law school."

"Why?"

"Why does anyone go to law school?" he says. "For a girl."

"Oh." I give him a knowing smile. "Well, at least your heart was in the right place."

"That's the thing," he says, suddenly serious. "As far as my career went, it wasn't. I mean, I was good at law. Quite good. I made it through law school with flying colors. Graduated top of my class, and even got hired to practice at a big firm in Boston. I was good. I had a whole career ahead of me, but . . ." He shrugs, contemplating his next sentence.

"But what?" I ask, hanging on his every word. The thing is, I won't admit it to Gavin, but our life stories, at least where our careers are concerned, seem to parallel each other.

"My heart wasn't in it," he finally says. "I was good at the work, sure, but when I gave my life a long, hard look, I realized that I hated law. I hated it so much. It just wasn't me. It wasn't what I was born to do."

I nod, letting his words sink in.

"So I moved out here," he says. "My parents thought I was crazy. And maybe I was, a little. I mean, who gives up on a law degree and a huge salary just like that?" He rolls out another line of gnocchi, then turns back to me. "But I found my way. I worked in several restaurants before getting the courage up to open this place."

I nod. "And the girl?"

He looks confused for a moment, and then grins. "Oh, she left me the day I quit my job."

"Sounds like a peach."

"Oh, yes," he says, smiling. "She was a plum."

I return his smile. "And did you ever find . . . love again?"

He looks conflicted for a moment and he opens his mouth to speak, just as the back door to the kitchen opens. A pretty, dark-haired woman in gray Lululemon leggings and a black jacket bursts through the door carrying a big box of eggplant with deep purple, shiny skin. At first she doesn't notice me. "Gav!" she says from the doorway, balancing the box in her arms. It looks heavy. "You wouldn't believe how gorgeous the eggplant is at Pike Place this morning. I know I bought way too much, but can you blame me when they're this perfect?" She speaks to Gavin in a familiar tone, as if she might launch into the details of her doctor appointment a moment later.

He runs to her side and lifts the box from her arms, and I feel, suddenly, that I don't belong here. She has striking features: full lips, big brown eyes, and high cheekbones. She's about my age, maybe a little younger. I wonder if she's Italian. Her long, shiny dark hair is pulled back into a ponytail. She doesn't wear makeup. She's the type of woman who doesn't need to. A natural beauty.

"Oh," she says as soon as she sees me seated at the table. She turns back to Gavin as if I'm not there. "I didn't know you had company."

"Adrianna, this is June," he says. "Our new neighbor."

She scrunches her nose. "Neighbor?"

"Her aunt, Ruby, passed away recently and left June the bookstore."

Adrianna forces a smile. "Oh," she says. "I think Lillian said something about a new owner." She finally turns to me. "I'm really sorry about your loss."

"Thank you," I say, still stunned by her presence.

Gavin turns to me. "Lillian and her husband own the toy store across the street, Geppetto's."

"Yes," I say cheerfully. "I knew them as a child."

Adrianna busies herself with the eggplant. She stands at the sink and begins running each under the faucet. "So I hear you're selling the bookstore," she says to me. Her tone is friendly enough, but her words sting somehow.

I'm startled for a moment. I haven't told anyone about my intentions for the bookstore, and suddenly I feel on the defensive. What will Gavin think? "No," I say quickly. "I—"

Gavin leaps to my rescue. "You shouldn't listen to neighborhood gossip, Adrianna."

I smile, but I feel a pit in my stomach, wondering what the locals must be thinking about me. Did someone overhear my conversation with the moving company? Were they tipped off by my profession? And then my mind turns to Gavin and Adrianna, their past and present.

"It's OK," I say quickly, trying to defuse the tension in the room. And I realize I don't have any idea who Adrianna is. His girlfriend? His sister? Please let her be his sister. "So you're Gavin's—"

"Business partner," he says quickly before she can respond. "Adrianna and I co-own the restaurant."

I nod. I feel immediately foolish. They're either married or dating, or maybe it's more complicated than that. In any case, I have the keen sense that Adrianna isn't happy to have me in her kitchen. I stand up and brush the flour off my hands. "Thanks for the cooking lesson," I say to Gavin. "But I should get back to the shop. I have so much work to do."

He frowns. "But you haven't gotten to taste any of it."

Adrianna eyes the table, then turns back to the freshly washed eggplant that she's setting on top of a cutting board at her right.

"It's OK," I say. "Another time."

"All right," Gavin replies, disappointed. "Don't be a stranger."

I nod as I walk out the door to the dining room, and then back out to the street. I unlock the door of the bookstore, and I walk inside. *What just happened in there?* I decide to keep to myself from now on. It's always easier that way.

❦

I spend the day sorting through boxes of books, alternating between trying not to think of what Gavin talked about in the restaurant's kitchen and analyzing his every word.

I work through lunch, stopping at two to eat a stale bagel I picked up at the café the day before. I think of Arthur, and how impersonal our working relationship is. He knows nothing about me, and all I know about him is that he's married to his job (which is likely why his wife left him ten years ago). Do I want to end up like that?

At five, I've successfully cleared out nine boxes, when my stomach growls. I think about ordering pizza, or maybe taking a cab to the Whole Foods Market a few miles up the road. I walk upstairs to grab my purse, when I hear a knock downstairs. But when I make it down the staircase to the door, there's no one there, just a large paper bag on the doormat. I reach for it, then latch the door again. Inside is a steaming hot takeout container with my name on it, beside a bottle of Italian wine. There's slip of paper folded in half. *June, you have a lot on your plate, and on your mind. Gnocchi always brings comfort. Enjoy + sweet dreams.—Gavin*

I smile and sink into the wingback chair by the fire, then pull out the box of gnocchi. There's a cloth napkin wrapped around a knife and fork, and I eagerly take a bite, closing my eyes as I let the flavors swirl in my mouth. Food has never tasted so good, and I finish the gnocchi, then run upstairs and find a corkscrew in Ruby's little kitchen. I bring it down with a tumbler and pour myself a glass.

In that moment I think of my sister. I think of our first dinner in the apartment we shared briefly in New York. I was so happy that she'd come out to live with me. I was thirty and she was almost twenty-six. A job as an assistant at a fashion house lured her east initially, but she didn't end up staying in that job, or any other, long. Amy was always letting herself be lured by greener pastures, only to find that the grass there was just as mucky as in the last place. But on that night, it was a new beginning for her. Her future was filled with new potential. I remember her talking about becoming a fashion designer. I made enchiladas, and we shared a bottle of wine. Ryan joined us at nine thirty, when we were both giddy and happy. I close my eyes. *Ryan.*

I shake my head as if to dismiss the memory, and I think of Ruby again. I feel an urge to read more of her story, and Margaret's. In her last letter, Margaret wrote about a revelation she was about to share. What? I remember the mention of *Make Way for Ducklings*, and wonder if this could be the location of the next set of letters. I go to the shelf and find the book, but there are no envelopes inside. I scan the surrounding books, and there is only one copy.

I sit down, deflated, and decide to turn back to the other two books I found letters in. I flip through their pages. What's different about these books? They're old, yes, but there are many old books in the shop. Then I think to look at the copyright page of each, and remember how Ruby taught me to identify first editions. I see the telltale "1" on the number line in *The Poky Little Puppy*, and then turn to *The Tale of Peter Rabbit*, with its copyright date of 1901 and the words "First Printing." That's when I know. Ruby chose the first editions to leave her letters in. Just as I thought, she *has* left me a scavenger hunt.

My heart races as I begin searching for a first edition of *Make Way for Ducklings*. I know it must be here, somewhere. And then I think, if I were Ruby, where would I keep the first editions? I remember that I found *The Poky Little Puppy* high on the shelf, so I walk to the ladder and decide to look there. After an hour of searching, I almost give up, when I spot a green dust jacket poking out over some shorter books. I reach for it, and sure enough, there is a duck and her six ducklings on the cover. I think of the scene at the lake today, and I feel a surge of emotion. I open the spine, and there, just as Ruby left them, two letters are tucked inside.

I reach for the first, from Margaret, and climb down the ladder to the chair, where I read with anticipation.

March 27, 1946

Dear Ruby,

Mother came to visit again yesterday. She cast a disapproving glance at a copy of <u>Runaway Bunny</u> on the table and indicated (in so many words) that I ought to go back to university to finish my degree, become a teacher. It's what the "spinsters" of her generation would do, she said. I didn't tell her that I gave up teaching after that disastrous semester as a student teacher. (The best thing about that experience was gaining your friendship.)

While I did not truly believe Mother's words, I absorbed them, and they all but deflated me. They had power over me. I woke up today with no zeal for my work. Her sentiments plucked the spirit and creativity right from me.

That's what I must tell you: I've decided to set writing aside, at least for now. Not because Mother has won, but because I feel lost, and I'm afraid I can't find my way.

That, and the voices of my characters just . . . stopped. I can't hear them anymore, Ruby. All I hear is my own grating thoughts. Is there anything more horrid than being trapped inside yourself with nothing but your own insecurities?

No word from Roberta. I'm thinking about sending her flowers if I don't hear from her by the end of the week. You're right about sisters. We must take them as they are, even if they drive us mad.

Well, I must be off now. Crispian is gnawing at my pant leg. It's an hour past his usual afternoon walk. So I will walk, and I will consider my future.

Maybe I should become a dog walker?

Your lost friend,
Margaret

I shake my head. How could she write that about sisters? We must "take them as they are, even if they drive us mad"? It's a sentiment I can't subscribe to, even when I press my mind to try. In the end, there's still the pain so raw, it almost stings. What would Ruby and Margaret have done in my shoes? Would they have felt the same?

I turn to the next envelope, from Ruby, and I pull out the pages inside.

April 11, 1946

Dear Brownie,

Oh, I wept reading your words. It breaks my heart to see you in such distress. I want to reach through these pages and embrace you, my friend. I want to let you cry on my shoulder. I want to comfort you and encourage you to carry on. How can I convince you to ignore your mother's sentiments? How can I make you see that her world is not yours, just as yours is not hers?

Can you imagine yourself as a housewife, with a maid and a cook and a gaggle of children running about? You'd go mad! No, it isn't a husband you need, nor a "respectable" job. You must be free to pursue the work you so love doing, work at which you shine, I might add, brilliantly.

Family relationships are the most challenging, aren't they? I know this well. After weeks of the silent treatment, I showed up on Lucille's doorstep yesterday. Miraculously, she let me in. We made small talk over tea, but we're talking. For now. It's a good step forward. I may never be able to share certain parts of my life with her (my relationship with Anthony, for instance, which she'd disapprove of emphatically), and I've come to terms with that. It is not worth upsetting her. And by upsetting her, I would, in turn, only upset myself. We feel our families' judgments more keenly. Even if we disagree with their declarations. It is because we love them, or in the most general terms, because we come from them, that we wonder if their words, even the most inflammatory of them, might be true. We question ourselves. We may even forsake ourselves to prove them right.

I will do anything in my power to see that my sister and I don't become strangers. Because I fear that would be a failure I could never recover from or forgive myself for.

Now, back to this nonsense about you ceasing to write. Think of all the children of the world who might stop reading, children one, five, ten, twenty years from now who are destined to hold a copy of one of your future works in their hands and be dazzled by those stories. If you stop writing, they lose that chance.

I'm sure that if you wait, your characters will start whispering again. They're still there; they're just a little frightened. Give them room to come out again, and give yourself the quiet space to hear them.

Every life, every story, has peaks and valleys. You are walking through a low spot now. Perhaps it's foggy in the valley. And maybe you can't see the path anymore. But it's there. Keep walking on it. You'll find your way. And when you come through the thicket, with little rabbits hopping about, there will be a clearing, and the sun will be shining down on you with rays that will warm you and inspire you again.

What if Einstein had stopped inventing? What if Bach had stopped composing? What if Edison had given up on the lightbulb? What I'm trying to say is that what you do is beautiful and worthy to children of the world (young and old), and you must carry on. Please, promise me that you'll press on, keep trying?

And, I have a bit of lunar inspiration to share with you: I was reading a passage in a collection of folklore. Of course, in our culture, we refer to "the man in the moon," but according to Chinese legend, it is a rabbit that lives on the moon. I was looking out my window last night, and, Brownie, I saw it! There is a little rabbit with floppy white ears leaning over a mortar and pestle. I shall never look at the moon in the same way again.

Keep your chin up, and when you've lost your way, look at the moon and think of me, for I believe in you.

Yours,
Ruby

Chapter 7

The next morning, after a long gnocchi-induced sleep, I kneel down along the south wall and reshelve the picture books neatly, the way Ruby would have liked. And then I shake my head. What am I doing? If I'm going to sell the shop, I need to take the books *off* the shelves, not put them back. I sigh and stand up, right before I hear Ruby's jingle bells at the door.

"Did you like the gnocchi?" Gavin asks, poking his head inside the store. I smile, and try not to worry what Adrianna will think of his being here.

"Yes," I say, nodding. "Yes, thank you. I loved it. Honestly, I don't think I've ever tasted anything so heavenly."

Gavin takes a few steps toward me. "Comfort food at its finest," he says. He rubs his forehead. "Listen, I'm sorry about yesterday."

I play dumb. "What do you mean?"

He scratches his head in an adorable way. "The way Adrianna acted," he says. "I hope it didn't make you feel . . . uncomfortable."

"No," I lie. And then I think of Ruby, and the confidence in her letters gives me the strength to face my feelings head-on. "Actually, it did make me uncomfortable," I say. "Because I . . ."

He takes a step closer to me. The bookstore is quiet, and I can hear the dripping sink upstairs. "Because you like me?"

At first I feel annoyed, but his smile defuses me.

He tucks a strand of my hair behind my ear, and my neck explodes in goose bumps. "Well, I like *you*," he says. There's a moment of pause, and my stomach flutters.

"But Adrianna," I say. "I don't want to interfere if—"

"You're not interfering with anything," he assures me, pointing to the chairs by the fire. "Want to sit down? I'll tell you the whole story."

I stare at the flames as he speaks. I'm afraid to look at him, for fear of what he'll say. Their past could dictate our future. *Future.* I turn the word over in my mind and let it whisper, taunt. "We were engaged," he begins. I gulp, taking in his words. *Engaged.* "I met her in culinary school. She was studying to be a pastry chef. We hit it off right away. She's from a big Italian family. And I didn't know anyone out here. They welcomed me instantly. We spent all our time together and after two years, getting engaged just seemed like the natural progression of things. So I proposed." He sighs. "It's funny, when I asked her to marry me, I remember having this sort of out-of-body experience. It was like I was seeing the whole thing play out like a movie, not like it was actually happening to me. I watched this guy get down on one knee and ask this girl to marry him."

He shakes his head. "But I didn't feel what I was supposed to feel. I kept waiting to, expecting those feelings to develop. I told myself I'd wake up one morning and it would all feel right. And then we opened the restaurant, and our futures were even more cemented. We would be married and we would be business partners." He stares ahead solemnly. "But six months ago, I woke up in the middle of the night in a cold sweat. I had a dream of being married, being happy. I looked over at Adrianna asleep beside me, and

I knew I had to tell her. She's a wonderful person. But she isn't the person for me."

"Wow," I say, suddenly feeling a surge of sorrow for this woman who was so cold to me just yesterday. After all, I know what it feels like to love someone who can never truly return your love.

"So we called off the engagement," Gavin continues. "Because we had the restaurant together, we had to figure out a way to make things work. At first Adrianna took it really hard. I mean, I know it's still hard for her. But she's accepted it."

"You don't think she's just waiting and hoping that you'll change your mind?"

He shrugs. "I don't know."

"It has to be so difficult on her to work with you every day, hoping that you'll decide that you made a big mistake."

"Honestly, I just try not to think about that," he says. "I actually thought she was over everything until I saw the look on her face when she walked into the kitchen yesterday."

"It can't be very healthy to work together," I say. "Considering your past."

Gavin nods. "I worry about that every day. But we both love the restaurant. We love our work. I keep thinking that we can rise above it all."

"But it's not that easy," I say, thinking of Amy. The wound is still raw, even five years later. "When you go through something as painful as what Adrianna has experienced, you don't just bounce back. She can't just flip a switch and see you as a friend after loving you for so long. A woman's heart doesn't work like that."

He nods again, solemnly. "I've been patient. I haven't seen anyone else. I knew it would be too hard on her. But we'd had a great month. She told me she met someone at Joe's and they were going on a bike ride around the lake. I thought she had healed. And when

I met you," he says, searching my face, "I can't explain it. . . . I was drawn to you."

I smile and open my mouth to speak, but no words come out.

"I know this is a lot to take in," he says quickly. "I'm not asking you to make any big decisions. I'm just asking if I can . . . get to know you better. Can I?"

I nod. "Yes. Yes, you can."

"Good," he says, grinning. "Listen, we're having a big night tonight at the restaurant. The first Friday of every month, we have a jazz band in, and we do a new pasta dish. Why don't you come, be my guest? I mean, if you want to." He stands up and eyes the door. "Tonight, then."

I return his smile. "Tonight."

The door closes, and I wish Ruby were here now. I want to run to her and let out a girlish scream and share the type of innermost thoughts that she shared with Margaret Wise Brown. It's true; I've had few strong female friendships in my life, but I always had Ruby. I wonder if she's here listening. I wonder if she's watching me, cheering for me. And then I remember the last pair of letters, the mention of *Runaway Bunny*. I begin my search with anticipation, and then I locate a first edition high on a shelf across the room. The dust jacket is brittle and cracked. I open the spine, and there they are, two letters waiting for me.

April 26, 1946

Dear Ruby,

You are not only a bookseller but a healer. That hangover of mother love (if you could call it that) I told you about turned into the flu, but reading your pages was like medicine, for body and soul.

Thanks to your encouragement, I'm back to writing, and I must say, this idea of the rabbit in the moon is an intriguing one. You've stirred up all sorts of inspiration. I'm envisioning a little bunny child in a nursery. And on each page, there will be the moon. It's not so much a concept as it is a feeling right now, but it is growing on me. It may come to nothing, but I will be patient and listen to the characters, and when they start whispering, I shall be ready to write their words down. If it ever becomes a book, I would like to dedicate it to you, my friend.

As I suspected, the flowers worked. Tulips, to be exact. I ask you this: Can anyone continue holding a grudge in the face of yellow tulips? I think not. Roberta received them and phoned me straightaway. She apologized for being so overly sensitive (and if I may add, critical) at our last meeting, and while relations between us are tense at best, at least we're speaking again. In time, I hope she'll grow to accept me as I am. It's all I can hope for. After all, in both of us are the wonderful memories of childhood that we created together, always arm in arm. Gazing at the stars, skipping through the forested acres beside our home, dreaming of life beyond the picket fence. Adulthood has suppressed those memories for her, I believe, but I think I can resurrect them in time. I think I can make her remember. And in turn, I think I can make her remember that beneath these adult bodies with their adult habits and preoccupations, we are still those same little girls.

You briefly mentioned Anthony in your last letter. I must admit, I'd hoped you'd write more. I have been worried about this relationship of yours. I know you are wildly in love with this man, but I must admit that I fear he will break your heart. It seems odd for me, someone so uncustomary, a rule breaker, to give such practical advice. But friends must be practical for each other, especially when we won't be practical for ourselves. So, I hope you will write me more about this man. In the end, if you trust him, I will too. But I do fear that going down the path of this love affair will only leave you with an irreparably broken heart. (And I've been down that path so many times, I'd be negligent for not mentioning it.) Promise me that you will protect yourself from such heartbreak?

I suppose my mood may be tinged with my own personal concerns. My doctor found a tumor in my left breast. I will need to undergo surgery next week, and then, well, I don't know what. Don't worry. I'll be fine. At least I'm writing again. And dreaming. And smiling, most of the time. That's all that really matters.

To lighten my spirits, the members of the Bird Brain Society hosted a Mad Hatter party last week. We all wore the most outrageous hats and had tea and crumpets and laughed until we hadn't an ounce of laughter left in any of us. That was nice.

Sometimes I fear we take ourselves too seriously. I looked at myself in the mirror the other day, and I saw my mother staring back. Wasn't it just yesterday that I was eleven years old in pigtails? I'm still her, of course—the girl in pigtails. I just have to remind myself that she's still living in this aging body of mine. I'll be damned if I lose touch with my inner child. It is my deepest fear, you know—that and being deemed utterly unlovable.

I shall be looking to the mailbox daily for your next letter, so write soon, my dear friend.

> With lots of love
> from New York City,
> Brownie

P.S. Today I received a telegram from one of my publishers addressed to "Miss Margaret Wise Brows." I'm thinking that this is a much better name for a children's book author.

April 29, 1946

Dear Margaret "Wise Brows,"

(Ha!) That is quite a typo. Tell me truly, how are you feeling? I cannot bear to think of you ill. I pray that this letter finds you resting and recovering from your surgery. Does the doctor worry that it's serious? Has the tumor spread? Oh, what you must be enduring at this moment.

I wish I could be there to nurse you back to health, but your muse has not forsaken you. You are writing again! Stories are the air you breathe, and that air is laden with sustenance and spirit.

And such a brilliant strategy to send tulips. I concur, they are the happiest of flowers. It is truly impossible to hold a grudge in their presence. I think I shall try this with Lucille. Wish me luck. And on that note, what you wrote about sharing childhood memories with your sister made me think of my own, specifically the time Lucille and I packed up our knapsacks and "ran away" for the day. We made it a few miles down a dusty road and spent our last coins on chewing gum before our father found us climbing a tree in someone's yard and brought us home. You know I saved the chewing gum wrapper from that expedition? I still have it in my jewelry box after all these years. It symbolizes my first adventure in the world, and I shared that with Lucille. I wonder if she even remembers?

I have some big news to share with you, and I must admit, I've been holding out on telling you. I know you're concerned about Anthony, as any good friend must be, and despite all the warning signs you see, and despite my better judgment, I have fallen head over heels.

And, I almost don't know how to tell you this. I'm giddy with excitement. You know how I've always dreamed of owning my own bookstore, a children's bookstore, specifically? Well, Anthony offered to buy me one of my very own. This turn of events is most unexpected, and I must admit, I'm still getting used to the idea, but it is true. He found space in a terrific brick building near Green Lake, with a darling apartment on the second floor. He wants to outfit it with furniture and books (my first order shall be to Doubleday, for a box of your latest release, The Little Island!). And guess what? I accepted.

I know what you must be thinking, but I assure you, Anthony's intentions are only to make me happy. He is the kindest man I know. He told me he loved me, and that this was his way of showing it. He said there are no strings attached and that if I decide to end our relationship, I may go on running the store (my name is on the deed).

I'm going to call the place Bluebird Books. What do you think? Oh Brownie, I can't wait for you to see it! It has a fireplace on the first floor (and radiator heating, of course, but the fireplace is a nice touch), high ceilings for lots of bookshelves (Anthony's bringing in a carpenter to install ladders on wheels so I can reach books on the top shelves), and big cheerful windows. Oh, and the upper-floor apartment is lovely. I'll need to learn to cook so I can make Anthony dinner.

Can you feel my happiness beaming off the page?

I'll write more soon and will think constantly of you and your health.

With love from Seattle,
Ruby

I smile when I think of Ruby keeping that gum wrapper all those years, and I instinctively open the little wooden box on the nightstand in search of it. I sift through a heap of jewelry—rings, bracelets, and necklaces with their chains snarled together—and then I see a bit of wax paper toward the back. I pull it out and press it to my nose. The scent of bubblegum has long since worn off, but its spirit has not. The memory of Ruby and Lucille's great adventure lives on. I can almost hear their girlhood voices giggling as they run along the dusty road swinging their arms gleefully as they go.

I laugh to myself, remembering the time Amy and I pulled the cases off our pillows and tied them to sticks (something we saw in an episode of *The Smurfs*), then packed them with all the essentials—stuffed animals, Amy's beloved blanket, a few picture books—and set out to the sidewalk, where we planned to run away. And we did. We roamed the neighborhood until after dark, when we were both so hungry, we considered climbing a tree to pick apples (my idea). In the end, we just went home. Nobody came looking for us like in the TV shows. And isn't that why kids run away, anyway? So their parents will come searching for them with open arms and a never-ending stream of I-love-yous? Yes, but Amy and I just walked in the door to a dark house, with sad hearts and empty bellies.

The memory of Amy haunts me. And maybe it always will. Maybe I'll just have to be OK with that.

There's something else haunting me too: the mysterious man in my aunt's past. I pull out my laptop and plop down on Ruby's bed. I key the name Anthony Magnuson into Google, and thousands of results come back. A *Seattle Times* obituary dated December 9, 1974, is the first link I click on:

ANTHONY MAGNUSON REMEMBERED
FOR HIS CHARITABLE LIFE

Seattle mourns the loss of Anthony Magnuson. He died Tuesday at Swedish Hospital from injuries he sustained in an ice skating accident at Green Lake. He was 62.

Magnuson is remembered for his work for the Magnuson Charitable Foundation, which his father founded a century ago. He is survived by his wife, Victoria, and his daughter, May. Magnuson's will stated that he did not want a funeral. Remembrances may be sent to the Magnuson Charitable Foundation.

I do a search for the Magnuson Charitable Foundation and click on a link that takes me to its website. The bios in the About Us tab identify Victoria Gerhardt Magnuson, wife of Anthony, as emeritus fellow, and their daughter, May Magnuson, as executive director. I click on the embedded e-mail address and draft a note:

Dear May,

My name is June Andersen. My aunt, Ruby, recently passed away, leaving me her business, Bluebird Books. I am writing because I came across some letters that indicate that your father and my aunt may have been close at one time. This chapter in my aunt's life is unknown to me. I apologize if I've stirred up any unpleasant memories from the past. I'm staying at the bookstore now while I sort through her estate. If you have a moment to talk, I'd be grateful.

Very best wishes,
June Andersen

After I send the e-mail, I scroll through my in-box to find a dozen or more e-mails from Arthur. He's fuming, as evidenced by his excessive use of exclamation points and all caps. He wants to know where I am and when I will be returning to work. Overcome with guilt—and maybe fear, I'm not sure—I hit the Reply button and with tingly fingers I type:

Arthur, so sorry for my delay. I've been consumed in matters
of my aunt's estate. I hate to say this, but I need more time
before I can return to the city. I thought I could wrap things
up in a week, but it's not looking likely. Please bear with me.
I'll keep you posted. —June

I'm overcome with a panicky flutter in my stomach when I consider the very real possibility that my employment is on the line. If I
lose my job, I lose all that I am. And I can't do that. No, I have to
speed up the process of liquidating the shop. I decide to start with
the attorney to get a sense of the financial health of my aunt's estate.
Is the bookstore mortgaged? Is there any outstanding debt? I'll
need these answers before approaching a developer. The attorney
has all the pertinent information recorded for me; I'll just need to
request it in an e-mail, which I do immediately.

After I've sent the message, I close my laptop and take one of
my pills. I lean back on Ruby's bed, close my eyes, and lie still until
my heartbeat stabilizes again and I consider my predicament with
Bluebird Books.

Uncertainty is weakness, or so Arthur always says. But maybe
he's wrong. Maybe uncertainty is simply *human*. I consider each sce-
nario carefully. There's my life in New York. A sure thing. I get up
in the morning, I go to work, I kick butt at my job, and for that I'm
paid well. But life here in Seattle? It's less sure. In fact, it's risky.
Didn't I just read a *Wall Street Journal* article about the forthcoming
doomsday for booksellers? Even if I do try to save Bluebird Books,
even if I put every drop of my blood, sweat, and tears into it, it
might still fail. I nod to myself. From a business perspective, it's like
the underperforming stock you know you shouldn't put more
money into. All the analysts say sell. So why can't I get rid of that
quiet voice inside that says buy?

I let out an exhausted sigh and close my eyes again, and when sleep comes, I don't fight it. I dream of a garden where books grow on trees, and Ruby is there, rocking in her chair, smiling at me as Gavin and I read. I see Amy, too, skipping across the garden on the arm of that doctor from the ER in New York, and the happiness fades.

I open my eyes, disoriented. How long have I slept? The sunlight is fading, and I look at the clock: It's nearly five, and I remember the dinner at Antonio's. I dress quickly, selecting a black pencil skirt and tights and a red sweater. I pull my hair back into a tidy ponytail, then slip into a pair of suede heeled booties. I don't know what to expect tonight, only that I'm showing up, and trusting Gavin.

I step out to the sidewalk, and I can hear jazz notes beckoning a couple about my age into the entrance to Antonio's. My heart flutters for a moment. What am I doing? I take a deep breath and walk to the restaurant, placing my hand on the doorknob. Through the glass door, I see Gavin in a crisp white shirt, with an apron tied around his waist. As he crosses the dining room to greet an older couple, he notices me standing outside. His eyes meet mine, and he rushes to the door.

"Right this way," he says cheekily, holding it ajar.

I smile and walk inside. A three-piece band is wedged into a corner. They play their instruments softly, and the melody seeps through the air, mixing with the aroma coming from the kitchen. I breathe it all in.

"I'm glad you're here," Gavin continues. "We're short staffed."

"Oh?"

He nods. "Adrianna has the flu, and one of our servers had to fly to California this afternoon for a family emergency." He hands me an apron. "Can you wait tables?"

"Wait . . . tables?" I shake my head. "I've never—"

"It's not rocket science," he says. "Just ask them what they'd like, bring out the food, then check on them every now and then." He doesn't wait for my response before handing me a little notepad and pen. His eyes are pleading, sincere. "Thanks," he continues, before I can respond. "I owe you, *big time*."

A moment later, he disappears behind the swinging door that leads to the kitchen. I turn to face the restaurant guests, and the clarinet player, an older man with a kind face, gives me a knowing smile.

I can do this, I tell myself as I tie the apron around my waist. I take a calming breath, then walk to the nearest table. "Good evening," I say. "I'm going to be running the dining room this evening for Gavin. May I bring you something to drink?"

❦

At half past ten, I've brought out the last order of tiramisu, when Gavin flips the sign in the door to CLOSED. I'm wiping the counter as the final guests file out the door, one a bit tipsy from too much wine. I watch as she trips on the sidewalk; her date catches her arm.

My feet are killing me, so I slip off my boots and collapse into a stool at the counter. Gavin leans over the counter beside me. "You were amazing tonight," he says. "May I hire you?"

I smile. "Well, I don't know if I'd say I was amazing. I'm sorry about the ravioli incident."

He laughs, recalling the plate I dropped on the dining room floor. "It's why we don't have carpet. Easy cleanup."

"Well, thanks for not firing me," I say.

"Are you hungry?"

"I'm starved. Nothing like waiting tables all evening to work up an appetite. I think I may have drooled a little when the guy at the corner table ordered the puttanesca."

As I untie my apron, he turns to the stereo system behind the bar and flips it on. Soft guitar music seeps through the speakers as he reaches for a wine bottle high on the shelf. He uncorks it with precision and selects two wineglasses, filling each halfway.

"To new beginnings," he says, holding his glass out to mine.

"To new beginnings," I reply.

"Come on," he says, taking my hand. "Now I get to cook for you."

I slip my shoes back on and follow him into the kitchen. The lights are dimmed, and the space has a different, more intimate feel than it did before. Gavin selects a pan hanging on the wall and drizzles olive oil inside before adjusting the flame on the stove. "This," he says, pointing to the pan, "is what I cook for someone who's grappling with a big decision."

I shake my head. "What do you mean? I—"

"You've just inherited a bookstore thousands of miles away from your home and work—of course you're going to be making decisions. Huge decisions." I watch the gas flame on the stove flicker as he adds garlic, then gives the pan a little shake. The basil goes in next, and then a heaping pile of chopped tomatoes. "Pasta arrabiata always helps." He mixes in a generous sprinkle of red chili flakes. "It's the spice that gives you clarity."

"I wish it were that easy," I say, smiling.

"It is," he says, letting the sauce simmer as he takes a seat beside me at the table. A moment later, he tops off our wineglasses, then turns to me again. "Tell me more about you."

"What do you want to know?" I ask a little cautiously.

"Well, I know that you grew up here, and that you left and pretty much never came back. Why?"

"Would you believe me if I said it was the rain?"

"No," he says with a smile. "I've lived here long enough to know that Seattleites aren't scared off by the rain. Affinity for moisture is in your blood."

"You're right," I say. "We also don't use umbrellas."

"I know!" he says, grinning. "What's with that? It can be a flash flood, and no one even bothers with them. And what's the deal with all the flip-flops—in January!"

I smile slyly, then shrug. "What can I say? We're an unusual bunch."

"So, what was the real reason? Why did you leave?"

I look away from him for a moment. "For the same reasons anyone leaves their home, I guess. I wanted to prove myself."

"Prove what?"

"I had a fight with my mother about that," I say. "She could never understand me. We're so different; always have been. I didn't want to grow up to be like her. She was someone who viewed work as an obligation, a burden, which I know now was because she never found her passion in life. It's hard to feel passionate about a job at the grocery store."

Gavin nods. "Unless you *love* your work at the grocery store."

"True," I say. "But she didn't love her work. She never did."

"So you wanted to find your calling?"

"Yes and no," I say. "I'd always thought I'd stay in Seattle, and help Ruby with the bookstore. In fact, as a child, that's all I wanted to do. But after the drama with my mom, I felt I needed to leave to find myself. Does that make sense?"

"Oh yes," he says. "I know this story all too well."

I nod. "So I decided to go as far away as I could. Ruby attended college on the East Coast, so I applied to some schools, and eventually settled on New York University. Along with my acceptance letter from the admissions office was an award of a full scholarship."

"Wow, you must have earned really good grades in high school, then."

I shake my head. "No. I mean, they were good. A's and B's, but I didn't have a 4.0. Not even close. The reason for the scholarship was never fully explained beyond that it came from one of the school's anonymous donors who wanted to recognize my merit as a student from a low-income home in Seattle. But I was grateful for the opportunity, grateful for it every day. Because of that scholarship, I got my degree in finance."

Gavin looks confused. "So why'd you pick finance?"

I sigh. "In my junior year, I had to choose a major, and I remember scanning the list of options, and I thought to myself, 'Finance, money. Yes. I'll learn about money so I'll never have to be poor again.' As it happened, I was good at managing money. And it all turned out all right."

Gavin doesn't look convinced. "Did it?"

"Sure," I say a little defensively.

"What did Ruby think of your leaving?"

My heart sinks when I remember the last time I visited Blue-bird Books. There were tears in her eyes, though she tried not to let me see them. "She didn't like to see me go, but she supported my decision. I don't know how to describe it other than to say that she got it. She understood. My mom? Not so much. She said I was a fool to traipse across the country to a fancy college in a fancy city. She said I'd be home within the year, and that if I wanted a better life, I'd be better off looking for a rich man."

Gavin's eyes are kind and tender, and somehow, even though this subject still hurts, he makes me want to open up.

My lip trembles a little. Even after all these years, the memory still stings.

"Don't you see?" he says, taking my hands in his. "Your mom's comments weren't about you. They were about herself. They grew out of her own disappointments about life. It's a terrible thing adults do; they color their children's lives in the same way they've shaded their own."

I bite my lip. I hear Gavin's words, and yet there's a seventeen-year-old girl in me who still has trouble believing them, believing she is worth it.

"When I left my job at the law firm, I went home for a few weeks, before I sorted out my application to culinary school," he says. "My dad took me out fishing, and I'll never forget the way he looked over at me and said I was a fool for giving up on law. He said that as a man, he'd lost respect for me. I was stunned. And then he made some joke. He just sat there with his fishing pole, carrying on as if he hadn't just completely pulled the rug out from under me." He sighs, and takes another sip of his wine. "It hurt. But then I remembered that my dad's dad probably had this same talk with him. History repeats itself, and if we don't fight against it, we'll do the same things our parents do. We expect the same things from our children that our parents expected from us. And when we're cornered or confused or scared, I think we dip back into that old familial thinking. The important thing is to remember that we can break out of those old molds. You know?"

"It's what you did, didn't you?"

"I did," he says. "But it wasn't easy. For years, I kept hearing my father's words in my head. They were always there. *You're a fool. A disgrace. I've lost respect for you.*"

"What stopped it?" I ask.

"My mom came out to visit, see the restaurant," he says. "She told me it was wonderful to see a man who loved his work after watching my father hate his throughout their entire marriage. That was news to me. My father worked for a large corporation. He worked his way up to vice president. You should have seen his desk. It was covered with service excellence awards. I thought he loved what he did. But then I realized that he didn't. At all. I forgave my dad that day. And I moved on." Gavin weaves his fingers through mine. "I think the important thing to remember is that your mom's preconceived ideas about life have no bearing on your own. We're each given one life, and it's our job to make it useful, beautiful, and fulfilling. There is no value in suffering through it, doing something we hate. There's no prize at the end for that kind of endurance. Just a spent life."

I wipe away a tear. "That's exactly what I'm doing. And I'm miserable."

"At the bank?"

I nod.

"Then leave it in your past," he says. "Start over. It's never too late to start over, to create the life you deserve."

"I don't know if I can," I say.

Gavin leans in to me, and whispers in my ear, "I know you can." He stands up then and returns to the stove, and with a flick of his wrist, tosses the sauce in the pan, then drains a boiling pot of pasta into a colander over the sink. "And this will help." He pulls two white bowls from the shelf and piles them high with wide pappardelle before spooning sauce over the top. He finishes with a generous amount of Parmesan cheese. It falls from the grater like snow, and when he sets the bowl in front of me at the table, fresh tears are in my eyes, and I'm not sure if I'm crying because I can't remember the last time anyone has cooked for me or if it's because I feel, for the first time in a very long time, well, *happy*.

"Dig in," Gavin says, handing me a fork.

"This," I say, "looks amazing. Arrabiata." I pause, letting the word sink in. "Yes." I take another bite.

We eat in silence until our bowls are empty and our bellies are full.

I haven't had feelings for someone since Ryan, and for a moment, that frightens me. I vowed never to be vulnerable with a man again after the way that relationship ended so badly. But this feels different, somehow. I think of what Ruby wrote about her Anthony, that she could crawl into his smile and sleep for a thousand years. And in this moment, I understand what she meant. Yes, I barely know Gavin, but all I want to do is know him. *More.* And more and more. When our eyes meet, I feel drawn to him. He's like a powerful magnet; his pull is too strong to resist. He cradles my face in his hands, then coaxes my mouth to his. I feel light and airy, like I might float away. I don't hear the kitchen door swing open in the background, not right away. But then Gavin pulls back abruptly, and we both look over to see Adrianna, staring at us. There's a distinct look of hurt on her face.

"I'm sorry," she says, shaking her head. "I didn't know . . . I didn't—"

Gavin takes a step back from me, and I try to make sense of the look on his face. Guilt? Regret? Worry? Something else?

Adrianna's wearing sweats. Her cheeks are pale. "My fever came down, so I, uh, just thought I'd stop in and see how the night went. And, well, I wanted to talk to you about something." She turns to the door. "But I see you're busy, so . . . it can wait."

"No," Gavin says, concerned. "What is it?"

Adrianna looks at me, then back at Gavin.

My mouth falls open as she pushes through the door to the dining room. Gavin runs after her. "Adrianna," he cries. "Please, don't . . ."

I feel foolish, embarrassed. And in their heated exchange, neither notices when I slip through the swinging door, collect my purse, and leave through the back door to the alley.

I try not to think about Gavin as I slide my key into the back door to the bookstore and then run up the back stairs. And when I hear a faint knock on the door downstairs a half hour later, I don't answer it.

Chapter 8

It's after eight when I open my eyes the next morning. Last night was beautiful and awful at the same time. My left arm hurts from holding heavy trays of food at Antonio's, and my heart hurts too. I can't ignore the dull ache inside when I think about the look on Gavin's face when Adrianna walked into the kitchen. We had shared a beautiful moment, but it slipped away. I'm not sure if I'm strong enough to wade through the murkiness of this complicated relationship. No matter what Gavin says, he and Adrianna still have unfinished business. That was written all over her face.

My phone rings a moment later. I don't recognize the number, and I pick it up cautiously. "Hello?"

"June?" I know her voice instantly, and it paralyzes me. "June, you picked up. I've been trying to call you for so long. Mom says you're in Seattle."

Amy's voice is nervous, hopeful.

"June," she says, speaking to me as if I'm standing on the railing of a bridge and liable to jump at any moment, except we both know it's the End Call button she's most concerned about. "June, don't hang up. Please forgive me, for everything. There's something I need to—"

"Amy, it's too late for that," I say, pulling the phone away from my ear. I stare at it for a moment. I think of Ruby and Margaret and their sisters. I think of the ways they kept trying. *Could I? Should I?* I shake my head and hit the End Call button quickly, before I can reconsider. I don't want to hear her apologies, or anything else. It doesn't matter. Her words can't change the past. If my work has taught me anything, it's to move forward decisively. I made my decision about Amy years ago, and there's no going back.

I sigh, and as much as I don't want to think about Amy, my mind goes there anyway. Her voice has caused all sorts of memories and emotions to rise to the surface. And at once, I am ten. Amy is six. We're at the bookstore. Ruby's upstairs making sandwiches, and Amy and I are playing a game of Old Maid on the floor. I cheat and let her win, as I always do, and then I praise her card-playing skills.

"June?" she asks. "What's an old maid?"

I scrunch my nose and think for a moment. "An old lady who doesn't get married, I guess."

"Like Ruby?" Amy asks.

"No," I reply. Even though Ruby never got married, I'd never think of her as an old maid. I think of her life as carefully planned. If she wanted to get married, she would have. "No," I say again. "Ruby's not an old maid, in the same way Mom isn't an old maid."

Amy nods. "Mom has lots of boyfriends."

It's true, there is no shortage of men in Mom's life, and yet, none of them ever stay. Amy's father left when she was two weeks old, Mom said—and mine? Well, I asked her once and she frowned and said something vague like, "He didn't want to be a father."

"I wonder why Ruby never got married?" Amy asks curiously.

I shrug. "Maybe she didn't *want* to. Not everyone wants the same things."

"Well," Amy continues, reaching for the doll beside her, "when

I grow up, I'm going to marry a handsome prince and live in a castle."

Amy and I suddenly notice a customer standing over us. A young woman. She has shoulder-length dark hair that's swept back with a headband.

She kneels beside Amy. "My mother grew up to marry a man that was as wonderful as a prince. They lived in a house that looked like a castle."

Amy beams at the woman, but I don't trust her. She addresses us with familiarity, but we don't know her. I remember something Ruby said once to me: "If anyone comes into the bookstore and asks you to leave with them, do not go. Come find me immediately." It frightened me at first, but I'd recently seen a story on the TV news about a little girl taken from her home by masked men, and I figured that my aunt was probably just protecting us from kidnappers.

"Did she live happily ever after?" Amy asks eagerly. "Your mama?"

The woman eyes me carefully before turning back to Amy. "No," she says. "No, someone ruined her fairy tale."

The woman hands me an envelope. "Can you give this to Ruby?"

"OK," I say cautiously.

I hear Ruby's feet on the stairs. The woman rushes to a car waiting on the street before Ruby can get a glimpse of her.

"Who were you talking to?" she asks.

I shake my head. "I don't know, but she asked me to give you this."

Ruby takes the envelope and tucks it into the drawer of her desk. She doesn't speak of the incident again.

A chime sounds from my laptop, jarring me back to the present. I see a new e-mail from May Magnuson, Victoria Magnuson's daughter, and I open it quickly.

Dear June,

I'd like to speak to you, but we must do so in person. I'm
traveling in Europe now, but will be back in a few days.
Would you like to come to my home on Queen Anne?
Contact my assistant, Kerry (copied here), for directions.
There are a great many things we need to discuss.

Best, May

I don't know what to make of the e-mail, but I immediately
send a note back suggesting a meeting Tuesday and inquire about
directions.

Later I go for a jog around the lake, but circle around on the
side street to avoid passing Antonio's. I don't want to face Gavin, or
Adrianna. Not yet. I don't know if I have the heart to insert myself
into their story. *Their* story. I shudder. How silly I was to think it
was Gavin's and mine.

It takes me a little while to find the first edition of *The Little
Island*, but when I do, the letters are there, waiting for me.

May 9, 1946

Dear Ruby,

I am feeling better, thank you. After two weeks of being an
invalid, I am out walking again. I can use my left arm, too, which
comes in handy more than you'd ever expect (try tying your left
hand behind your back for an hour, and you'll experience my
personal misery!). It amazes me how much we long for something
we previously did not appreciate when it is gone.

Roberta and I went to the zoo! I admit to employing a bit
of trickery to get her there. (I'm calling all of this Operation

Sisterhood, I should add, and I'm having a great deal of fun coming up with ways to melt the ice between us.) We were walking along Sixtieth, and I suggested we take a shortcut to the café where she thought we'd be dining. And voilà, the entrance to the zoo just happened to be on the next block. I coaxed her into coming in with me, and you know, we ended up having a marvelous time. Side note: Just like it is impossible to feel grumpy with someone in the face of yellow tulips, it is also true of monkeys. I implore you to take Lucille to the zoo and have a heart-to-heart in front of the monkey cage. Just try it!

And now, on to the matter of this bookstore. Your bookstore! I must say, I am flabbergasted, if not wildly happy for you. My only regret is that I didn't wire you the funds to open the shop before Anthony did. I do hate the idea of this man being so intertwined with your life and work; though, as you say, you do love him. And I need to trust you on this count.

It is difficult for me to trust men, especially men I am feeling romantic toward. I seem to have such abysmal judgment when it comes to reading their character. When I feel they are being honest, true, it usually turns out that they are not. For instance, Bill Gaston, a man I fell truly, madly, deeply in love with in Vinalhaven last summer, turned out to be married. When he left his wife, I thought it might be for me. But by the time I returned to the island the next season, he'd moved on to someone else, who, I might add, is about half my age.

I suppose the consolation prize I received was a long-standing love of Vinalhaven—and all of the Fox Islands area, for that matter. It's hard to understand exactly why I am enamored with this place. The climate is harsh (and I often think of myself as the young Marguerite in Calico Bush as I tend to the grounds). And the locals, mostly lobster fishermen and a few retired quarry workers (the area once supplied granite to most of the post offices in the country), think of me as quite an eccentric. Nevertheless, I've just purchased my first, and only, house here. For that reason, I have taken to calling it the Only House, as I have no interest in owning multiple dwellings. No matter how much wealth I accumulate, I abhor the idea of collecting homes like pieces of jewelry. I shall only have one home, and for me, it's a simple cottage with small rooms and no modern utilities. My "boudoir" is outside in the back, where I've set up a pitcher for fresh water, a mirror, and an assortment of French milled soaps. I keep my butter and eggs in the well, where the ground temperature chills them, and, for convenience, I bury my wine bottles in the banks of the nearby rivers (you should have seen the look on my friends' faces when we went out for a walk and stopped at the riverbank, where I pulled out a perfectly chilled bottle of chardonnay).

Sometimes I think of my life as a great big story. Each silly thing I do is a new paragraph. And each morning I turn to the next chapter. It's fun to think of life that way, each day being an adventure of the grandest proportions. If I can give you any advice, my dear, and I am unworthy, at best, to be doling out such wisdom, I might just say this: Whenever you're down on your luck, and when things aren't going the way you like, remember that you are the author of your own story. You can write it any way you like, with anyone you choose. And it can be a beautiful story or a sad and tragic one. You get to pick.

Every time I see my story tinged with unfortunate events, even when such unfortunate events seem to simply happen to me, I remember that I am ultimately the author of my life. My dear friend, in many ways, you've helped me see that I can end a bad chapter early. I can start a new one. I can write myself a fur coat, and a lovely little hotel room in Paris with a view of the Seine.

And so can you. Just remember, all right? We are both au-thoresses.

Well, I am rambling on when I intended on packing this letter with all the important questions of your new venture, most important: May I come to do a book signing? It cheers me to think of paying you a visit, opening a bottle of cham-pagne after the store closes (or perhaps before?), and toasting your good fortune.

Remember: monkeys.

> With love,
> MWB

> May 15, 1946

Dear Brownie,

It cheers me greatly to know that you are on the mend. I can't imagine not using one of my arms, just as I cannot imagine a world without you in it.

Monkeys! Oh, you are genius, indeed. I'm already dream-ing up an Operation Sisterhood of my very own. I fear that things between us are more far gone than the troubles you describe with Roberta, but I do think it's worth a go. If I could just get her to laugh more, to see me as she used to, to trust me again. I've never stopped loving her, and I suspect she feels the same about me. I just need to excavate those feelings. And the zoo sounds like the ideal place to do it. Come to think of it, I have a neighborhood friend who runs the pri-mate cages at the Woodland Park Zoo here in Seattle. I won-der if he could arrange a private viewing?

Life in Seattle is well, very well. Though we will never marry, Anthony and I feel like a couple of newlyweds. It's silly, I know, carrying on this way about a man who will never be my husband. But we share a bond, a love, that may not be matrimonial, but it is beautiful and, I feel, everlasting.

Anthony comes over every evening for supper. I cook for him in the little apartment over the bookshop. Last night I made trout and deviled eggs. I'm not much of a cook, but I'm trying, and Anthony is a dear. He'll eat anything I make, even the horrible Swiss chard casserole I baked last week (or, more accurately, "Swiss *charred* casserole").

I love our evenings together. We read by the fire, or we'll shelve the books that have just come in. I can't reach up to the top shelves, so he tucks them away (at least, until the new rolling ladders are installed next week).

When the clock strikes eight, though, our little world crumbles. He hasn't stayed over yet, though I wish he would. He always goes home to Victoria.

I try to be understanding. I try to trust him, believe in him. And I do. Especially last night when he took me into his arms in the doorway of the shop and said, "You are the only woman I love, and the only woman I will ever love." But it never gets easy seeing him walk out the door. And I always watch with tears in my eyes. Each night, he leaves our world to go to another, one I do not understand.

Well, enough of matters of the heart for a moment. I'm happy to report that Bluebird Books has officially opened its doors. Oh, Brownie, it is just the sort of store I've always envisioned. Floor-to-ceiling bookcases. A big roaring fire with two wingback chairs to warm yourself while reading. Anthony had a carpenter make little chairs for the children for story time, which I host every Wednesday morning at ten, and there's a rocking chair for me.

It is late, and I'm about to turn the lights out and head upstairs. I almost hate to go out on a serious note, but the strangest things have been happening in the evenings. I saw the flash of a camera on the street yesterday, and then a car sped off. This afternoon, a man came into the shop. He was looking around in a way that seemed his intentions were other than looking for children's books. I hate to sound paranoid, but this activity worries me. I hate to think that . . . Well, I don't know what I'm getting at other than to say I'm a little put off by it all. I don't want to worry Anthony, so I've decided not to mention it.

This world can be wonderful and worrisome at the same time, can't it, Brownie?

Wish you were here. Yes, please come to Seattle. I will host the most lavish party for your reading.

With love,
Ruby

P.S. Thank you for what you wrote about being the authors of the stories of our lives. I have never heard anyone put such a thought into words so succinctly and so wisely. I shall remember it always, especially during the rainy season.

I set the letters in a little basket by Ruby's bed, where I keep each pair I discover, and I think about why she might have selected these pages for me to read. She's trying to tell me something. She's trying to teach me something she wasn't able to before she died. I lean back against the headboard of the bed and tuck my knees into my chest. Operation Sisterhood. Is this what Ruby had in mind for Amy and me? Was it her hope that we would salvage our relationship because she wasn't able to do the same with her sister? Or maybe it's something else, something more personal, directed only at me. I think about Margaret's words. *Whenever you're down on*

your luck, and when things aren't going the way you like, remember
that you are the author of your own story. You can write it any way you
like, with anyone you choose. And it can be a beautiful story or a sad
and tragic one. You get to pick. Yes.

Her words gnaw at me for some time. I think of my office in
New York, Arthur, and the rest of the team at the bank. I can picture them sitting around the conference room table. I see myself
there too, with a shrewd, tense look on my face. My heart rate
quickens when I realize that this isn't the beautiful life story Margaret alluded to, nor is it the story I want to write for myself. I take
a pill from the prescription bottle and wash it down with a sip of
water. "Ruby?" I whisper into the air. "Are you there? Are you listening? I want to rewrite my story, but what happens if I don't
know how?"

Chapter 9

I stand in front of May Magnuson's house at nine thirty on Tuesday morning and from the front stoop, I gaze up at the massive white Georgian colonial with Ionic columns reminiscent of the White House. Precisely trimmed boxwood hedges frame the front garden, which is lined with white and pink impatiens, not a petal askew. I've always thought of them as beautiful flowers. Ruby used to keep them in terra cotta pots in front of the bookstore. As a child, I once asked her why they are called "impatiens," and she looked up from the rusty green watering can and said simply, "because they remind us to be patient. Nothing good ever comes from rushing." I close my eyes and sigh—*yes*—then ring the front doorbell. My heart beats rapidly as I hear footsteps inside.

The door opens and a young woman stands before me. "You must be June," she says in a businesslike tone. "I'm Kerry, Ms. Magnuson's personal assistant."

"Yes, hello," I say, following her inside the home.

The woman indicates a room across the hall, and I follow. "Please have a seat," she says. "Ms. Magnuson is just finishing up in her office and will join you momentarily." I'm struck by her formality. "Would you like a cup of coffee while you wait?"

"No, thank you," I say. "I'm fine."

Alone in the room, I survey my surroundings. There's a fireplace, unlit, on the far wall. Hanging above is a formal family portrait: a man in a suit, a beautifully dressed dark-haired woman, and their young daughter. No one is smiling. There's a Jack Russell terrier seated at the foot of the man. Even the dog looks stiff.

A crystal vase of lilies rests on the coffee table in front of me, and I pause to admire them.

"Mother loves lilies," a woman says from behind me. "We keep them in every room."

I turn around quickly to see a middle-aged woman standing in the doorway. She's slim and wears a navy-blue pantsuit. Her brown hair is cut blunt at her shoulders and a floral scarf is tied around her elegant neck in a tidy knot.

"Does your mother live here, with you?"

"Yes," May says a little guardedly, as if my question has raised her hackles. She takes a seat on the sofa across from me. The vase of lilies on the table stands between us like a referee. "Mother's in good health, for ninety. She still gets around, with the help of her nurse." May arranges a stack of magazines on the table so their spines are perfectly aligned. "And she likes things to be just so."

I think about Mom, and even though I've spent my life annoyed by her laid-back, forgetful ways, I find myself grateful for her in light of the alternative: rigidity.

"So," May continues. "I must say, I was quite surprised to receive your e-mail."

"Oh?"

She nods. "Of course, I'd heard of Ruby's passing, and let me say, I am sorry for your loss."

She has kind eyes, but her expression is distant, guarded.

"Thank you."

"June," she says, "how much do you know about your aunt's past?"

"Well," I say a little nervously, "I know that your father and my aunt were—"

"Lovers?" she says, without emotion. "Yes. They were."

A silence falls on the room, and I see that Ruby and Anthony's relationship is still a sore subject for May. And then, suddenly, I can see her as she was in 1946. A little girl in braids wearing a private school uniform and patent leather shoes, caught in the middle of her parents' unhappiness.

"It killed Mother," she continues. "The way they carried on all those years." She sighs. "Mother used to drive by the store, with me in the back. She'd park outside just to watch her, just to try to see what she had that Mom didn't. Well, thankfully, her memory loss has diminished that burden. It's the only welcoming thing about dementia."

The pain of the past is obviously still raw. I decide not to say anything and just listen. For now.

"I was thirteen when I put it all together. I asked Mother, and she told me. She didn't spare any of the vulgar words she used to describe your aunt, either." She sighs. "Daddy spent all of his time with her at the bookstore. It was their love nest, you know. Our family life, at home, was just . . . a formality."

"I'm sorry," I finally say. "I didn't know that." Hearing May's perspective casts a shadow on the beautiful love story I've conjured up in my mind. And I wonder if there is a dark side to every great love story. With great love comes great hurt. I wonder if it's inevitable.

"I always wanted to know what was so wonderful about Bluebird Books that Daddy would want to spend all his time there," she says. Her eyes are stormy, and she looks like she might cry or laugh. "I remember one night," she continues. "It was my birthday. My tenth birthday. It's a tender age, you know, an age when a girl needs her father. And Mother had prepared a big dinner, and a chocolate cake for dessert. We waited until the food got cold, and he never did come. Of course, he brought a gift the next day, but it . . . well, it hurt."

"Oh, May," I say, my words flooding with emotion. I don't know what to say, and yet part of me feels that I ought to apologize to her, for Ruby. I know she would have never wanted to hurt young May. "That must have been so hard for you."

"Well," she says stiffly, expertly navigating away from any sentimentality between us. "You've obviously come here for a reason. How can I help you?"

"Yes," I say cautiously. "I hoped to learn more about my aunt's life. I left Seattle when I was quite young myself, and there was so much about my aunt I didn't know. I owe it to her to learn about her past. For instance, I had no idea that she and your father were in love."

"Love," she says. "It's such a funny thing. You see, he was supposed to love us, but apparently we couldn't hold his attention the way your aunt did."

"Did you ever meet her, my aunt?" I ask, remembering the brief reference to May in the letters.

"A few times," she says. "But my loyalty was with Mother."

"Forgive me for asking this, but why didn't your mother divorce him?"

"She loved him," May says simply, as if there was no other explanation. "Even in spite of it all. She made a vow, and she never dreamed of breaking it."

"And your father?" I ask. "Did he want a divorce?"

May shakes her head. "He needed her fortune to shore up his work in the community," she explains. "You can put a pretty spin on it, but in actuality, what he did was use her."

"But surely your mother could have gotten a divorce if she really wanted to."

May shakes her head. "There was great shame in divorce in those days. She didn't want her marriage to fail."

I wonder if this is the truth or merely a story May has told herself over the years. Ruby's letters described Victoria as a foreboding woman who was very much in charge of her affairs. If she really wanted a divorce, at least according to the picture Ruby painted, she could have gotten one. I look up at the striking dark-haired woman in the painting over the mantel and wonder, suddenly, if Victoria refused a divorce to *punish* Anthony and Ruby. By agreeing to a divorce, she'd allow them to be married, and perhaps she was too prideful to let that happen.

"And then there was the ultimate betrayal," May continues, "when Ruby got pregnant."

I sit up straighter. "What do you mean?"

May nods. "I had a feeling this would be news to you."

I shake my head, speechless.

"It was a shock to everyone, really," May adds. "Father was in his sixties then, and Ruby had to be in her forties. I got the news from Mother when I was traveling in Europe. She left a message at my hotel. I'll never forget the way the maître d's lip trembled when he came to my room to relay the news."

I shake my head. "I don't understand. Ruby never told me she was a mother. Are you sure?"

May sighs. "Perhaps she didn't want anyone to know. She gave the baby up for adoption. He would have been about your age now. To think she has a son out there. And I have a brother." She shakes her head as if this is a very disturbing thought.

I'm simply . . . stunned. "All these years," I say. "I had no idea."

"Well," she adds, "Father never got to meet him. He died while Ruby was pregnant. They went out ice skating on Green Lake, and he fell. They thought it was a simple concussion. But he died four hours later."

"How horrible," I say. "For everyone." I want to say, *Especially for Ruby*, but I don't. I think of my aunt, pregnant, hovering over Anthony on the ice. I think of them together in the back of an ambulance, him reassuring her that everything will be fine. And then I picture her crying over his lifeless body in a hospital bed. Alone.

"So you have a brother somewhere," I say, as if somehow, by uttering the words aloud, I'll come closer to understanding a part of my aunt's life I never knew existed.

"Well, a half brother," May says.

"Did you ever . . . meet him?"

She closes her eyes for a moment, then opens them again. "No, I never did, and never will. It was a closed adoption. Ruby wanted it that way. I think because she didn't want the Magnuson family meddling in his life. It was her way of keeping control. To think there was a little boy that was the flesh and blood of Father, and we couldn't even know him." May lets out a deep sigh. "Mother hired a private investigator to tail Ruby and Father for years, and after the baby was born, I know she had her PI keep a close eye on the bookstore. Maybe it spooked your aunt."

"Why would your mother do that?"

"Listen," May continues. "If there was a *Magnuson* being raised in the bookstore by her husband's bohemian lover, then she wanted to be sure the child was raised well." She sighs. "Yes, I think the ongoing surveillance compelled your aunt to give him up."

I shake my head. "I can't imagine Ruby giving up her only child as . . . revenge."

May smirks. "Then I guess you never knew your aunt."

For a moment, I begin to think that May could be right. If Ruby could hide a friendship with the legendary Margaret Wise Brown, what else could she hide?

"I don't know what to say," I finally concede.

"Well," she continues, "we might be able to work together. We share a family member. He's out there somewhere, and if we combine our efforts we might be able to find him."

I think for a moment, and consider the fact that if Ruby wanted to find him, wanted us to find him, she would have included him in her will, or left a letter about his whereabouts, if she even knew.

"As curious as I am, there are Ruby's wishes to consider," I say.

May sighs to herself. "There have been far too many secrets kept in my family," she says to me. "Please, help me."

"And if we find this long-lost brother," I say, "which would be my . . . cousin, I suppose—what then?"

"Honestly, I don't know. I just think it's time I found him. He's my brother, after all. Surely you can understand that."

I think of the store then, and consider the fact that this long-lost son of Ruby's might make a claim on Bluebird Books. With no sentimentality about a mother he never knew, he might try to sell it. And even though my intentions for the store are equally questionable, the business side of me is poised for a fight. Ruby left the store to me, not him.

"Your aunt must have kept some documentation about her child," she says.

"But you said it was a closed adoption."

"Yes," she says. "I've been thinking about this for so many years now and I've come to this conclusion: This was the son of my father, the greatest love of her life. Would she really give the boy away and cut off all contact with him forever?" May shakes her head. "I don't think so. It was her last tie to Anthony. She would have found a way to keep her son in her life, from a distance, and in a way that fooled everyone else." May nods to herself. "Mother received word through our attorney that the boy had been given up for adoption, and that the proceedings were sealed. In some ways, it helped Mother attain closure. She stepped back. But I never could."

Though I feel uncertain of May's intentions, I think she's right about Ruby: She must have kept in some kind of contact with her son.

"I thought, maybe, I might come over, to the bookstore, and have a look around," she says. "There has to be some old paperwork that would lead us to her son."

I think of the pain Victoria, and possibly even May, might have caused Ruby over the years, and I decide Ruby, if she were still alive, might not be thrilled about one of them riffling through her possessions. "I'll keep an eye out, and I promise to let you know if anything turns up."

She seems vaguely disappointed by my response, then turns to the doorway, where her assistant stands.

"Excuse me for interrupting, Ms. Magnuson, but you're wanted on the telephone."

"Please take the call," I say quickly. "I was just leaving."

"Shall I show you out?" the young assistant asks me.

"No," I say, gathering my purse. "That's all right."

"Well, good-bye, June," May says.

"Good-bye."

She and her assistant disappear into the hallway, and I stand there for a moment, a little stunned, before making my way to the doorway, where I nearly collide with an old woman, who I instantly realize is May's mother, Victoria. Her gray hair is short and curled close to her head. The tired skin sags on her face like wrinkled silk, but even so, I can tell that she once was very beautiful, perhaps more beautiful than her daughter could ever have been. I wonder what kind of effect this had on May, growing up in her mother's shadow.

"Oh, excuse me, ma'am," I say, a little startled.

"Well at least they've done something right," the woman mutters to herself. "They finally remembered I like lilies. Last week they set up tulips everywhere. I hate tulips."

"You must be Victoria," I say.

The old woman looks at me as if she's just noticed my presence. "Do we know each other?"

"No," I reply. "I was just, well, here to see your daughter. I'm June Andersen, Ruby Crain's niece."

Victoria looks shaken, and I know that after all these years, my aunt's name still has power over her. Of course it does. For the majority of her marriage to Anthony, Ruby was "the other woman."

Victoria looks right, then left. "What did my daughter tell you?" she asks quickly, as if we might not have much time to speak.

I decide to be vague. "Not much, really," I say. Besides, I've already said enough. She's an old woman, and I worry that memories of my aunt may not be good for her nerves.

"Listen, my dear," she continues, lowering her voice to a hush. "Please, you must be careful with my daughter."

"What do you mean?" Surely she doesn't think I came here to disturb her in some way?

"My daughter's like a dog with a bone," Victoria says bluntly. If there's any love hidden in her meaning, I can't detect it. "She won't give up on the past. She won't give up until she's found . . ."

"Found what?"

She looks up at the stairs and then back at me.

"I've tried to tell her to move on with her life, to put it all past her. I've done that for myself. But she won't. She won't rest until she has it."

"Do you mean information about Ruby's son?"

Victoria looks confused, and she shakes her head. "No. No, it's something else. Something she believes is in the bookstore."

I look back when I hear the faint sound of voices behind me, and then May and her assistant round the corner.

"Mother," May says. "What are you doing out of bed? You should be resting before your surgery tomorrow."

Victoria flashes her a dutiful smile. "Just on my way up," she says. The assistant takes her arm, and escorts her down the hallway. I hear her mutter, "Lilies. I like lilies, not tulips," as she disappears into a darkened corridor on the right.

"I hope Mother didn't say anything upsetting," May says to me. Her words are less of a statement and more of a question.

"No," I say guardedly. "No, she didn't."

"Because she's very confused these days. She doesn't know what she's saying. Some days she doesn't even know my name."

"We were just talking about how much she loves lilies," I say, adjusting the strap of my purse on my shoulder. "Well, I've taken up enough of your morning. Good-bye, May."

Before walking back up to Queen Anne Avenue to catch a cab, I cast one final look at the house, and see May watching me from the window. I look away quickly.

Back at the bookstore, I sort through the contents of two boxes of Ruby's paperwork, scanning each page with greater zeal than before. If there's any trace of Ruby's son under this roof, I'll find it. But after two hours sprawled out on the floor, I have nothing more than a stack of useless old book order forms for the shop. They sit in a defeated heap destined for the recycle bin.

I hear a knock at the back door. I haven't seen Gavin since the night at the restaurant, and honestly, I'm not prepared to talk to him, not yet. Whatever has been said, or left unsaid, between him and Adrianna has created a rift between us. We're like a cherry tree branch on the verge of blooming, but we'll never bear fruit. It seems smarter to clip off the buds now and save us both a lot of headaches.

I walk to the door hesitantly and turn the lock, opening it just enough to peer out to the alley, and I'm shocked to see Adrianna standing there.

"Hi," she says. "Sorry, am I disturbing you? I wasn't sure if the front door was open or not."

"No, no," I say, a little surprised by her civility toward me given the iciness of our past encounters. "I mean, no you're not disturbing me. Come in."

Adrianna follows me inside the bookstore, and I point to the wingback chairs beside the fireplace.

"Sorry, it's a bit of a mess in here," I say as we both sit down.

"Please," she says with a smile. "I guess Gavin hasn't mentioned that I'm a total slob. Messes are sort of my thing."

I grin, surprised by her warmth toward me.

"Listen," she says. "I came here to apologize. Gavin probably told you about us."

I nod.

"We were engaged," she says. "And then we weren't. I kind of got my heart broken."

"I'm sorry."

"No," she replies. "That's the thing. You have nothing to apologize for. Gavin is single. I'm single. What we had is . . . over. It's just taken me a long time to realize that."

I look at my hands in my lap, digesting her words.

"When I saw you two together the other night," she continues, "I realized for the first time that it's really, truly over between us. And you know, it was so weird, I thought I'd feel sadder than I was. But I had this epiphany. I was putting so much effort into the hope of getting back together that it was killing me. It was literally killing me. And now that I've acknowledged our end, I honestly just feel relieved."

I nod again.

"I'll probably always love him," she says. "I mean, look at the guy. How can you not?"

I smile cautiously.

"What I'm trying to say is . . . Gavin really likes you. I think you two have a real chance, and I'd hate to think that my presence ruined your chance at happiness."

I blink hard. "Wow, I don't know what to say." I shake my head in bewilderment at this unexpected show of kindness.

"You know, I completely misjudged you," she says.

"I don't understand."

"I thought you were some high-powered New Yorker who'd waltz in here in your stiletto heels and sell the bookstore to the highest bidder." She shakes her head. "But you really love this place. I see that now."

"Well, I—"

"I don't know how I read you so wrong."

I smile awkwardly. Of course I love the bookstore; I always have. But I don't tell her that the future of the bookstore is still uncertain. In fact, even though it pained me, I called a commercial real estate agent this morning to get an assessment of the property's value.

Adrianna smiles nervously. "We're more alike than we thought," she says. "We both care deeply about family businesses. My grandmother's restaurant in San Francisco is at risk of closing. She's too old to be doing the cooking and neither of her daughters is interested in carrying on her legacy." She pauses for a moment as if she's considering a very weighty matter. "I haven't told Gavin yet, but I'm going to fly down and assess the situation, see if I can help."

"Wow," I say. "So you'd take over the business."

"Maybe," she says. "I still have to think it all through, especially how my leaving would affect . . . Antonio's."

I nod.

"Well, Gavin's in the kitchen right now," she continues. "He doesn't know I'm here. I think you should go over and see him today. Talk to him. The two of you need a fresh start without me in the picture." She pauses for a moment. "I'm not sure what I'll do after San Francisco, but I think a few days away will give me clarity." She stands up and smiles. "But I have to warn you, Gavin snores. And he's a bear in the mornings. And he doesn't do the dishes, unless you beg him, and he will probably forget your birthday. And Valentine's Day. But other than that, he's about the best guy you could ever find." She takes a long look at me and before she turns to the door, I think I detect a glint of moisture in her eyes. "Best of luck to you, June. I really mean it."

Before I can say anything else, she's gone.

The real estate agent arrives at two. He's about my age, with hair that's slicked back. His smile reveals unusually white teeth. "You must be June," he says in the doorway. "I'm John from Coldwell Banker Bain."

"Yes," I say. "Hi, John. Come in."

"Quite a place this is," he says. There's an excited glint in his eye.

"Yeah," I say a little nostalgically. "Isn't it something?"

I can see by the look on his face that he doesn't share my sentimentality about the store. "Imagine all the work you'd have to put in to get this place functioning again," he says, shaking his head. He picks up a book lying on top of a shelf, then tosses it down like a piece of junk mail. "You're smart to think of selling. Nobody's making money at books these days. It's an uphill battle. Might as well cash out now." He surveys the shop and points up to the ceiling. "The place has good bones. It'll likely appeal to a condo developer, though they'll most likely be interested in bringing in the wrecking ball."

I know I've invited him here, and I know he's simply assessing the store from a place of dollars and cents, which is his job, but I don't like it. I don't like it *at all*.

He points to the rug with the cushions splayed out on the floor, where Ruby used to hold court for her daily story time, and laughs to himself. "Do kids even go to bookstores anymore?"

"Of course they do," I say, annoyed by his bravado. "This bookstore is beloved by generations of children."

"Maybe not this generation," he retorts. "My sister has kids, and they don't read books. They do everything on their iPad."

I feel my cheeks redden. How dare he walk in here and declare my aunt's legacy meaningless. How dare he imply that books are dead. This man embodies the type of thinking that Ruby despised. And even if I am going to sell the shop, I don't need to work with someone with such a cavalier attitude about literature. Real estate agents are a dime a dozen, anyway. I'll find another.

"You know," I say suddenly, "I don't think this is a good fit."

The agent looks confused. "What do you mean?"

"I mean that I don't think this is going to work out. I'd prefer to work with someone who has a vision for this space. And you clearly don't."

He looks panicked. "Oh, I think you misinterpreted me. I didn't mean to insult you."

"Well," I say, flipping on my business face, "you did." I extend my hand. "Thank you for your time."

He shakes my hand regretfully. "Well, you have my card. If you change your mind—"

"Yes, thank you," I say, walking him to the door and closing it behind him.

I sink into a wingback chair and make a promise to myself: If I sell the store, I'll need to find an agent who respects the legacy of Bluebird Books the way I do.

I remember the last mention of a book in the previous pair of letters: *Calico Bush*. I read it when I was eleven. I search the shelves until I find the first edition and open the cover, where the letters are waiting.

May 25, 1946

Dear Ruby,

I don't like the sound of the suspicious visitors to the shop. But try not to dwell on it. Keep your doors locked at night. Be diligent, but don't let a few odd incidents rob you of your joy. The type of happiness you have is what everyone wants. If you leave it out for the taking, it will be taken. Guard your joy, and don't let anyone snatch it.

Oh, how I do envy what you have with Anthony! Of course, I am so very happy for you, even if my own prospects are a bit dire.

I talk a lot about how unconventional I am, which is true, but I will let you in on a secret: I do dream of the happily ever after too, Ruby. But with each passing year, I have to wonder if it's in the cards for me. I've had so many failed love affairs that I'm afraid the pile of wilted roses might reach the height of the Empire State Building.

Even still, I haven't given up on love just yet. Your happiness gives me hope.

Meanwhile, the wheels keep turning. They're doing an article about me in Life magazine. Evidently I have sold nearly one million copies of children's books over the past years, which was news to me. (I can only keep track of what is directly in front of me, and today I just received finished copies of Little Fur Family, which, I must say, came out quite well. Don't bother buying it. I'll have Harper send you a box.) Well, back to Life. Apparently, they think people want to know more about the woman behind the stories.

I find it curious that I am scheduled to be in the issue with Ingrid Bergman on the cover (or so the rumor is). Ingrid Bergman and me! Maybe my father will finally take my work seriously after he sees the issue (though I won't count on it). I suspect Roberta will find it all amusing. She's coming around, by the way. She sent me a postcard from her recent trip to Niagara Falls, and that cheered me. Another step forward for Operation Sisterhood.

Ursula, my editor at Harper, arranged the Life interview. A photographer and reporter will meet me at Cobble Court (you know, the little cottage in Manhattan that I rent as my office), where I imagine I must look presentable and answer questions intelligibly, and hopefully intelligently.

I am really quite shy, as you know, so this doesn't bode well for me. But I will smile, and I will answer the reporter's questions. I'll probably have to defend my work, as I always seem to be doing at parties these days. At a friend's party last week, I sat beside the head of Random House. He looked over at me through his spectacles and made a comment about an award one of his authors won, and then he smirked and said something like, "But you wouldn't know anything about that, writing baby books." Baby books. He laughed heartily. His ample belly shook beneath his starched shirt. And what did I do? I poured my drink on his lap and walked out with a satisfied smile on my face.

Well, you wouldn't believe what showed up at Cobble Court the next morning: a flower arrangement with a card that read, "Forgive me."

I have decided to use the Life magazine interview to explain that I do what I do because it is a vocation just like any other—granted, one I fell into. But sometimes one must fall into their life's work this way, like Alice stumbling into the rabbit hole, simply because we, if left to our own devices, would only take more sensible paths, and ruin our destinies.

I'm always feeling as if I must defend my work, defend its worthiness. What I might say to the Life reporter is that I do not write for accolades or awards, for money or praise. I don't even write for children, not in a direct way. I write because of the child that is still in me.

For example, yesterday, I woke up after dreaming a tale of a dog who built himself a house, and did not think to myself, "The children of the world will love this story!" I thought to myself, "I love this story!"

Still, I carry with me the sentiments of others who see my work as unimportant, those who, like the Random House executive, refuse to take me seriously. In these moments, I do wish I could be like Virginia Woolf or Gertrude Stein. I often think about the respect they commanded upon entering a room.

Clem and Posy are coming over for drinks this evening at Cobble Court. As you know, Clem is the illustrator I work with most closely. Tonight we'll talk about a new idea, one partially inspired by your prodding to write something about the moon. I think we will.

> With all the love and affection
> in the world, my dear friend,
> Brownie

June 2, 1946

Dear Brownie,

Life magazine! You will do fine in the interview. Just tell them what you wrote me. Speak from your heart and everyone will love you as I do.

I do wish you didn't have to run up against such scrutiny in literary circles. They're snobs. Ignore them. (And, in all of your idolization of Gertrude Stein, remember her ill-fated attempt at publishing a children's book? I know you loved the book, as you love everything she's written, but I will remind you that children did not. As a bookseller, I saw firsthand how the copies languished on the shelf. My point being: Just as you aren't a novelist, she is not a proficient teller of children's tales. We all have our gifts.)

I have been well. Though, Operation Sisterhood isn't going as well over here as it seems to be on your side of the country.

Lucille told me the idea of having a zoo outing was utterly childish, and, naturally, I got my feelings hurt. I've learned that it isn't as easy as it sounds to put oneself out there repeatedly and to be continually denied by the other. I suspect there will come a time when I grow weary of such rejection, but I'm not ready to quit just yet.

The shop is flourishing, and I'm counting my blessings. I love to read to the children on Wednesday mornings at story time. I love everything about Bluebird Books. It is, as Anthony had hoped, my haven.

A real estate developer came into the shop yesterday and told me I ought to sell so they could build a department store in the space. He offered to pay me one and a half times more than what Anthony paid for it. You should have seen this man in his fancy suit and Italian leather shoes. He just waltzed in with paperwork and assumed I'd sign. When I refused, he laughed and said I was a fool to think I'd make any money selling books to children. I was too stunned to respond and he left before I could tell him off. But I still have the last word, at least here, to you, Brownie. For we know the importance of the book industry. We know the importance of literature. It doesn't always come with monetary reward, but just the same, I feel deeply that what we do, you and I, in our own different ways, is worthy.

Well, that's all for now. Until your next letter, I'll be thinking of you, my friend.

Yours,
Ruby

P.S. I got a shipment of the most delightful new books today. I must admit, I'd all but ignored the Little Golden Books imprint as the owner of Elliott Avenue Books had dismissed them as "fluff," but you know, I do believe she was wrong! In looking through the latest titles, like <u>Baby Looks</u>, I wonder if more simple storylines might be refreshing to children. I often worry that we're filling their heads with fairy tale after fairy tale, when in reality, I think they want to read about their own lives. In stories, children look for reflections of the world, so they can process and better understand it. Isn't this what you've always called the "here and now" style of writing? Well, I see its value now more than ever.

I tuck the letters in Ruby's desk drawer, and think about her words: *I've learned that it isn't as easy as it sounds to put oneself out there repeatedly and to be continually denied by the other.* Is that how Amy feels? Denied? Rejected? I remember the tone in her voice the last time she called—tired, sad, *weary.* What if she stops trying? What then? For so long, it's been enough to know that she's trying, even if I'm not reciprocating. There's a sad sort of comfort in her letters, her calls. But when that one-way communication line goes completely dark, will I feel better or worse?

If I search my heart, I already know the answer, and it scares me.

Chapter 10

I wait until the next morning to knock on the door of Antonio's. I want to be sure Adrianna has had time to say her good-byes. And even despite all she's said, I'm not certain that Gavin feels for me the way I think I do for him. And what if he still loves her, as she does him? Still, I venture over to Antonio's at ten, and I'm startled to see a sign on the door: CLOSED.

Closed. My heart sinks. While the restaurant doesn't open for lunch until eleven thirty, Gavin's always there early, with the door open. I peer through the window, and see a light on in the kitchen. I knock on the door, and a few moments later, Gavin appears through the swinging door. He smiles when he sees me.

"Hi," he says, opening the door.

"Hi," I reply, stepping inside. "The closed sign's up—feeling introverted this morning?"

He shrugs. "Adrianna came to talk to you, didn't she?"

"Yes," I say, "but what does that have to do with the closed sign?"

He nods. "With her leaving, I'm not sure if I can keep Antonio's going by myself." He looks around his beloved kitchen, and places his hands on the table. "I came in this morning and my confidence sank."

"That doesn't sound like the can-do guy I know."

Gavin shakes his head. "Adrianna needs some time away, and I think I do too. I've been working so hard lately, and honestly, I haven't had a day off since we opened this place."

I nod. "Then take a break—but don't give up on what you love."

His eyes meet mine. "This past year, I've been so hell-bent on making the restaurant a success that I've forgotten to just take a deep breath, you know? To just live. There's more to life than Antonio's."

"Sure there is," I say. "But you're talking as if you're thinking of closing . . . for good. I know you'd regret it."

"I might," he says. "But for now, it feels like the right time to turn the page to the next chapter."

His eyes pierce mine, and I look down at my feet. Somehow I know that if I let his gaze hold mine, it will be like stepping off a cliff. No turning back. But I feel his fingers on my chin, tilting my face up to look at his.

"Adrianna told me what she said to you. About us."

I search his eyes.

"And I want you to know that I'm willing to give this a go if you'd like to." He grins. "Sorry, I'm a little out of practice. What I mean is, I *want* to give this a go, and I hope you do too. The truth is, I'm crazy about you. I am. I want to take you to meet my friends, my family. June, I hope you want that too."

"I do," I say. "At least, I think I do. It's been so long since I trusted someone."

He pulls me closer to him. "Trust me," he whispers in my ear.

I nod, and he presses his lips lightly against mine. Our lips fit together perfectly, and I feel a surge of warmth. For a moment, everything is right with the world.

"Let's spend the day together," Gavin says, kissing my forehead.

"I'd love that," I say. "What do you have in mind?"

"Let's take a ferry to the island."

"Bainbridge?" I've always loved the little island, just a half-hour ferry journey from Seattle. I hesitate for a moment, thinking of all I have to do at the store. The clock is ticking for me. My job is waiting in New York, and then there's the issue of Bluebird Books. If I sell, I'll need to find the right buyer. Someone who, even with plans to demolish, would respect its past, its legacy. I shudder inwardly, and look into Gavin's eyes, so warm, so happy. I decide not to think about the store. Just for today.

"Yeah, Bainbridge," he says. "We can park downtown and walk on, maybe have lunch in Winslow. I know a little café that makes a mean crab melt. Then maybe we can walk along the waterfront, find a little park bench somewhere and just listen to the birds chirp. It'll be good to get out of the city."

"You had me at crab melt," I say, grinning.

It's a clear day, and Gavin and I choose to sit on the ferry's top deck outside. It's windy, and my hair will be blown to bits, but I don't care.

"I love seagulls, don't you?" he says, tossing a cracker from his pocket out onto the deck, where a half dozen seagulls swoop in and peck at it.

"Yeah," I say. "It's one of the things I missed most about Seattle. I love their calls. It's a combination of a shriek and a scream, which sounds like it would be horrible. But, you know, I think it might actually be one of my most favorite sounds in the world."

"The sound of the sea," Gavin says.

I nod.

"I'm glad to hear you speaking in nostalgic terms about Seattle," he says. "It means you're going to put down roots here."

I smile noncommittally, noticing his choice of the future tense, as if I've already parted ways with my old life in New York and am poised to begin my new life in Seattle as a children's bookseller. If only it were that easy.

"Do you think you'll stay above the shop?"

I think of myself living as Ruby did, rising with the sun streaming through those big old double-hung windows, making a simple breakfast, then running downstairs to reunite with her beloved Bluebird Books. I know why she loved it so, because I love it in the same way. And for the first time since arriving in Seattle, I realize that I can't sell the shop, not to a developer, not to anyone. I can't sell it, because I love it too much, and I see a life for myself here.

"I have to tell you something," I say to Gavin.

He looks startled. "What?"

"I haven't been honest with you about . . . my intentions for the bookstore." He holds silent, so I continue. "I'm a banker. You know that. But what you don't know is that I'm the kind of banker who specializes in shutting down businesses in default. Cafés, little craft shops, even bookstores. You name it, I've closed it." I shake my head, unable to make eye contact with him. "As a finance student, I would never have been able to imagine myself performing such excruciating tasks in the name of business, like looking in the eyes of a seventy-year-old woman who has been late on her mortgage payments for eleven months and saying, 'I don't care that your business has been in the family for six generations. I'm shutting you down. Sayonara.'" I sigh. "But that's the kind of person I've had to be. And I was good at it. *Am* good at it. I'm paid well to clean up these kinds of messes."

I turn to face Gavin, but he's staring off at the horizon. I'm not sure if he's just taking it all in, or if he's thinking about how he's grossly misjudged my character. "I'd hardened over the years," I continue. "I didn't realize that until I came home to Seattle and the old memories came rushing back. I honestly thought I could spend a few days, sort through my aunt's estate, and sell off the assets, just like in my work life." I shake my head. "I had a real estate agent come out yesterday to appraise the store, and I couldn't stand the way he looked at the place with dollar signs in his eyes. I began to realize then that I could never sell the store, because I love it too much. And I know I always will."

Gavin's silence makes my heart race in anticipation. Will his feelings for me change now? Is he formulating his exit strategy? I fold my hands together tightly and bite the edge of my lip, as he turns to face me again. "That," he says, "took a lot of guts to tell me."

I look away. "It's the sad truth."

He takes my left hand in his, and I turn back to face him. "No, there's nothing sad about this story," he says. "It has a happy ending."

"Well," I say, "not yet."

"You're the prodigal niece," Gavin continues with a smile. "You left home and forged a life you thought you wanted, but it didn't fulfill you. It took coming home, seeing all the love waiting for you here, before you could face your past, face yourself."

I smile, ignoring the stinging sensation in my eyes. "You make my life sound poetic, when it's really quite a mess."

"Nah," he says. "It's not a mess. So you have a job to quit, an apartment to sell. You've had bigger fish to fry. You can get this done." He kisses my hand lightly. "And you'll have me to help."

"Thank you," I say, smiling again. "Isn't it fascinating how a situation can feel infinitely more difficult when it's part of your own life?" I shake my head. "I don't know how I'm going to tell Arthur."

"Arthur?"

"My boss. He's the one who trained me into this profession, groomed me, made me into the corporate woman I became. He's not going to see this coming."

"He's already seen it coming," Gavin says.

"How do you know?"

"Because it's impossible not to see how unhappy that job has made you," he says. "This Arthur has seen it all along, and he's ignored it."

I nod. "Frankly, I think the job makes him miserable too."

"Then tell him," Gavin says. "Soon. The sooner you get this off your chest, the better you'll feel." He squeezes my hand. "The sooner you can focus on what's next."

I tousle his windblown hair. "Where did you come from?"

"Next door," he says simply.

"Why couldn't you have been next door before I left Seattle?"

"Because we wouldn't have been ready for each other then," he says. "We had a lot of hurdles to jump first. And we did."

One of the seagulls from the flock meanders closer to me. "Sorry, little guy," I say. "That's the last of the crackers."

He bobs his beak as if he understands and hops backward, then swoops into the air, letting out a shriek as he flies against the wind.

"I love how they do that," Gavin says, pointing to the bird. "It's like they're suspended in the sky."

I grin. "I've always thought that it's a game they play, like they're trying to beat the wind." Then I remember something Ruby said about being envious of birds because they can take off and fly anytime they want. "My aunt loved birds, all kinds. I once asked her why she named the bookstore Bluebird Books, and she told me about an old song she used to love called 'Bluebird of Happiness.'"

"The Disney one?" He strains to remember the tune: "There's a bluebird on my shoulder . . ."

"No," I say, smiling. "It's a different one. But come to think of it, bluebirds have inspired a lot of happy songs, haven't they?"

"What makes *you* happy?" he asks, his face more serious now.

I pause for a moment, caught off guard. "I don't know," I say honestly. "I've spent so many years avoiding that question."

He gives me a face as if he doesn't understand.

"As a kid, I used to think I'd grow up and everything would sort itself out. When I left Seattle, I thought the perfect life was around the corner. And for a while, it sort of was. I thought I was happy. I thought I had everything I could ever want, and then, bam, I lost it all. Well, all but the job, and that sort of took over my life."

"What happened?" Gavin asks.

I look away, counting the seagulls overhead. One, two, three, four. No, I'm not ready to tell him. Not yet.

The ferry's horn sounds, and the seagulls scream and shriek overhead, sounding their disapproval. "We'd better walk down now," I say. "We're almost to the terminal."

He smiles at me with a "we're not finished with this conversation" look, and we walk together to the front of the boat. The ferry rocks and jostles a bit as it makes contact with the dock, and I lose my footing. Gavin places a steadying hand on my waist, then takes my hand in his as we walk off the boat down the ramp to the sidewalk that leads to the island's main street shops.

It's a warm day, and birds are chirping in the trees overhead. "I love Bainbridge Island," I say, breathing in the salty air.

"I have a friend who lives on the island," Gavin says. "His name is Jack. He and his wife live in an old colonial right on the water-front. He fishes every day, and crabs."

"Oh, I've always wanted to go crabbing."

"The Dungeness are amazing out here," he says. "I've been meaning to come out and get some crab for the restaurant." He scratches his head. "But, I don't know. Maybe not, since . . ."

I squeeze his hand. "Buy the crab," I say with a smile. "Don't you see? Cooking is your passion. Sure, things are hard now, but giving up on the restaurant isn't what will help."

He nods, but I can still see hesitation in his eyes. "Maybe, but it will be different. I thought I could do it, but I don't really know if I can ultimately run this place without a partner."

I want to tell him, *You can push through this,* but I know he's right. I know if I had tried to work with Ryan after . . . well, it would have killed me. Not a quick, clean death, but a slow, painful one. I can see why Adrianna wants out.

We round the corner to a crosswalk that leads to downtown Winslow, the only "city" on the island.

"What will you do, then?" I ask soberly.

"You could hire me to be your assistant in the bookstore," he says with a mischievous grin.

"It's not a bad idea," I say. "Especially if we knock down a wall and turn Antonio's into a café."

He's quiet for a moment, and at first I worry that I've offended him, but he turns to me and stops on the sidewalk, and his eyes flash. "Yes," he says. "That's a perfect idea. A bookstore-café. We could specialize in family fare, kids' food."

"Well," I say. My heart skips a little picturing a new sign with the words BLUEBIRD BOOKS & CAFÉ. "I wasn't actually serious when I suggested it, but now you've got me thinking we're onto something."

"I think we are," Gavin continues. "I talked to Joe yesterday. He's closing his café in two months."

"Oh, no, why?" I ask.

"He wants to retire, sail to Mexico. And without Joe's the street will need a new café."

"I don't know," I say. "What about Adrianna? She'd have to weigh in, and we don't know what her plans are for the future."

Gavin pauses, and his eyes look momentarily stormy, as if he's stopping to let a squall pass. "She told me that if I wanted to buy out her half of the business, I could. Of course, I told her no. I don't want her to think I'm trying to force her out."

"But maybe she *wants* out," I suggest. "Listen," I say quickly. "Let's not think about this now. We're stowaways on an island. Let's make a day of it. No serious talk."

He smiles, and weaves his fingers through mine. "Where to, then?"

I see a sign that reads BLACKBIRD BAKERY across the street, and I point to it. "Coffee and a scone first?"

We sit at a corner table and talk and laugh over Americanos and blackberry scones, then continue our tour of Winslow, stopping at a wine store. Gavin buys a case of local cabernet for the restaurant, and an extra one for me. When I notice a bookstore, Eagle Harbor Books, across the street, we walk there next.

"I love this bookstore," I say, breathing in the air as we step inside.

"You've been here before?"

"Yeah," I reply. "With Ruby. She knew the owners, and used to take my sister and me over on the ferry for events. We once saw Maurice Sendak read here."

"As in, *Where the Wild Things Are?*"

"Yeah," I say.

"What was he like?"

"Grumpy and wonderful, and wise," I reply. "Ruby was sad that he couldn't make it to Bluebird Books as part of his tour, but she was determined to take us to see him. She closed the store, and we came over on the ferry." I point to the children's section, remembering how dozens of children crowded in to get a glimpse of the foreboding author with his bushy eyebrows and serious face. "I stood right here," I continue, pointing to a place along the far wall. "And he said, 'You there, little girl. May I ask you for your assistance?' And so I went up to the front, and he asked me to hold the book for him as he read. He also asked me to make the growling sounds for the monsters. At first I was nervous. But then I kind of got into it, and I just let it out. After that he told me I had the very best monster roar he'd ever heard."

"I love that story," Gavin says. "Do you still remember how to roar?"

"Still do," I say with a wink. "It's one of my most well-honed skills, in fact."

We scan the bookshelves independently for a few minutes, and I select a novel from the "staff picks" table. Gavin returns to my side with an illustrated book about birds. A barrel-chested bluebird appears on the cover. "I thought you could keep this in the store," he says.

"I love it."

We pay for our purchases and meander down the sidewalk. "Can you imagine a world without bookstores?" I say.

Gavin shakes his head.

"Before she died, Ruby left a letter for me in the apartment. She said she was afraid that the store was in its final act. She feared for the future of the store." I shake my head regretfully. "She said she worried children didn't love books the way they used to." I turn to him. "Do you think that's true?"

"I don't know," he says thoughtfully. "I think they have more choices today. There are books, and then video games, TV, which provide instant gratification. But with books, you have to work for it."

"But that's why reading is so wonderful," I say, shaking my head. "You're a participant."

"Yes," he says. "But it's not just books versus TV, that's the problem; it's bookstores versus the Internet."

I nod. "Ruby was afraid of the Internet. She didn't even want a website." I pause to remember the tech-savvy young customer who offered to set up a website for her ten years ago, but she resisted vehemently. "Gavin, what if Ruby was right? What if people stop going to bookstores? What if they abandon them entirely? I believe this was Ruby's greatest fear."

"And it will be your greatest challenge," Gavin says, pointing back to Eagle Harbor Books. "Think of the memories you have of meeting Maurice Sendak, listening to him read his stories. Think of all the time you spent in Bluebird Books. You love books; you love bookstores because you made important memories in them as a child." He nods. "The only way to save bookstores is to keep children coming to them. All you have to do is keep the doors open, and welcome children and families. You will be planting a seed, then letting it grow."

I nod. "I guess you're right. The dishwasher never rendered restaurants obsolete."

"Neither did the microwave," he says.

I laugh. "If anything, the microwave *improved* business."

Gavin smiles. "Technology is not the enemy of bookstores." He points to his heart. "It's deeper than that."

"You're right," I say.

We walk in silence for the next few minutes, until we cross the street and stop in front of a café on the corner. "You haven't lived until you've had a crab melt from Cafe Nola," he says.

I smile and we sink into a booth; we set our purchases down on one side and sit together on the other. He holds my hand in his under the table, and it makes my stomach feel fluttery, which surprises me. I tell myself it's just hunger.

Our conversation is easy, and at times I find myself wondering if I've known this man all my life. We're both firstborns. Our favorite color is green (the color of the Puget Sound, we both say, almost at the same time), we adore the movie *The Princess Bride*, and we both hate lima beans. All silly, small things, but when you add them up, and combine them with this feeling in my heart, it equals something wonderful, and a little frightening.

Gavin pays the bill, and we hear the horn of the ferry ahead. "If we're quick, we can make the three thirty," he says, looking at his watch.

We gather our bags and run ahead. Good food is sloshing in my belly, and there's a huge smile plastered on my face. We climb the steps to the terminal, then make our way, a little out of breath, to the long, dimly lit corridor where walk-on passengers wait to board.

"Good," he says, exhaling, "we'll make it."

I lean against the railing beside Gavin as hundreds of passengers from the Seattle side stream off the ferry and into the terminal.

A few minutes later, a ferry worker unclicks the gate and motions for us to board.

We move to the right, to make way for a couple of passengers who are late to exit, and at first I don't hear my name.

"June?"

I look behind me, and then to my left, and that's when I see her. I stop in my tracks, like a rock lodged in a creek bed. The people, like rushing water, continue on around me. I can't take my eyes off her.

"Amy?" My sister looks different. She was always thin, but she looks gaunt now. While she once wore layers of makeup, now her skin is bare. She's beautiful, even more so without a painted face, and yet there's a hollowness to her cheeks, sadness and longing in her eyes. She wears gray leggings and a black wool cape sweater. Her blond hair is pulled back into a tidy ponytail.

Amy takes a step forward. There are tears in her eyes, and I feel mine sting. My first instinct is to run to her, to embrace her, but my legs don't move. They feel like they're set in dried cement. And when I try to open my mouth, no words come out.

"June," Amy cries. "I can't believe you're here. I can't believe I actually ran into you." She looks at Gavin as if to beg for his help at thawing my icy exterior. He turns to me and then back to Amy, confused, waiting for me to make a move, to say something.

Tears stream down Amy's face now, the way they did in the apartment in New York so many years ago, the day we parted ways forever. *Operation Sisterhood*, I think to myself. I imagine how Ruby and Margaret would have behaved, throwing their arms wide open for their sisters. I feel a flicker of warmth inside, but it isn't enough to melt the ice. And I know in that moment that I . . . *just can't*.

"I'm sorry," I say finally. "We'll miss our ferry. Let's go, Gavin."

I barely recognize my own voice, stiff and cold. I bristle at the sound of it. It's as if I'm on autopilot and the operating system has completely overridden my heart.

I don't look back as we round the corner to board the ferry.

"What just happened back there?" Gavin asks as we sit down in a booth facing Seattle.

"Listen," I say in a faltering voice, "if it's OK with you, I'd rather not talk about it."

He nods, and tucks a protective arm around my shoulder. As the ferry pulls out of the harbor, the seagulls outside the window swoop into the air in a frenzy. They shriek and cry as if begging me to turn back. But I can't, and I don't think I ever will.

Chapter 11

Gavin and I don't discuss my run-in with Amy on Bainbridge Island, and I'm thankful that as the next few days pass, I've almost forgotten about it.

But then, the following Tuesday, as I'm cleaning out the contents of Ruby's desk, Gavin comes over with lunch from Antonio's and sees a framed photo of Amy and me.

He's quiet for a moment, and I know he recognizes her.

"That woman at the ferry terminal," he says in a tentative voice. "Amy. She's your sister, isn't she?"

I sigh. "Yes," I say after a long silence.

I watch him eyeing the photo of us. I'm six, and she's barely two. We're both wearing floral sundresses. My arm's draped around her chubby shoulder. He looks back at me, and I read his mind. *Why can't you forgive her for whatever she did? You're family.*

"Don't," I say defensively, plucking the frame from his hand and tucking it away in Ruby's desk drawer.

"I didn't say anything," he says, a little hurt.

"But I know what you were *thinking*."

"OK," he says, "if you already know, then I'll just say it."

I rub my forehead.

"She's obviously distraught that you won't speak to her. Maybe it's time to . . . move on? Put the past in the past."

"It's not that easy," I snap. "Listen, can't you just trust me when I say that I *don't want* her in my life?"

He takes a step closer to me. His eyes are filled with concern. "I can, but I saw the way she looked at you. I'm just worried you may be making a decision you'll regret one day, that's all."

"How can you even say that?" I counter. "You don't know her. You don't know what she did."

"No," he replies. "I don't. But I know that you're expending a lot of energy on whatever pain happened in the past. That's taking a toll on you." He sighs. "And her. I saw the pain in her eyes that day on the island. June, she's—"

"She's nothing to me," I say quickly, turning back to Ruby's desk. "Are we done here?"

Gavin takes a step back. He looks a little stunned, and I regret my choice of words as he moves toward the door. "Yes," he says, closing it behind him. Ruby's bells jingle, but they sound lonely and distant now.

I feel like a child who wants to throw herself on her bed and sob, but instead I look for comfort in another pair of Aunt Ruby and Margaret Wise Brown's letters. I recall the mention of *Baby Looks* in their previous correspondence, and find the next set waiting for me in the first edition of a Little Golden Book with a plump, cherubic baby on the cover. I smile to myself as I thumb through the familiar pages, and I can almost hear Ruby's soothing voice in my ear: "Baby found a buttercup, found a little clover. Leaned way down to sniff them, then he tumbled over." I lean back in Ruby's desk chair and read.

June 14, 1946

Dear Brownie,

I know you must be busy, because I haven't heard from you this week. So, I will keep the torch burning and write to you again. I hope you aren't growing tired of my letters!

Operation Sisterhood has been a miserable failure, I'm afraid. I invited Lucille to visit the bookstore, which I deeply regret, especially when Anthony walked in the door unexpectedly. He kissed me on the cheek, so I had to explain our relationship. It did not go over well. To make matters worse, apparently Lucille once worked at a nursery school where Anthony's daughter, May, attended. So she knew about his marriage to Victoria. Imagine the look on her face when she put it all together. We've taken a giant step back, and, to be honest, I'm not sure if we can move forward again, and that is heartbreaking for me.

Anthony left on a business trip to Chicago, and I admit, I've missed him terribly. I've come to love our little routine. He comes over after work, and we have a late dinner together in the apartment above the bookstore. I'm getting better at cooking, too. I've been studying my copy of <u>Betty Crocker's Cookbook</u> at night and actually trying to learn. It's rather funny, actually. Imagine me, hovering over a cookbook! And, yes, it is all for a man (I may be struck down by lightning right this second).

Oh, but Brownie, he is a wonderful man. Gentle and kind, and he loves me so. He tells me, of course, but I also can see it in his gaze. I love to feel his gaze on me. We talk about the future, our life together. It is our unspoken understanding that our relationship will never be recognized by church or court, but I have his heart, and I believe I always will.

Last week, after I'd closed the bookstore, we were sitting by the fire together, and I asked him if he'd like to bring May to a story hour sometime. Brownie, you should have seen how the very mention disturbed him. He immediately rejected the idea. And he was angry at me for suggesting it. It was our first disagreement, if you could call it that.

I'll never forget what he said. "Don't you understand, Ruby? I must keep these two worlds separate, for your sake, and mine. And for May."

I could not understand his reasoning, and I felt hurt that he wanted to keep me away from his "other" life. "But don't you want me to know your daughter?" I pleaded.

He shook his head, and then he said the thing that made me understand, finally. "No, Ruby, I don't. Because she's a smart little girl. And she'll see the way I look at you and she'll know that I love you in a way I will never be able to love her mother. And I worry that will break her heart."

I understood then. And this is why I will never get to know May. Still, I mourn the loss of this relationship that is never to be. I saw the way she behaved when I first met her at Elliott Avenue Books, and I couldn't help but wonder if she might soften a bit if someone took an interest in her. I could have done that. But I will honor Anthony's wishes.

I try not to think about his life outside of the one we're building together. I know he goes home to Victoria. I know they share a bed, and every night when I set my head on my pillow, alone, I think of him lying beside that woman. I try not to think of her undressing in front of him, or her hands on his skin. But what right do I have to protest when their union is legally binding?

No, this is the arrangement I agreed on. I knew it wouldn't be easy, but I went into it with eyes wide open. I did it for Anthony. Because I trust him. I just need to remember that.

I don't see him as often as I'd like. His life is busy and full, but he makes room for me. I've come to view myself as a little mouse, happy to take a found crumb here and there. Oh, but they are such delicious crumbs!

Before he left for his trip, I got a shipment of new books in, and he helped me unpack them all onto the shelves. Afterward, we had dinner on the rug by the fire, like a picnic. We had this moment where we just looked in each other's eyes for a long while, and then I asked him, "Why did you do all this for me?"

He reached up his hand to my cheek and said, "Because I knew it would make you happy."

And I am happy. So terribly so. Sometimes I look at him and wonder if my heart might burst. And yet, I wonder if I'll always feel this way. I wonder if years will pass and I will grow discontent with our arrangement. I wonder if I'll gradually want more and more. What if I'm not satisfied until I have all of him? This is the human condition, you know, to keep yearning for more. But with Anthony, there will never be more. This love he offers is constrained.

So that is my dilemma, my great paradox. Brownie, what would you do in this situation? I'd love to know.

Well, I've been going on and on, and I haven't even asked how things are in your world. Writing? Love? What are you dreaming about these days? You always have the most amazing dreams. I wish my mind entertained me the way yours does. When I close my eyes, it's as if the curtain closes on my imagination and I'm out like a light.

Brownie, I will sign off now. Please write soon.

With love,
Ruby

June 29, 1946

Dear Ruby,

I've been holed up in Maine for a few weeks writing. How your letters cheered me, though, when I returned to New York and found them waiting.

First order of business: Your cooking. I don't know whether to be shocked or amused that you have become a proficient cook. In any case, I hope when I do finally make a trip to see you in Seattle that you'll make me a nice pan of biscuits like the ones my mother used to make in the cast-iron skillet. Do you wear a red-checked apron, too? (I'm only teasing.)

Next, dear, I am so troubled about this upset with Lucille. Don't give up on Operation Sisterhood just yet, though. You have experienced a significant setback, yes. But think of it this way: Lucille now has seen all of your "faults" and can accept you as you are, if she chooses, rather than the false, idealized image of you. And isn't that the ultimate goal? To love each other through all of our flaws? And to do that, we must show each other who we really are. Give her time; I bet she'll come around. It's 1946, for crying out loud! It's silly to think that relationships between men and women should be so scripted, when in actuality, our world has become so very complex.

In slightly better news, Roberta and I are considering making a trip to Europe together. Maybe you and Lucille could join us? Don't lose heart.

I am flattered that you think my sleep life is appealing, but I assure you, when you wake up for the thirteenth time in a month with a dream of a white rabbit sailing on the high seas, with sharks in hot pursuit, you will wish you could dream like normal people do. The truth is, my mind never shuts off. I think it's wearing me out, actually. The mind needs rest, just as the body does. I fear that my imagination only knows how to go, go, go. It's so tiring, really. I don't suppose someone who has an active imagination burns through their years faster than ones who do not? At this rate, I fear I'll be dead by fifty.

A new experience has descended upon me without warning. I'm absolutely fixated on my mortality. Will I die on my walk to the café? Will I slip into a manhole on my way to a business meeting? I'm plagued with thoughts of my death, as if it's near. Does this happen to you? Am I off my rocker? (I suppose we both already know that the answer to that question is yes.)

Frankly, I'm frustrated with my lot in life right now. Yes, I've cobbled together a career (fell into it accidently, I should say), and I've seen some success. I ought to be grateful, I know. But why am I not? I've come to see that I won't be able to rest until I write my first real book. A book for adults.

I've shared my concerns with you before that the literary crowd, which includes the group of publishers, writers, poets, and other artists of my acquaintance, finds me amusing, at best. "There she is, Margaret Wise Brown," they say, "the baby book writer." Nobody thinks of me as a real writer. At parties, they simply smile and ask, "What new nursery rhymes are you working on, Margaret?"

I would be lying if I said this didn't hurt me. It does. And I long to be taken seriously as a writer. I long to walk into a room and have people think, "There she is, Margaret Wise Brown, the *novelist*."

Regarding Anthony, I hope you will remember that no two love stories are the same. Each plays by its own rules. Each takes different twists and turns, has different joys and challenges, different heartaches. There is no perfect story, just as there is no perfect man or perfect woman.

Society tells us that we must do this, or do that. Sign this paper, or that. Vow this or vow that. But none of that matters, not really, not from the perspective of the heart.

I have come to believe that the truest expression of love is when two people can come to each other honestly, and simply love. That is what you and Anthony have, no? My advice is that you celebrate that, live in that, become drunk in that love. For it's more than most people get in a lifetime. And you should consider yourself the luckiest of women to have found it. After all, I'm still looking.

I should add that I do not mean to diminish your concerns. All that you have shared is valid. And yet, I want to remind you that there is a downside to every good thing. Our challenge is to not let the bad corrupt the good.

And maybe this is why I'm so fixated on my mortality these days. After all, life is short. We must pursue the people, places, and things in life that bring us the most joy. This is the challenge I've given myself of late.

To explore it fully, I'm going up to Maine again soon. It will be just me and the frogs, for a month, maybe more. I'm hoping I will be able to hear myself think a little clearer up there. Maybe I'll finally begin the novel I've been dreaming up.

Though this will be my last letter for a while, when I return, I hope to find a letter from you waiting.

> With all my love, your friend,
> M.W.B.

When I set the letters down a great sense of clarity comes over me. I eye my laptop on the desk, then open it up and pull up my e-mail. I know what I need to do. I know what the next chapter holds, but taking that first step, oh, it's hard. Buoyed by Margaret's words—*After all, life is short. We must pursue the people, places, and things in life that bring us the most joy*—I write the words I should have written years ago:

Dear Arthur,

Please accept this letter of resignation from my position at Chase & Hanson Bank. You took me under your wing and showed me the ropes of the bank. You made me who I am, and my success in our profession is owed solely to you. But, speaking frankly, Arthur, I don't like who I've become. I don't like the woman who's learned to feel no emotion, the woman who can sell a beloved business on the auction block without blinking an eye. Yes, positions like ours are integral to the success of business, to capitalism, to the world, even. I just don't want to be the one who carries out that work anymore. It's time for me to turn the page. You're a good man, Arthur. You're the nicest asshole I've ever met.

Yours,
June

I stare at my in-box for a while. It's after seven New York time. I know that Arthur's still at work, combing through paperwork, thinking about what restaurant he'll order in from. I know he's reading my e-mail right now. I know he's seething. But I don't predict his speedy response. The chime of my in-box makes my heart rate quicken. I feel the familiar numbness in my hands, and I realize I haven't taken my medicine. *Don't be afraid*, I hear Ruby say then. *Don't let anyone stop you from being your true self.* My true self. Is that who Ruby saw? Amy? I know one thing for certain: This person sitting here in Bluebird Books is the real June Andersen. But *that* person, the VP of Chase & Hanson Bank, who's she? I don't know her. I take my medication, then exhale deeply before opening up Arthur's e-mail.

June,

You've let me down.

Arthur

He's right, but the thing is, I'm no longer willing to let *myself* down.

Chapter 12

The next morning, I hear a knock and see a mail carrier standing outside. "Hello," I say, unlatching the door so we can talk. "I'm Jim, the neighborhood postman. You must be June."

"How did you know?" I ask.

"Your aunt told me you'd be taking things over."

"She did?"

Jim nods. "She talked an awful lot about you. She was proud of you. Very proud. It's sad to see her gone now. The street isn't the same without her."

My eyes sting. "The world isn't the same without her," I say.

"You're right about that." He hands me a large stack of mail. "Well, I saw the lights on in the apartment yesterday, and I figured I should restart the mail service. After I learned of Ruby's passing, it didn't seem right to let the mail pile up. So I kept it until you got here."

"Thanks," I say, eyeing the stack of catalogs and various hand-addressed letters.

"There's one for you in there too."

"For me?" I shake my head. "But no one knows I'm here."

He shrugs. "Well, good luck with the bookstore. Ruby would be happy you're here."

"Thanks," I say, turning back to the store.

Inside, I sit down at Ruby's desk and sort through the mail, mostly publisher catalogs of new books, which I make a mental note to look through later. I set a few personal letters from friends of Ruby's aside. They probably don't know she died. I'll have to write to let each of them know. Later.

Beneath another catalog, I see a card addressed to me. I recognize the name and address on the envelope immediately—May Magnuson—and I tear open the envelope with anticipation.

June, thank you for coming to see me last week. I found this old photo of your aunt with her baby in my files. Given that the chances are small we'll ever find him, I thought you'd like to have this picture. —May

Beneath the front fold of the card is the photo, which May wrapped in a sheet of white paper. I pull out the grainy color photograph, wrinkled and weathered over the years. The background is the interior of the bookstore, but the shot is distant, perhaps taken by someone standing on the other side of the street. Ruby didn't like to be photographed, and given the secretive way she handled the adoption, I could guess that she was probably unaware the camera had captured her image. I squint to make out the scene. There's Ruby, holding an infant swaddled in a blue blanket. They're sitting near the dollhouse. I can't make out the baby boy's face, just Ruby's. She's smiling—beaming, actually. She cradles her infant with such love, whoever was looking through the lens must have felt it. I feel it now. And I know in my heart I must find this boy. I must find him and I must tell him what an extraordinary person his mother was. And no matter what sort of life he's had, no matter what pain he felt when his adoptive parents told him about his past, he'll see this photo and know that his mother loved him, with all her heart.

I sigh to myself and set the photo down, which is when I notice a familiar logo on the corner of a stark white envelope addressed to Ruby, one I've come to know well over the past eleven years. I tear open the flap in anticipation, and pull out the letter inside.

Dear Ms. Crain,

We regret to inform you that your bookstore, Bluebird Books, will enter foreclosure on August 1, if you do not remit the outstanding balance of your delinquent payments. I've enclosed a detailed payment sheet to show the amount owed. If you cannot cover this debt, we will proceed with foreclosure and seize your assets and sell them at auction to recoup what is owed.

Regards,
Arthur St. Claire, VP of Small Business Affairs,
Chase & Hanson Bank International

I shake my head. Is Arthur really coming after Bluebird Books? After a dead woman? Of course, he doesn't know of the connection to me. It's a form letter. Bluebird Books is just one of thousands of pesky small businesses in default, in need of discipline from his department. And if he knew that I inherited the shop? It wouldn't change his course of action. Business is business. I can almost hear his voice in my head.

I flip to the second page, and see that not only is Ruby behind on payments, but she took out a primary and secondary mortgage on the shop years ago. I shake my head. The attorneys mentioned they'd be sending over an accounting of Ruby's estate, and they hinted that she had some debt, but nothing of this magnitude. I sigh. Even if I sell my apartment in New York, which is what I'm planning to do, and empty out my savings, there's no way I'll have the funds necessary to save the store. That's the brutal fact.

Bluebird Books will have to close. Tears sting my eyes, and I wonder about the June Andersen who used to run an arm of Chase & Hanson Bank, the June Andersen with a heart of steel. She'd laugh at me now, an out-of-work owner of a bookstore in foreclosure.

I feel foolish. If I'd only received the letter from Arthur yesterday. But would it have changed things? Would I really have left Bluebird Books in foreclosure, left it on its deathbed, then returned to New York to my old life as if nothing had happened?

And then I remember my journey. I remember the reasons why I decided to part ways with my career. I crumple the letter into a ball and toss it in the wastebasket by my feet. The foreclosure notice changes nothing. In fact, it gives me a *purpose*. I will fight for Bluebird Books in the way I used to fight for Chase & Hanson Bank. I will use everything in my arsenal to save the bookstore. My heart beats strong and sure, not erratically, the way it used to when under stress. Yes, I will fight for the bookstore, and even if I fail, I will go down having given it my all.

The disagreement Gavin and I had earlier seems insignificant now. I need to tell him about my plans for the bookstore; I need him to help me fight.

I run out to the sidewalk without even bothering to lock the door. I see that there's an OPEN sign on the door of Antonio's. *Good*, I think. *He's decided to keep it open.* The idea to combine the bookstore with the restaurant and create a bookstore-café is appealing, but maybe Gavin would prefer keeping Antonio's intact. And the restaurant he's built is worth preserving. I see the band setting up in the corner of the dining room, and I assume he's having them back ahead of schedule to attract more customers. Maybe I can help him. The bookstore is sinking in a quicksand of debt, but I could wrap an apron around my waist and wait tables until I figure out my next steps. Restaurant work is exhausting, but fun, and oddly satisfying. I feel a pit in my stomach when I think of the possibility of the bank repossessing Bluebird Books, auctioning off Ruby's prized possessions. They'll sell it to a developer who will demolish the place and turn it into a row of shoddily built townhouses or, worse, condos. Seattle does *not* need more condos. It will be me against Chase & Hanson Bank. David vs. Goliath.

I sigh, walking into the restaurant. The scent of sauce simmering and bread baking comforts me. "Hi," I say to Ned, the saxophone player. "Is Gavin here?"

"Yes, but he's—"

"Thanks," I say, making my way back to the kitchen. I burst through the double doors. "Gavin, I got a letter in the mail and . . ."

My voice trails off when the scene before me comes into view. The edges are blurry at first, but they quickly become crisp and clear, soberingly so.

"Oh," I say, catching my breath.

Adrianna, her feet bare, is wearing a black cocktail dress that's half-zipped in the back. Gavin stands behind her, with his hand on the zipper. The dress is low-cut, and I can see the outline of her ample breasts and the lace of her camisole beneath the fabric. Suddenly everything Adrianna said, everything Gavin said about their past, their present—it doesn't matter. All that matters is this moment, this emotionally charged, intimate moment.

Gavin projects extreme discomfort. "Adrianna got back from her trip a little early," he says awkwardly. "I was just helping her with—"

"I came home early," Adrianna says, fumbling for words. "My grandmother found a buyer for her restaurant. I have a—"

"I should go," I say quickly. "I'm sorry. I . . . I didn't mean to interrupt."

I run out the door, through the dining room, and then out to the street. I'm mad at myself, for being a fool, for thinking I could actually step into Adrianna's shoes, for letting her convince me she was ready to move on, when she clearly isn't. And maybe it's too soon for *Gavin*.

I'm grateful I have my running shoes on, because all I want to do is sprint. I turn to the lake and find my way to the path, where I sift into the steady stream of bikers and joggers. I want to run until I can't feel anything anymore—not my hands, not my feet, not my legs, and not my heart.

Chapter 13

I don't even know how long I've been running, how many laps I've completed, when I notice the bench ahead. It's the same bench where I met Gavin a few weeks ago. I sit, tucking my knees to my chest, and think about Gavin and Adrianna. How foolish I've been to not see that he still loves her. My cheeks flush when I think about how beautiful she looked in that dress. What could he ever see in me? I shake my head and stand. I feel a raindrop on my cheek as I make my way to the street. By the time I pass Joe's Café, it's an all-out downpour. I look into the window of Joe's, packed with regulars, and feel sad, remembering what Gavin said about Joe retiring, closing the shop. Why must things change? Why can't everything just go on as it is? As I pass Antonio's I can't distinguish the raindrops from my tears. A black SUV peels out of the parking spot in front of the bookstore, and when I see the door to the shop left ajar, my heart beats faster.

Suddenly, Gavin appears. "June!" he cries. "I was looking everywhere for you! I went to go find you at the store and"—he pauses to point to the open door, and as frightened as I am about the prospect of burglary, I can't help but think of how adorable he looks standing in the rain, when I probably look like a soggy, drowned rat—"June, someone broke into the bookstore."

I come to my senses as he runs ahead. I follow him through the store, and I gasp. Bookshelves have been overturned, boxes ripped open. Books and papers are scattered all over the floor. Even the air feels disturbed, violated.

"Who would have done this?" Gavin asks.

"I don't know," I say.

I'm shaking as I kneel down and begin sorting through the books and papers—days of my hard work ruined in the span of minutes.

He places his hand on my back. "Let me help you."

"No," I say quickly. "I'll be fine."

"June," Gavin says, "I'm staying whether you say yes or not. I won't leave you here like this. What if the people who did this come back? You need to file a police report."

"I will," I say in a shaking voice. "Gavin," I cry. "I got a letter today from Chase and Hanson, from my old division. My aunt was in a lot of debt, apparently. Bluebird Books is almost in foreclosure."

He looks as if my words have knocked the wind out of him. "What?"

"I don't have much time," I continue. "There's a chance, a small one, that if I sell my apartment for a profit, and drain my savings, I might be able to keep the shop afloat. But even then, I'm not sure if it will all work. It might not be enough."

Gavin nods. "I have some savings," he says. "I mean, it's not a lot, after buying out Adrianna's share, but please, let me help."

"No," I say quickly. "I mean, that's kind of you, but you have the restaurant to consider."

"When will you know if . . ." He swallows hard. "If you'll have enough?"

"Soon," I say. "I'll probably catch a flight out tomorrow, and I'll talk to my friend, Peter, in New York. He's an accountant, and this will take some serious number crunching. We'll plot it all out."

"And this," Gavin says, indicating the mess left by the intruders. "Does this frighten you? If someone is looking for something, what if they come back?"

"Yes, it does frighten me." For the first time, I tell him about the letters between Ruby and Margaret Wise Brown, the way Ruby left them out for me to find, with clues, one after the next. And then I tell him about Anthony Magnuson, my aunt's baby boy, and the cryptic warning from Victoria Magnuson about her daughter.

"There must be something of considerable value here in the store," Gavin says. "Do you have any idea what it could be?"

I shake my head as I survey the shelves where most of the first editions are housed. None have been touched. Then I glance at the papers and books on the floor. "Whatever it is, I don't think they found what they were looking for." I stand up and take a closer look at the shelf filled with valuable books. "If they were after valuables, they would have taken these old books," I say. "But they didn't. They must have been looking for something else."

"Maybe you could sell some of the first editions," he suggests, as if struck with a brilliant idea. "I mean, to help pay back the debt, to keep the store afloat."

I shake my head. "I would hate for it to come to that. It would be like selling off part of the store's soul."

He nods as if he understands. "Then what?"

"I don't know, but I think you're right about there being something else of value in the store." I take a deep breath and stare at the disarray. "If it's here, I'll find it."

I stand up, and turn to the stairs that lead to the little apartment above the shop. "I'd better go pack."

"Wait," Gavin says, walking toward me. "Not until I tell you what I need to say. What you saw in the kitchen at the restaurant . . . it isn't what you think."

I look away. "You don't have to—"

"I do. I do have to say this. Because you have it all wrong. Adrianna and I are over."

"But I thought—"

"She's going on a *date* tonight."

"A date?"

"Yeah," he says, grinning. "She returned from her trip early, and met someone on the plane, and"—he shakes his head at the absurdity of our conversation—"and they hit it off. He's taking her to Canlis. She bought a couple dresses and really wants to look great, so she came over to get my opinion."

"Wow," I say, smiling. "I have to admit, when I saw you unzipping her dress—"

"*Zipping* her dress."

"Oh," I say, still smiling. "Well, when I saw you standing together, I felt like such a fool."

He nods. "We both know it's time to move on from each other, in life and in business. We'll always care for each other, but we need our own space to just be without the other one always looking over our shoulders. It's why she offered again to sell me her share of the restaurant, and I accepted."

"You did?" My question comes out a little more like an exclamation.

"Yes, I did," he says, smiling. "Of course, I'll always be grateful for her help in building Antonio's into what it is. But it's time to turn the page." He pauses and searches my face. "Remember how we talked on the island about the idea of joining forces? Combining the bookstore and the restaurant into a store-café model?"

I nod, feeling my heart pound with excitement.

"Well, if you still want to do that, we could," he says. "I mean, if you feel it's in the best interest of the store."

"I do," I say a little guardedly. "But, I . . ."

He rubs his forehead. "But what?"

"Well, I don't even know if I'm going to be able to save it," I continue. "Believe me, I'm going to try. But that's all yet to be determined. I wouldn't dream of yoking the store's debt with Antonio's—what if it caused you to go under too?" I know from professional experience that combining business efforts in this way is risky. "Also, you already tried to run a business with . . ."

"Someone I love?"

My cheeks flush. *Is he saying he loves me?*

"You're right," he says. "There's that. I see how you'd be worried that we'd make the same mistakes that Adrianna and I did." He takes both of my hands in his. "But please, you have to know that what we have . . ." He clears his throat. "What we're building together is so different. June, it's so different, I don't even want to compare. What I'm trying to say—and this is going to come out awkwardly, because I've never been one to sound smooth when I tell a woman I love her, which isn't often. I've done it three times, and the first time I was eleven years old. But, I'm rambling."

I smile and bite my lip. "Did you just say what I think you said?"

He nods. "I'm telling you, yes, that I stand here before you in this terrible mess of an old bookstore, staring at a girl I met not even three weeks ago, who probably thinks I'm completely nuts—but still, I cannot let you leave Seattle without knowing that I have found myself falling so hard for you."

I giggle and cry at the same time, which sort of comes out

sounding like a snort, but I don't care. Nothing can ruin this moment. "I don't know what to say."

"Say that you're crazy about me in the same way I am about you."

I lean into his arms. "I am," I whisper. "And after everything I've been through, I didn't think I could feel this way again."

He gives me a little smirk. "Which, by the way, we need to cover in a future installment." He kisses my forehead, then my nose, then my lips. "You're a great mystery to me, June Andersen, a mystery I cannot wait to solve."

"You will," I say. "I promise."

"Good," he says, glancing at the clock on the mantel. "Does that really say four o'clock, or am I hallucinating?"

"Yes," I reply.

"Well, darn. I burned the bread. The loaves are probably on fire in the oven right now, unless one of the servers took pity on me and took them out. Let's hope."

"Oh, I'm sorry!"

He takes me in his arms again. "Never will burned bread taste as good as it will tonight," he says, beaming. "To be continued," he adds, running to the door.

"To be continued."

Chapter 14

The next morning, I have a half hour before the cab will pick me up for the airport. I hate to go, to leave the shop, more now that Gavin and I are on a solid path ahead. I blush when I think of him telling me he loves me.

The police came by yesterday evening to survey the bookstore, fingerprint the door, and ask questions about the break-in. "Was anything stolen?" a young female officer asked a bit disinterestedly.

"I don't think so," I said. "At least not that I can tell."

Her eyes lit up when she saw a book on the floor, splayed out facedown. I hated to see the books disheveled like that, but Gavin had encouraged me not to alter the "crime scene" until the police arrived (some bit of knowledge he mined from *Law & Order*, no doubt). "Is this Eloise Wilkin?" the officer exclaimed.

"Yes," I said, looking over her shoulder.

She thumbed through the pages of collected stories from Wilkin, then stopped on a page where a little girl glides through the air on a swing over a grassy lawn in front of a beautiful home with a gabled roof. "I used to daydream about this scene for hours," she said, without taking her eyes off the page. "I would pretend that this was my life, my swing, my house." She shook her head nostalgically. "You know, I don't think I've seen this book since I was nine years old."

"Why don't you keep it?" I said.

"No," she said. "I couldn't."

"I insist."

She finished writing up the incident report, and left with the book tucked under her arm. Somehow I think it was meant for her.

I can tell my blood pressure is elevated, so I take my medication. I've done my best to tidy the mess before I leave this morning. Gavin said he'd keep an eye on the place, but what if whoever broke in comes back when he's too busy at the restaurant to notice? What if this time they find whatever they came looking for before?

I feel a chill spread down my neck to my back as I reach for my suitcase and lock the door.

At the airport, I hand my ticket to the man standing at the gate. He sends it through a scanner, then says, "Have a nice trip, Ms. Andersen."

A trip? I think to myself, this is *definitely* a *trip*. Here I am now, the unemployed owner of a bookstore in Seattle on the verge of financial failure. I left New York on top of the world—on paper, at least—and now I'm returning with nothing. And I desperately need to get my roots touched up at the salon.

Part of me wants to turn around and run back to the comfort of the bookstore, to run back to Gavin—to just leave New York in . . . New York. And yet, the practical side of me knows that getting on the plane is the first step toward a better future—for me, and for the store. I have to put one foot in front of the other. And that's hard.

"Ms. Andersen," the ticket agent says. "You may proceed to the airplane now."

I nod. "Sorry. Right."

I head down the terminal to Delta flight 208. I have an appointment with the real estate agent tomorrow morning, and then the movers come that afternoon, followed by drinks with Peter, my accountant friend, to shed light on my financial picture. I just hope I can pull together enough funds to keep Bluebird Books afloat.

As the plane takes off, I reach into my bag and pull out the new pair of letters, which I found on the top shelf in Ruby's kitchen, in an old copy of *Betty Crocker's Cookbook*. I read with anticipation.

July 5, 1946

Dear Brownie,

Thank you for your wonderful advice. As always, your words soothed my ache like medicine. I will give Lucille more time. Maybe we'll have our European tour . . . someday.

I want to go to one of these literary parties you wrote of. I'd like to have a few words with anyone who finds your work "amusing." How dare they belittle you! How dare they question the importance and brilliance of your work!

Just yesterday, a little boy and his mother came into the bookstore. You should have seen this child, so dejected and sad. His mother told me his father had died two months ago and he was having trouble at school. She said he didn't have many friends, and she hoped to get him some books to cheer him up. So I led him to a bookshelf and pulled out a copy of <u>When the Wind Blew</u>. I told him I knew the author—you, of course—and his eyes lit up. I read the story to him. And though I've read it before, it hit me then that this was a story about finding happiness in the loneliest little corners of life; that even a cat or a dog can be a companion, which leads one to the notion that we are not as alone as we feel we might be. What a transformative message, for a child and an adult.

Well, Brownie, the little boy turned to me after I finished reading and he smiled. "Boxer's my best friend," he said.

"Boxer?" I asked.

"My dog," he said cheerfully.

Next time you feel that your work doesn't have merit, remember how your words cheered this little boy, how they lifted his spirits during a dark time in his life. Let the others be the serious "literary" types. Let them write big important novels and give each other accolades. But, in all of it, remember that you are doing very important work. And there are very few in this life as uniquely talented as you to do this work.

Margaret, I hope you'll take what I've just written and put it in your pocket and save it. When you're feeling down about your work, your purpose, may you take it out and remember just how important you are.

With all my love,
Ruby

P.S. Anthony invited me to accompany him on a business trip to Miami. He says he'll get a car to take me to Key West for a day or two while he's tied up with work. Key West! I admit, all I've been able to think about in the past few days is a) I need to find a swimsuit, and b) What are the chances of running into Ernest Hemingway?

I study the letter carefully and see that Margaret must have heeded Ruby's advice, because the letter has obviously been folded many times. Its creases are very deep and worn, as if she might have done just what Ruby suggested. *I hope you'll take what I've just written and put it in your pocket and save it.* She must have done just that.

July 12, 1946

Dear Ruby,

Your letter arrived just before I left for Maine, and I'm so grateful it did, for you saved me from myself. I might have spent the entire monthlong holiday trying to be someone I will never be. And when I say that, I mean a novelist. I suppose there will always be a part of me that wonders if I could do it. And maybe I could. But what you say is true. I have been granted a special talent, and it's one I shouldn't be ashamed of. Thank you for reminding me of that, my dear friend.

Maine is lovely. Warm and quiet, just me and the creatures. Frogs croaking at dawn; jackrabbits hopping through the morning mist; dragonflies buzzing in the tall grass; crickets chirping at dusk. Time passed slowly. In fact, I was oblivious to it entirely, which is always the best time spent. I would find myself lying on a blanket in the grass with a book, and I'd doze off. When I awoke, I didn't know if it was the next day or an hour later. Everyone should experience such marvelous laziness.

I thought of you often, Ruby. I'd look up at the moon at night and think of you staring at the same moon. When do you leave for Miami? I must say, I'm tempted to find a swimsuit and join you both there. I'm dying to meet Anthony, and then there's Ernest. Did I ever tell you that we met at a party in New York last year? He'd had far too much to drink when he told me I looked like Lana Turner, but I have to admit, even despite his inebriation, I did find him altogether charming. What a pair we'd make. The hotheaded literary don and the children's book author. It's almost too hilarious to think about.

Well, I'm off to a meeting with my editor. I suppose we'll be talking about all things <u>Little Fur Family</u>. In keeping with Operation Sisterhood, I will bring Roberta the very first copy, with a yellow ribbon tied around it.

Write soon, and let's make plans for Key West.

> With all my love and adoration,
> M.W.B.

Sharon, my real estate agent, stands in the kitchen of my New York City apartment. She wears a black suit jacket and skirt, with heels so high, they make my feet hurt just looking at them. "Well," she says skeptically, "it will be a challenge."

Sharon helped me buy the apartment five years ago, which, sadly, was the peak of the real estate market. I paid more than the asking price because there had been a bidding war. But now? Sharon explains that the market is flooded with similar listings and there will be no bidding wars. In fact, we'll be lucky to get even one full-price offer.

"You're going to have to lower your expectations for the sale," she says, walking to the living room. She runs her finger along the edge of the old mantel, which I intended to have repainted but never did. She attempts to smooth a bubble of peeling paint, then frowns. "It's a buyers' market now."

I gaze out the big windows that look out to the balcony and views of New York City beyond, and I shake my head. "Sharon, I have to sell the co-op for what I paid for it, or more."

She sighs. "Well, if you want my advice, I'd suggest sitting on it for a while. Maybe get a renter in here. Then, in a few years, maybe there'll be less inventory to compete with and you can get your price."

I shake my head and tell her about the bookstore in Seattle. "I can't. I need to cash out. I need the money for Bluebird Books."

"Well," she says, obviously disappointed, "I can't promise you success, but I will certainly do my best."

"That's all I can ask, I guess."

"When do you want the listing to go live?"

"Tomorrow," I say.

"That quick? You sure you don't want to think about options a little?"

I shake my head. "It's clear to me what I need to do." I try to project confidence, but my heart is fluttering, even though I made sure to take my medication before Sharon arrived.

She nods. "OK then, will we need to stage it?"

"No," I say. "I'll leave the furniture. Moving it to Seattle isn't practical, as my aunt's place is furnished. I'll just pack my personal belongings. The movers are coming later today." I don't tell her that I don't want any reminders of my old life, my old self. I want to shed my New York self like molted skin.

"OK," she says. "The furniture will help. I can have a photographer come by this afternoon, so I can get the photos for the listing. Will that work?"

I nod, and her business face melts for a moment. "Remember when I first showed you this apartment?"

I smile to myself. I'd just been promoted at the bank, and I had the feeling of invincibility. I walked into the open house and fell in love with the apartment instantly. It didn't matter that there was a six-way bidding war; I knew I'd make this place mine.

"You've changed," Sharon says, clutching her Louis Vuitton purse. She looks at me curiously.

"I have," I say simply. "I want different things now." We stand together in silence for a moment. "Or maybe I always wanted those things, but I just didn't know it yet."

❦

The movers arrive at two, and at my direction, they box up my closets and drawers, clear out the books from my shelves. "All the furniture stays," I say.

They shrug as if they've heard stranger things from people before. The lead guy, who introduced himself as Jose, has kind eyes. He works meticulously to tape my boxes of clothing and shoes. I remember him admiring the glass entryway table. The piece was picked out by my decorator when I first moved in; I always hated it.

"Hey," I say, pointing to the table. "Would you like to have this one?" I see a gold wedding band on his left hand. "Maybe for your wife?"

"Really?" he says, surprised.

I nod. "It's yours if you'd like it."

"Thank you, ma'am," he says, beaming, before returning to the task at hand.

☙

Peter texts me that he's going to be late, so I slide into a booth at the Fifty-sixth Street Bistro and order a gin and tonic for me and a martini for him. I gaze out the window and think about how long it takes to build a life. The many ladder steps you climb in a career. The laborious task of setting up a home, buying furniture and throw pillows, and curating the collection like a museum. Then there's the art of honing your identity—your favorite restaurants, where you shop for groceries, get your coffee in the morning. And then, just like that—in a single afternoon, really—you can simply light a match and let it burn.

Peter arrives just as I finish my drink and the waitress brings me another.

"My girl!" he exclaims, leaning in to give me a big hug.

"It's so good to see you," I say, smiling. "How's Nate?"

"Good as ever," he says with a smile. Peter and his boyfriend, Nate, recently purchased a brownstone in Brooklyn, and they had me over for dinner the month before I left for Seattle. "We finally got the living room paneling done."

"I bet it looks amazing," I say, thinking about what it might feel like to put down roots the way Peter and Nate have. This is to be their only house. They spent a fortune on the place, which ultimately became affordable when Nate's parents gave them the money for the down payment. In some ways, I envy them. I envy the certainty of their lives, when mine feels more like a box whose possessions have been scattered all over the floor. Picking them up and setting everything back into place feels exhausting now.

"Aw," he says, "what's with the sad face?"

He leans in to hug me again, and then sets his overcoat on the hook on the outside of our booth.

"I was just thinking about how much things have changed," I say. "I never thought I'd leave New York. I thought this was *me*."

"It still can be," he says. "I mean, I am slightly biased, but I'm here to tell you that you don't have to go. Do Nate and I need to launch a Keep June in New York City campaign?"

"You're adorable, you know?" I take a sip of my drink, and grin. "No, I have to go."

"You've fallen in love with the bookstore, haven't you?" he asks. I already filled him in on the situation by phone from Seattle.

"Yes," I say. "And I think I've also fallen in love with a man."

He raises his right eyebrow and gestures to the waitress for a refill for both of us. "The plot thickens," he says. "Cute?"

"Very."

"Good heart?"

"*Huge* heart."

"Then you have to go," he says. "As much as I hate the thought of you on the other side of the country, you know I'm a sucker for true love."

"Then you should hear about my aunt Ruby's story," I say.

Peter looks intrigued.

"She was in love, all her adult life, with a married man, who bought her the bookstore," I explain. "His name was Anthony."

"So she was a *kept* woman?"

"No, nothing like that," I say. "It was . . . somehow sweeter than that."

"And did they ever marry?"

"No," I say. "His wife refused to give him a divorce. So he divided his time between his life with her and with my aunt. And yet, Ruby loved him fiercely, until his death."

"How'd he die?"

"This is the tragic part," I say. "My aunt got pregnant in her forties, which I think was a shock to both of them. And Anthony died one day when they were ice skating. He fell and hit his head. Just like that."

"Just like that," Peter says, rubbing his forehead. "It's tragic."

I nod. "Their relationship was obviously far from perfect, but if we could all find an ounce of the love that Ruby and Anthony shared, we'd be doing very well."

"Sounds like you've found it."

"Maybe I have," I say. "Time will tell. But first I have to save Bluebird Books." I glance out the window at the New York street beyond. "I can't explain it," I continue, shaking my head. "I think I've always known, deep down, that I belong in Seattle, at the bookstore. I just didn't feel it was a purpose, a calling, until now. Peter, I desperately want to save the store. I hope it wasn't a pain for you to crunch all those numbers."

He holds up his hand as if to say, "Nonsense!" then reaches for his brown leather messenger bag and pulls out a file folder. Peter was my friend before he became my accountant, but I soon learned that he's as good with numbers as he is with friendship.

He sets a spreadsheet on the table so we can both see it.

"If I clear everything out, will it be enough? I mean, enough to save the store and to live on?"

"Honey," he says soberly, "I hate to be the bearer of bad news, but I don't think so. I took a look at your aunt's debt, and here's the thing—you're going to have to sell the apartment at a profit. You were mortgaged pretty high on that place, and you no longer have an income. Even if you clear out your savings and IRA, which I would not recommend doing—even then, you still might only make it work by the skin of your teeth."

My heart sinks. "Oh."

Peter pauses for a long moment. "You could ask your old boss . . . Arthur. Maybe he could help."

I shake my head. "Are you kidding? No. I could never do that. It would be like crawling to Potter."

"To Potter?"

"You know, in the movie *It's a Wonderful Life*, when Jimmy Stewart has to swallow his pride and ask Mr. Potter for the money to repay his debt."

"Oh stop," Peter says. "You're overdramatizing this. Just send him an e-mail. Tell him the trouble you're in. You worked for the guy, for what, like, ten years? He's got to have a heart."

I shrug. "I don't know."

"Sure he does," Peter says. "What did you always call him? The best jerk in the world?"

"The nicest asshole I've ever met."

"See?" he says.

"But I don't think it's a fifty-fifty thing. I think the asshole side outweighs the nice side, by a long shot."

Peter takes a long sip of his martini. "Still, I think it's worth a shot. What do you have to lose?"

"My pride," I say. "It takes a lot to crawl back to Potter."

He grins and grabs my hand. "The thumb-wrestling champion makes the call. You win, you do it your way. I win, you go to Arthur."

I roll my eyes but play along, mostly because I always beat Peter at thumb wrestling.

"On your mark," he says, "get set, go!"

He goes in for the (thumb) jugular. I wriggle free from his grasp and put the clamp down, but not hard enough—he extricates his thumb and is back in the running.

"I'm not going to lose," he says. "I won't let you give up on your destiny."

"My destiny, eh?" I say, trying my hardest to pin him (er, his thumb). "And who says my destiny isn't to marry Ryan Gosling and have six children?"

"Because, *shhh*, don't tell Nate, but it's *my* destiny to marry Ryan Gosling," he says with a victorious grin, before clamping my thumb down with his and holding it down.

"No," I say. "Rematch!"

"No rematch. I won, fair and square. Now, you have to talk to Arthur."

I lean back in my chair and realize that Peter's right. "OK. I'll send him an e-mail. But you know he's just going to rub my face in it."

"So what if he does? At least you'll give it the old college try."

I roll my eyes. "Who says that?"

Peter folds his arms across his chest. "Smart people."

"Smart people from 1982."

We pretend to be angry at each other for about three seconds before we hug.

"I'm going to miss you," he says.

"I'm going to miss you, too," I say as my eyes well up with fresh tears. Suddenly I'm questioning everything. I left Seattle when I was eighteen. I'm a New Yorker now. "Maybe this is a big mistake. Maybe I'm not supposed to move to do this."

"Honey," he says. "Don't second-guess yourself. Even though I haven't met Gavin, I can tell that he makes you happy. Trust yourself, OK?"

I nod. Turns out, it's harder than you think to trust yourself. It's easier to trust Peter. So I do that.

That night, my last night in my New York City apartment, I pull
out my laptop and address an e-mail to Arthur. I think of all the
previous times I've e-mailed him to report on a successful foreclosure
or an ambush on a small business, one that resulted in less loss for
the bank. I shiver. This time it's different, of course. This time it's
personal. I close my eyes tightly, then open them again. And then I
type:

> Dear Arthur,
>
> So . . . I don't know exactly how to put this. But, here
> goes . . . I've gotten myself into a bit of a mess. You see, I
> inherited a bookstore in Seattle, a beloved children's
> bookstore, where I spent the only happy hours of my
> childhood. And I didn't know it when I flew out to Seattle to
> get my aunt Ruby's estate in order, but I realized that I want
> to make a life of this. No, I *need* to make a life of this. I want
> to be a bookseller. I want to read to children, and I want to
> try to teach them the same love of literature that my aunt
> taught me. But the bookstore is on the brink of financial ruin.
> It's kind of ironic, given my (former) line of work. I got a form
> letter from you, Arthur. You (a.k.a. Chase & Hanson Bank) are
> foreclosing on Bluebird Books. My aunt Ruby's Bluebird
> Books. *My* Bluebird Books. The funny thing is that after all
> these years doing what we do, I somehow trained myself to
> stop feeling. I trained myself to just get the job done. Like a
> robot. And now I'm on the other side. And it turns out, it
> really sucks.
>
> I don't know what I'm saying here. I don't know what I'm
> telling you. Actually, I do. And this is the hard part. I'm ask-
> ing you to help me, Arthur. Please, help me save Bluebird
> Books. I don't expect you to move mountains, but I know
> you can press the Pause button on the foreclosure

proceedings. Just give me a few more months. I'm selling my apartment, cleaning out my savings, but even then, I don't know if I'll have quite enough. Could you just give me a little more time?

Do it for me, please, or prove me wrong, that you're not the nicest asshole I've ever met. I'd be eternally grateful.

Yours (even though I'm no longer your employee, can we still be friends?),

June

I press Send, and then I lay my head on my pillow with a thud, like it's a bowling ball. Arthur's my last hope. Please let him say yes. I just need time.

Chapter 15

Gavin picks me up at the airport the next day, and when I sink into his arms, I feel like I am home.

"How'd it go?" he asks.

"Well," I begin, "it will be an uphill battle. I'm not even sure that if I sell the apartment I'll have all the cash I'll need to save the bookstore." I pause for a moment, as he navigates his car onto the freeway. "I e-mailed my old boss at the bank, to see if he can help."

"That's a great idea," Gavin says. "Do you think he will?"

"I'm not sure," I reply. "I don't want to get my hopes up. But, I think . . . maybe. I know somewhere under all those layers of spreadsheets that he has a heart. I haven't checked my e-mail since last night, so maybe the answer is already waiting for me in my in-box."

Gavin nods. "Either way, we'll find a solution. Together."

I shake my head. "I won't drag you into my financial mess."

"But it's much nicer if we could call it ours," he says.

I grin. "I do like the sound of that."

Gavin spends the afternoon at the restaurant, which he's managed to keep open as sole proprietor, for now, and I unpack upstairs in the apartment. I think of the boxes that will be coming on the moving trucks soon, and look around the apartment with new eyes. It's home now.

I throw some clothes in the washing machine, then cautiously open up my laptop, and I see Arthur's reply waiting for me. I was careful to take my medicine in New York to quell my bursts of rapid heartbeat that had surged in reaction to the financial and real estate stress.

When my heart begins to race again, I regret not taking a pill this morning. I click open the e-mail and hold my breath:

June,

I'm sorry, can't help. It's too bad, but it's the way the cookie crumbles.

Arthur

I close the laptop quickly. For a few minutes, I just sit there, stunned. *The way the cookie crumbles.* My cheeks feel hot. I regret baring my soul to him. *What was I thinking?* And then I come to my senses. No, it's not Arthur's job to save this bookstore; it's *my* job. And I will give it everything I've got.

I turn to my laptop again. It's time to get to work. My aunt had a son. He must be out there, somewhere. Maybe he can help. I don't know how, but I'm going to find him.

I pick up my cell phone. "Mom, it's June. I need your help."

"What is it? Honey, are you in some sort of trouble?"

"Well," I say, "yes, maybe. Bluebird Books is in financial trouble. I just got back from New York. I'm selling my apartment. I'm going to try to save the store."

"Honey, you know Rand and I don't have any money, I—"

"Mom, that's not why I'm calling. Listen, I know about Ruby's baby."

"What? You know about . . . ?"

"Mom, I know. I went to see Anthony Magnuson's daughter, May. She told me about Ruby's baby boy."

"Ruby's baby boy . . ."

"You know, don't you, Mom?"

"Yes," she says solemnly.

"Why didn't you ever tell me?"

"It wasn't my place to. It was Ruby's wish to keep it quiet."

"Well," I continue, "so much time has passed. The reasons she had for hiding him aren't real anymore. Besides, I think I had it wrong. Instead of being a competitor, it's more likely he'd want to help me save his mom's store. And, who knows, he could even have the financial means to invest in Bluebird Books."

"Oh, June," Mom says. "I really don't think you should go down that path. Besides, this person may not be who you think he is."

"I have to do something," I say. "Listen, where do you think he might be living? Do you remember anything? Any clue? A name? Anything to help me start my search?"

"No," Mom says. Her voice sounds edgy, distant. "I can't help you with this, June. I'm sorry."

I can't tell if she truly has no information or if she's being deceptive for other reasons. How could she be so uncooperative? There's a man out there, my cousin, and he may not even know how wonderful his mother was. He began his life here in the bookstore, and maybe he could come back, to help me save it.

After I end the call, I open my laptop. I feel a deep sense of conviction as I search the listings for the King County records department.

"Hello," I say to the operator. "If I were trying to find out the name of someone who was born in Seattle in 1970, someone whose records were sealed in a closed adoption, could I get that information? Could I see his birth certificate, or would it be part of a closed file?"

"All birth certificates are a matter of public record," the woman says. "You can come downtown and put in a request, or you can look it up. We just got our files digitized, so if it's a quick answer you're looking for, I can save you a bit of time and look it up right now for you."

"Really?" I say, grateful. "Yes, that would be wonderful."

"Do you have the child's mother's name?"

"Ruby Crain." My heart beats faster as I hear her clicking on her keyboard over the phone.

"And you said the birth year was 1970?"

"Yes," I reply.

"Here we are," she says a few moments later. "Ruby Crain, delivered a child on . . ." She pauses for a second. "Looks like the type has smudged. Let me get my glasses." I hear her set down the phone before she returns and picks it up again. "Yes, the baby, J.P. Crain, was born on May 12, 1970."

"J.P.," I say to myself after thanking the operator and hanging up. I think of Ruby's son then. He'd be tall and slender like her. He'd have light hair, maybe a dusting of freckles on his face. He'd have kind eyes and a quick smile. Smart and gentle, and literary, just like his mom. The moment he got wind of Ruby's store, he'd help me. And I'd welcome him, just like family. Gavin could host a dinner for him. We'd toast the next chapter of the bookstore.

"I'm going to find you, J.P. Crain," I whisper as I lace up my running shoes and head out for a jog.

Gavin's in the kitchen chopping cauliflower when I poke my head in later.

"Did you just get back from a run?" he asks.

I nod and pop a piece of raw cauliflower in my mouth. "I found Ruby's son," I say. "At least, I found his name."

"What do you mean, *Ruby's son?*"

"Ruby gave birth to a baby boy the year I was born. My cousin. Or second cousin."

Gavin looks equally confused. "Great-cousin?"

I shrug. "In any case, I'm related to him. Ruby gave him up for adoption. But I keep thinking that if I can find him, maybe he can help save the bookstore."

Gavin shakes his head. "What makes you think this guy will have any sympathy for a mother who gave him away?"

"Ruby had her reasons," I say. "I'm sure it was excruciating for her to make the call, to make it a closed adoption, but I know it's what she felt she had to do. I'll explain that to him. He'll understand. And he'll fall in love with the bookstore. He'll love it like I do."

"I don't know," Gavin says. "What if he has no interest in knowing about his past? What if he's a drug addict or a con artist?"

"Aunt Ruby's son?" I say. "Not a chance."

He grins. "Don't be so sure. Someone in my family line won a Pulitzer Prize, and yet the gene pool is equally peppered with degenerates."

"Well, I just *know* that J.P. is not a degenerate."

Gavin drizzles olive oil on the cauliflower spread out on a sheet pan before sprinkling a dusting of kosher salt on top. "Listen, I just don't want you to get your hopes up. The guy could be a big disappointment."

"Or the best thing that ever happened to Bluebird Books," I add cheerfully.

As it turns out, J.P. is a very popular name. There are more than a thousand men in the Seattle area who go by the name J.P., and even then, I can't be certain if his name is still J.P. Wouldn't his adoptive parents have given him a new name? And then what? I can't search under Ruby's last name, Crain, as he'll certainly have a new family name.

I decide to search on a website called Adoption Connector, where there are message boards designed to connect the grown children of closed adoptions with their birth families.

I take a deep breath, complete my registration on the site, and then post:

> I am in search of the biological son of my great-aunt, a wonderful woman who passed away recently in Seattle. The child was born in Seattle on May 12, 1970. The name on his birth certificate is J.P. Crain. I can't be certain of the exact date, but I believe he was adopted sometime after his birth, in a closed adoption. If you have any information, please e-mail me through this site. Thank you!

I flip on the old stereo and fiddle with the dial until I find my favorite jazz station, 88.5 FM, KPLU. I used to listen to it in high school and dream of smoky New York City jazz clubs. Little did I know that I'd end up sitting alone at those very tables years later wondering if I'd made a mistake in leaving home.

I find *Where the Wind Blew* after some searching (the first edition hid on a lower shelf), and pull out the next collection of letters:

July 19, 1946

TELEGRAM
TO: Margaret Wise Brown
FROM: Ruby Crain

Bought red gingham swimsuit. Will arrive in Miami on July 23. Staying at the Savoy. Key West together on the 26th?

July 20, 1946

TELEGRAM
TO: Ruby Crain
FROM: Margaret Wise Brown

Bought green swimsuit. Key West has no idea what it's in for.

Beneath the telegrams are two letters, and I open the first hoping for an account of their time in Florida.

August 5, 1946

Dear Margaret,

I've only been home for a week, and yet I miss you and Florida so much. That sunshine! Anthony really liked you. He told me so several times. He said I am lucky to have such a devoted friend, and he's right.

Oh, what fun we had in Key West! It was enough fun to last a lifetime, and take my mind off Lucille, who is back on no-speaking terms with me again. I'll set that aside for now and just say, if I never do anything exciting again, at least I'll be able to think back to those two days and smile to myself. The beaches! The dinners! Those drinks with the lime wedges in them and the salt on the rims of the glasses. The coconuts hanging from the palm trees.

I can't believe we walked up to Ernest Hemingway's home and rang the doorbell, just like that, like a couple of salesgirls. To think he'd answer his own door like he did and invite us in for a drink (or ten!). He was a hoot, wasn't he? And such a gentleman, too. He obviously had eyes for you, Brownie. Did you see the way he looked at you? I'd say you should write him, but I don't know that a man like that would be good for you. I fear he'd drive you mad. Or perhaps you'd drive each other mad. You both burn hot. You're both so alive. I suppose the type of woman Ernest needs is the type of man you need: someone mild and peaceful. Besides, isn't he married?

Well, needless to say, that night will go down in history as one of my very favorites. (Though, how strange Ernest's cats were! They seemed almost human in the way they'd look at you. And one had six toes. Did you see that? It was the one with blue paws. Poor kitty must have gotten into a bucket of paint.)

Off to go shelve a new shipment of books. Wish you were here this afternoon. It's raining, and I'm already missing the tropics. And you.

With lots of love,
Ruby

I smile to myself as I turn to the next letter.

August 14, 1946

Dear Ruby,

Key West was divine, wasn't it? If I had more confidence in my ability to be a wife, I think I'd marry Ernest. But you're right, we could never make each other happy, not in any sustainable way. We'd drive each other mad, that much is certain. But it would be great fun for a while, wouldn't it? Can you see me yukking it up in Key West with him and all those cats? I'd live in long sundresses and straw hats. I'd go barefoot and my skin would be covered in freckles.

But no, I could never do it, for two important reasons, the first being Ernest's beard. I know he'd never shave it, and I would despise the scratchy feeling on my face. The second reason is, of course, hurricanes. The thought of them coming as unexpectedly as they do would frighten me to no end. So there you have it, beards and hurricanes: the two reasons why Ernest Hemingway and I will never be lovers.

But I do think those cats will always stay with me. I loved that little fellow who got mixed up with a can of paint. Blue paws. I can't get them out of my head. I think I shall write a book someday about two kittens who get into mischief with buckets of paint. I could call it <u>Color Kittens</u>. What do you think?

I'm writing to you on a drab day in New York. I'm looking out my Cobble Court window and the wind's blowing the little white picket fence gate so hard that it flings open every few seconds, then slams shut again. While it was good to come home, to sleep in my own bed again, I realize how lonely I am here sometimes. I'm like the gate, swinging in the breeze when I long for someone to just secure the latch and stop me from flailing about.

Perhaps this is how you feel about Lucille. When we lose touch with a person we love, I suspect it feels that we lose a part of ourselves. As I've always said, don't lose heart. But prepare yourself for the day that you must mourn your loss and move on, rather than let it paralyze you. I hate to think of you stymied by the choices of another.

Well, I should be getting back to work. My editor wants a new idea soon, and I'm afraid none feel good enough to share just yet. I keep coming back to the moon concept you mentioned months ago. I think there's something there.

Sending love and sunshine and another one of those tart key lime margaritas (which they, obviously, named after me),

M.W.B.

I think of what Margaret wrote about the cat at the Hemingway home, and realize it's proof of the inspiration for the book *The Color Kittens*. Of course, I read the book dozens of times as a child in the bookstore. I think of Aunt Ruby and Margaret sipping cocktails with Ernest Hemingway, and I smile to myself.

I take a deep breath, pondering Margaret's more serious words: *Prepare yourself for the day that you must mourn your loss and move on*. What if I'm not ready to move on? What if there's still hope after all? I place my hand on the phone, then pull it back again. Tomorrow. Maybe tomorrow.

Chapter 16

Gavin walks into the bookstore the next morning with a cup of coffee for me. "I'm going to miss Joe's," he says.

"Me too," I say, taking a sip of the Americano, mixed with the perfect amount of half-and-half.

"Any luck finding the mysterious J.P.?"

I shake my head. "It's a little harder than I thought. But I posted something on an adoption website, and I just have to hope that if he's looking to find more about his past, he'll see it. Sometimes fate plays a role in these things."

My cell phone buzzes on Ruby's desk, and I run to retrieve it. It's a New York number.

"Hello?"

"Oh, hi, June, it's Sharon. Can you talk?"

"Just a sec," I say, then cover the phone and turn to Gavin. "It's my real estate agent."

He nods, and I turn back to the phone. "So, do you have a juicy offer for me? Please, tell me you do."

"Well," Sharon says, "we do have an offer, which is encouraging, but I'm sorry to say it's not juicy."

"How much?"

"It's ten percent below asking," she says, "which isn't bad in this market. I think we should take it, June."

"But I'm already selling it at a loss," I protest, a little panicked.

"It's a good offer, June. All cash. Quick closing."

"Can we counter?"

"We can do anything you want to, but in a market like this, I don't want to scare off a buyer. I suggest you take it."

I sit down in Ruby's old swivel chair and look at Gavin standing beside a bookcase, so strong, so sure. His smile tells me it's going to be OK. And somehow, I feel that it will be.

"OK, Sharon. If you think we should take it, let's take it."

"Good," she says. "I'll fax over the paperwork to you this afternoon."

I set my phone down, a little stunned. "I just sold my apartment in New York."

"Great news," Gavin says. "This calls for a celebration."

"Not really. I'm selling it at a big loss."

"Oh."

"I don't think I'm going to have enough to save the store." I feel like crying, or laughing, or both. And suddenly, out of nowhere, I begin to laugh. It pours from me like a river. I laugh until I'm crying.

"What?" Gavin asks. "What's so funny?"

"My life," I say. "It's a total mess."

He smiles at me. His eyes sparkle in the morning light streaming through the window. "It's a *beautiful* mess."

❧

That afternoon, I borrow Gavin's car so I can drive to a salon on Queen Anne Hill to get my hair done. No matter how dire things get this month, I can at least go about my business with nice hair.

After a partial foil and a trim, I start back to Green Lake, when I realize how close I am to the Magnuson home. I decide to drive by the old mansion again.

I pull the car up in front of the home, and I think about the break-in at the bookstore and Victoria Magnuson's cryptic warning about her daughter. Was May really behind the break-in? It's possible, yes, and yet I don't believe it, not really. After all, it was kind of her to send me that note with the photo of little J.P. I shake my head. No, it couldn't have been May.

I take the keys out of the ignition. What if I just went to the house and met with her again? Maybe she knows more about him. Maybe she remembers something that she can share. I step out of the car and walk up to the iron gate in front of the brick walkway that leads to the house. This is not the kind of residence one just drops into. You make an appointment. But there's no time for those formalities now. I need to find J.P.

A Hispanic woman opens the door. "How can I help you?" she asks in a heavily accented voice.

"My name is June Andersen, and I was hoping to speak to May, if she's home."

The woman looks at me skeptically, then shakes her head. "Ms. Magnuson isn't home. But I can—"

The door opens wider, and suddenly May's mother appears. "I can take it from here, Julia," Victoria says with surprising command. She looks lucid, aware, somewhat different than she did when I saw her before.

"But, ma'am," the younger woman protests, "Ms. Magnuson said you must stay in bed today."

"Ms. Magnuson doesn't make the rules," Victoria says. "I do. After all, this is still my house, isn't it?"

"Yes, ma'am," Julia says, stepping back.

"Now," Victoria continues, "I will show you in, Miss . . . ?"

"Andersen. June Andersen."

"June," she says, staring at me curiously, as if she may or may not remember meeting me two weeks ago.

"Yes."

We sit down in the library, and Julia looks at Victoria. "I'll be upstairs if you need me."

Victoria waves her away, and as soon as the library doors click shut, she turns to me. "I'm glad you came."

"Thank you for inviting me in," I say. "I wasn't planning on stopping by, but I was in the area. There's something I'd like to discuss with you."

Victoria folds her hands in her lap and looks at me expectantly.

"I realize it may be hard for you, to revisit the past," I say.

"I should have let him go to her," the old woman says distantly. Her eyes search my face, then look away, to a far corner of the room, where perhaps she's seeing her late husband and Ruby in the shadows. "I should have let them be a family. I didn't love him like Ruby did. I could never love him the way she did, so completely. When I learned about the baby, I was jealous and I felt scorned."

"You were hurt," I say. "It's a natural response."

"Yes, but it was bigger than that. I wanted to make them pay. All along, I wouldn't agree to a divorce. I said he'd get nothing." She dabs a handkerchief to her eye. "That worked for a long time, but by the time Ruby got pregnant with the child, he didn't care about the money anymore. He was going to leave me, leave everything he had to be with her. Of course, I wasn't going to let him go that easy. I told him that I'd go to the newspapers. I'd disgrace him. I was desperate, but it didn't matter. He'd already made up his mind. He was going to tell her his plans to leave the night he died. Even after he was gone, I just couldn't let go. I threatened your aunt. I wanted to make her life miserable."

I listen, though it's hard to hear. Her words sting. I am a surrogate for Ruby's pain.

"It seemed unthinkable to me that she could bear his child," she continues, "that she could keep such a beautiful piece of him. I hated that."

"But you had May."

"Yes, but May was grown. She had her own life to live. I was alone. And here your aunt had a chance to start all over again. I wanted that desperately."

I nod, nervous for what's to come.

"I drove your aunt to give away her son, you know," she says. "It was all me and my threats. I made her think that I'd have the child followed. I told her the child deserved to grow up as a Magnuson, and that my attorneys would see to it that he was raised the way Anthony was, in the best boarding schools. Well, as you can imagine, she didn't want me in her son's life. And she made it so I never would be. She arranged the private adoption. She duped me."

I shake my head. "Would you have really tried to take the baby from his mother?"

Victoria sighs. "There was a time when I think I actually might have. I think Ruby knew I was capable of it. God knows, I have enough money to get things I want. But as the years passed, my heart began to soften." She leans toward me. "What I want you to know, June, is that I have deep regrets about the way I behaved in those years. My actions kept two people from each other, and then tore apart a family. I never should have intervened the way I did. And I shall go to my grave with those regrets. I just pray that Anthony has forgiven me."

I wipe a tear from my cheek and move to sit beside Victoria. I take her hand in mine, and I look her in the eye. "I *know* he'd forgive you," I say. "As would Ruby."

She shakes her head. "My actions are unforgivable."

"No," I say. "Your heart is in the right place now."

"I wish I could turn back time," she says. "I wish I could fix things."

I think of Bluebird Books and my eyes widen. "There is a way you can," I say. "The bookstore is in financial trouble now. It will close if I can't raise enough funds." It feels strange to make this appeal to her, after the years of pain she endured. And yet, her story has come full circle in a way that feels right. "Would you consider making a contribution to keep the business going?" I pause. "In memory of Anthony, and Ruby."

"Of course I will, dear," Victoria says. "How much do you need?"

Her answer comes so quick, it startles me. And then I hear the library doors open, and I turn around to see May standing in the doorway. She looks startled, a little angry.

"Mother? What are you doing downstairs? You should be resting."

"Everyone's always telling me I should be resting," she says. "When you get to be ninety, you'll realize how tiresome it is to be told this at every hour of the day."

May walks over to her mother and eyes her territorially, then turns to Julia, who's standing in the doorway now. "Julia, take Mother upstairs. I'll be up in a moment."

"Outnumbered," Victoria says, winking at me. "Well, you be in touch now, all right?"

"I will," I say, smiling. "Thank you so much."

After the doors have closed behind us, May looks at me with intense eyes. "Let me be clear," she says. "You will not be in touch with my mother."

"But I—"

"I know what you're here for," she says. "I heard you asking her for money."

"No," I say quickly. "It's not like that. It's for the bookstore. I—"

Her eyes are searing. "You will leave now, and Mother will have no further contact with you."

I shake my head. "But she said she—"

"She has dementia," May says. "She doesn't know what she's saying." She shakes her head. "Shame on you for trying to take advantage of an old woman."

"But, May, I wasn't. I was only—"

"You were only looking out for your own interests. Good-bye, June."

Back at the bookstore, I feel deflated, discouraged. I find *The Color Kittens* and long for the letters that I know will cheer me.

August 21, 1946

Dear Brownie,

As much as I miss the sunshine of Florida, I must admit, it is nice to be home. I suppose Seattle will always suit me more than warmer climates. There's a certain madness to sunshine, I think. Warm weather makes people think they should be doing something, always. There is no rest in warm weather. And yet there is something so comforting and peaceful about the dark clouds and rain. Everyone goes inside and cozies up with books.

Lucille surfaced, in the form of a card, announcing that she and her husband are expecting their first child this winter. My sister is going to be a mother! Of course, I'm exceedingly happy for her, but I will admit, only to you, that it caused me to examine my own life in greater detail. Will I ever be a mother? Anthony's made it clear that he cannot and will not become a parent again, and yet, I would be lying if I said that there isn't a certain part of me that longs to hold a baby, my own baby, in my arms.

Yet, this isn't the path I chose when I decided to love Anthony. But sometimes I wake up in the middle of the night in a cold sweat. The dream is always the same: I have a baby in my arms that someone takes from me.

It's silly to read into dreams, so I try not to think of it. Besides, I may never have children of my own, but I have plenty who I've had the privilege of getting to know through the bookstore. Little Loretta Franco brought me a wreath for the door last week, and another little boy wrote me the sweetest thank-you card. This ought to be enough for me, and yet my heart longs for the type of motherly love I know I may never be able to experience.

Well, I worry that I'm wearing on your nerves, so I will change the subject. Oh! I had an idea this morning. I've decided to make a calendar of events for the store, which I'll post in the window. Each day I'll have something new to entice children to come in. I was thinking that on Tuesdays I'd do young author workshops. I'll give children pens and paper and paint to make their own little picture books. Together we can come up with concepts for their stories, and then they can work on the art. Imagine how fun that could be!

Write soon and tell me about this new book idea that you have in mind!

With love,
Ruby

P.S. Anthony will be traveling to Chicago over my birthday weekend, which means I'll be spending it alone.

August 25, 1946

TELEGRAM
TO: Ruby Crain
FROM: Margaret Wise Brown

Catching flight to see you in Seattle. Won't let you be alone on your birthday.

Did Margaret Wise Brown come to Bluebird Books? I reread the telegram, and then Aunt Ruby's letter, but there are no book titles mentioned, no further clues. What next? The story of the bookstore's past beckons, and yet, I don't know how to turn to the next chapter.

Chapter 17

I walk into Antonio's with slumped shoulders, and slide into a chair at the table in the kitchen.

"It looks like someone could use some wine," Gavin says, reaching to the shelf and plucking a glass. He uncorks a fresh bottle and pours its crimson liquid. "What happened?"

I sigh. "I went to the Magnuson house again. I talked to Victoria Magnuson."

He grins. "The Queen Mum?"

"Yes," I say. "I told her about the plight of the bookstore, and she offered to help. It was beautiful. She said it would be sort of a repayment for the way she treated Ruby over the years."

"That's good news, then, right?"

"Well, it was," I say, "until her daughter walked in and accused me of trying to swindle money from an old woman."

"Oh," he says.

I take a sip of wine. "May doesn't get it. I think she still has a ton of anger that her father abandoned her."

"That makes sense," Gavin says diplomatically.

"I don't know," I say. "I don't even know my father, and yet I don't have any abandonment issues."

He looks at me curiously, as if he knows me better than I know myself, maybe, which is vaguely unnerving. "You don't?"

"I don't," I reply. "I don't know anything about my dad except that he and my mom met at a bar, and it was a one-night stand. At least my sister's father had it in him to stick around until a couple of weeks after she was born. Anyway, I have no interest in finding my father, nor do I feel as if he abandoned me. It is what it is."

Gavin nods as though he's not altogether convinced.

"It's different with May," I continue. "She grew up with a father who she loved, desperately so, and yet he was never around. And then as if she didn't feel unloved enough, he goes and starts another family with Ruby." I swirl the wine in my glass. "I get why she's hurt. I get why she sees the bookstore as the impetus for her pain. I wish she'd see its value, from a community perspective. And I guess most of all, I wish she'd see that my intentions are good."

"Don't feel so bad," he says. "This is bigger than you. You're just the messenger. I bet she'll come around."

"I'm not so sure," I say. "You should have seen the look on her face."

"Well, then we'll have to think of a Plan B."

I throw up my hands. "Got any brilliant ideas, Watson?"

"Yes," he says. "You know the letters you've found between your aunt and the children's book author?"

"Margaret Wise Brown."

"Well, I was thinking that maybe we could really spruce up the shop and host a party. A fund-raiser. We can sell tickets. I'll cater it. Maybe you can hint that we have a big announcement to make about the literary history of the store, and then we can unveil the letters between your aunt and the author."

"Actually, that's genius," I say, the wheels in my mind turning so fast I can hardly keep up with them. The bookstore has been featured in local media before. Ruby kept a framed *Seattle Times* article about the shop hanging over her desk. Surely the story of saving a beloved Seattle institution would appeal to modern-day media.

"I can see the headline now," Gavin says, "'Fund-Raiser Held to Save Historic Seattle Children's Bookstore Believed to Be Birthplace of *Goodnight Moon.*'"

I think of the last set of letters between Margaret and Ruby, and I worry that I've hit the end of the scavenger hunt. I shake my head. "I don't know that Bluebird Books was the inspiration for *Goodnight Moon*, just that my aunt encouraged Margaret to write about the moon."

"Do you know if she ever visited the store?"

I nod. "I think she was planning to. I found a telegram stating that she planned to come. I just don't know if she ever did. I can't find the next set of letters."

"Surely there's a clue that you've overlooked," Gavin says.

I pull the letter and telegram out of my pocket and hand them to him. "No. No books mentioned," I say. "So now what?"

He's silent for a few moments as he reads, and then he smiles. "Wait a second. What about this mention of the children's home-made books, here?" He points to the page, and I reread it: *I was thinking that on Tuesdays I'd do young author workshops. I'll give children pens and paper and paint to make their own little picture books. . . . Imagine how fun that could be!*

"I think you're brilliant," I say.

Gavin leaves a pot simmering on the stove and together we race over to the bookstore. I climb a ladder to a high shelf where I remember Ruby tucking in the treasured "books" her youngest customers had made especially for her. They're bound in all fashion—staples, glue, tape, yarn. I pull out one with a colorful cover held together with masking tape that's yellowed over the years. "A Tugboat's Dream," the title reads. "By Jenny Hamilton."

I feel a bulge beneath its pages and there they are, the letters. I almost squeal as I hold them out for Gavin to see. "Found them!"

"Good," he says, turning to the door. "I've got to get back to the kitchen before the sauce boils over, but come over as soon as you can, OK?"

It's good to see him moving ahead with the restaurant, confidently, and I think of what a pair we'd make as co-owners of a bookstore-café. But I don't want to rush things. "Go make your sauce," I say, grinning. I race to the wingback chair and read expectantly.

September 2, 1946

Dear Brownie,

You just stepped into the taxi that will take you to the airport, and oh how I hate to see you go home to New York. This has been my very favorite birthday of my life, and I shall be forever grateful to you for traveling across the country to share it with me. Your friendship is more than a friendship; it's a sisterhood.

I'm so delighted that you love Bluebird Books as much as I do.

I pause and gasp. Margaret Wise Brown *did* come to Seattle, to Bluebird Books, and she loved it.

I knew it the moment Anthony brought me to the space (blindfolded at first!). Certain buildings just have good feelings to them, don't you think? The apartment upstairs isn't much, but I'm going to fix it up in time. I have a paint color picked out for the walls, and one day I'd like to have part of the space framed in for an office, or maybe a bedroom, though I do love the openness of the space, and sleeping at the center of it all. Walls are so stifling.

Anthony will be sad to have missed you. He was so glad to know you were coming to stay with me. In all the excitement of your visit, I didn't even notice the little box tied with ribbon tucked into my desk drawer. I found it just now and opened it straightaway. It's a watch, from Anthony. Cartier. He must have seen me admiring it on our trip to Miami. I admit, I'd forgotten about it entirely until I found it. Oh, Brownie, but it's not so much the watch as what he had engraved on the back of it. It says, "I will love you until the end of time."

I still have tears in my eyes. It's the most beautiful sentiment I've ever read. I may not ever get a ring, but I will wear this watch proudly.

Oh, before I forget, you left your sketches for the new moon book on the table upstairs. Would you like me to mail them back to you? Or did you intend for me to keep them? I must admit, I love getting a little more time to linger over the pages and see your brilliant creative process. Do you always think of ideas for the illustrator? Are they receptive to your artistic suggestions?

I have a good feeling about this moon book. There's a palpable sense of comfort in the nursery. But, if I may make a suggestion, I do think the walls should be a bright emerald green. It's such a happy color, don't you think? Also, in the nursery of my dreams, there would be a bookshelf and big picture windows so you can see the stars from the bed. And maybe a telephone—to symbolize a connection to the outside world—and a bowl of something warm on the nightstand. A little snack. Food. Warmth. Love. What more could a child ask for? What more could any of us ask for?

Whatever direction you and your illustrator take with the story, I know it will be a resounding success. I cannot wait to see it when it's finished (and, of course, to sell stacks of copies on your behalf!).

Anthony is scheduled to return tomorrow on the 11 a.m. train. I'm going down to the station to greet him even though I know there's a small chance that I may run into Victoria there. If she comes, it will only be to upset me. The life she's living is a charade. She refuses to agree to a divorce, and yet she carries on with other men. I don't think I told you this, but Anthony said he came home one night and found one of them at the house. They're both miserable, and yet sometimes I feel as if each is intent on making the other even more so.

I had better sign off. Story time begins in fifteen minutes and I need to prepare. I expect at least a dozen children today.

Missing you already,
Ruby

P.S. I tucked a copy of <u>Pippi Longstocking</u> in your suitcase. Read it when you get a chance. I discovered it at a book fair in Seattle a few months ago. It's a translation of a book that's quite popular in Sweden. My prediction is that it will become a sensational hit with children in America before too long, but don't mark my words.

September 12, 1946

Dear Ruby,

I managed to catch a cold on my journey home to New York. It is two in the afternoon, and I just now got out of bed to fetch the mail and what should I find but a letter from you. How it made me smile.

Roberta is expecting a baby. She phoned me this morning to give me the news. Funny you should describe how this news made you feel, because I had the same response. For all my life, I've said I didn't want to be a mother. And now? Well, Roberta's news made me question everything. It helped knowing you feel the same, that this news caused a collective twinge in our hearts. See, we are secret sisters, indeed.

My editor rang me up this morning, and she heard the gravelly tone to my voice, and she told me instantly that I'm not caring well enough for myself, which is rubbish, of course. She said I ought to sleep more and play less. Well, what sort of life would that be?

I should be on my feet in a day or two. And my week in Seattle was well worth this pesky cold. I loved seeing you in your element. The bookstore is exactly as I imagined it, and perhaps even lovelier.

Yes, the mockup of the moon book is yours to keep. We'll be making changes to the text, of course, but I wanted you to have it—after all, you've been integral in its very creation. Maybe someday when I'm rich and famous you can sell it for a thousand dollars. Ha!

I've been thinking about your suggestions, which are very good. I've decided to change the opening lines of the book from "in the great room" to "in the great green room." Doesn't that have a happier ring to it? It practically chirps off your tongue. Like the little bluebirds you love so much.

And yes, there will be a telephone. A bookshelf. And a balloon. Perhaps, red? And there will be a bowl of porridge. And maybe a painting of a cow jumping over the moon, just like the one hanging over the hearth at Bluebird Books.

Well, I'm still sorting it all out, but as loose as it all is, I have a feeling about this book. It has a soul that some of my other projects didn't. And I don't worry about getting it just right, because I know the words will find me. I know the story will be written the way it's meant to be written. That gives me great peace. I know I'll wake up one morning and pick up a scrap of paper and write the words down, and that will be that.

Oh, and yes, I found the Pippi book. Thank you! And you are right, I do think American children will be wild about this little redhead. She has such spirit, such heart! She is the girl I longed to be as a child, strong and sure, kind and steadfast. I only wish I'd thought of her first. Alas, I shall keep with my bunny rabbits and dogs. And moons.

> With love from foggy New York,
> M.W.B.

My mind is reeling when I set the letters in my lap. Aunt Ruby not only helped Margaret Wise Brown come up with the idea for *Goodnight Moon*; she actually helped her shape it. And somewhere, under this very roof, there are sketches—an early mockup, perhaps—of the story for me to find. I can hardly wait to tell Gavin.

Gavin's fiddling with an enormous food processor when I return to the restaurant. I tell him about the revelations in the letters, and he beams. "Just think of all the Seattle celebrities and notables who would come if they knew the history of the bookstore."

I feel a surge of confidence now. "If we could really reach the people who grew up coming to Aunt Ruby's story times, her young author workshops, if we could appeal to them, surely they'd want to help to save the bookstore."

"That's exactly what I'm thinking," Gavin says. "If we can get people to come back and show them how important the bookstore is, talk about its legacy and its future, they're bound to contribute."

"You're amazing, you know?" I say.

"Not really," he says. "I just think I was a publicist in a former life."

"So where should we start?"

"Well, let's get the store spiffed up first. Maybe a few new shelves? Some fresh paint? Nothing extravagant, but if we're going to lure people in, we have to make the place shine."

"I agree," I say.

"What do you think about timing the event?"

"We're going to have to do it soon," I reply. "I'm afraid we don't have much time before the bank pounces. And they *will* pounce."

"Yes," he says. "I have a buddy who's a graphic designer. I'm sure he can help us with the invitations, posters. I can write the press release."

"Wonderful," I say. "We'll have to think of a good name for the event. Maybe 'Inspired by the Moon' or something like that." I inch closer to Gavin. "Can't you just imagine how happy Ruby would be right now if she were here?"

He smiles.

"And if this is all a success," I continue, "if we can keep the shop afloat, maybe we can pursue our plan to join forces. I mean, if you really want to."

"I do," he says. His words are sincere, but his eyes are distant.

"What?" I ask suddenly. "What is it?"

He rubs a stain on his apron compulsively. "It's nothing." He pauses for a moment, and then looks up at me. "Listen, there's something I've been meaning to . . ."

I search his eyes, but he doesn't make contact with mine. "What is it?"

Just then, the kitchen door swings open and a man with clipboard appears. "Sorry to interrupt," he says. "I knocked, but there was no answer. The door was open so I just came on in. I've got your wine order. Just need you to sign right here."

"Of course," Gavin says, hurrying toward him. He rubs his brow nervously before he takes the pen in his hand.

"Where should I leave the boxes?"

"By the bar is fine, thanks," Gavin replies, turning back to me as the man disappears through the doors to the dining room.

"Well, I . . ."

I decide not to press him, especially while he's working. If he needs to tell me something, he will. In time. "Are you coming over tonight?" I ask. "After you close?"

"I can't tonight," he says a little distantly. "I have to . . . make the marinara for a wedding I'm catering this weekend."

"Oh," I say. "Can I help?"

He smiles. "Thanks, I've got it covered. But I'll bring lunch over to the bookstore tomorrow. Sound good?"

"OK," I say. "Call me if you want help."

"I will." He kisses me softly before I turn toward the door.

I spend three hours tidying the store, energized by the idea of the fund-raiser. I think of *Goodnight Moon*, and decide that I'll contract a painter; I'll try to match the exact color of the emerald-green walls of the nursery in the illustrations. And maybe I can have the drapes replaced. They've gotten so sun-bleached over the years. We already have a rocking chair, and the old telephone, plus the painting of the cow jumping over the moon, hanging over the fireplace.

It's nine before I stop for dinner. I can smell the aroma from Antonio's next door, and my stomach growls. I think about going over and eating in the kitchen, but I don't want to bother Gavin. So I walk up the stairs to the apartment and make a frozen dinner. I stocked the freezer before I left for New York. I flip on Ruby's old TV while I eat the little dish of cheese ravioli. I wonder how many times Ruby sat in this chair and watched television over a frozen dinner, alone. And my heart hurts so much, I have to clutch my chest then and blink away the tears. I think of how she was always knitting. Scarves. Sweaters. Mittens. She was never particularly good at it. If you inspected her handiwork closely, you'd find a dropped stitch here, or a small hole or lump there. But it was impossible not to love something Ruby had made. "Made with love," she'd say.

After I eat, I reach for my laptop. I checked my messages this morning, a little disappointed. It was a small chance that J.P. would find the message, and yet, I held on to hope and had to fight the urge to check the adoption website hourly. But I tell myself that a quick check before bed wouldn't be a bad idea.

I key in the website and pull up my dashboard. I see that there's a mail icon next to my profile name. I click on it eagerly, and read a message with the subject line titled "Hello from J.P."

Hi, I saw the message on Adoption Connector. My name is J.P. I live in Seattle, where I was adopted by my parents, a kind and wonderful couple who raised me with love. I am thirty-five years old. I had a wonderful childhood, but recently learned that I was adopted (my parents kept this from me for fear that I'd do just this: try to find my biological family). I assured them that I have no interest in replacing them. They are my parents. No others could fill that role. And yet, I can't rest until I know where I come from. I have little information about my birth mother, just that she was in her forties when she had me, and that she was a single mom and educated. She named me J.P., also, and my parents kept the name because they liked it. Anyway, I work downtown, at the main branch of the Seattle Public Library. I'm director of reader services. I'd love to meet, to discuss all of this. Maybe we could have coffee. Look forward to hearing from you. —J.P.

I practically squeal when I finish reading the message. *This has to be him.* A librarian? Thirty-five? The son of an educated single mother in her forties? It all fits.

I reply to his message immediately:

Dear J.P., How amazing to hear from you! I cannot wait to meet you and discuss more! Are you free on Tuesday for coffee at ten? I can meet you at the library. Thank you, June

I check my messages incessantly for the next hour until I see his reply:

Dear June, SO good to hear from you. Yes, Tuesday at ten. My office is on the third floor. Just go to the reception desk and ask for me there.

I leap out of my chair and throw on a sweater. It's after ten. The restaurant just closed, but I know Gavin will still be in the kitchen working on the marinara, just as he said he would be, so I head to the back door to the kitchen. I reach for the handle, but it's locked. That's strange. I peer through the window. The kitchen is dark and I feel the familiar flutter of my heart rate quickening as my anxiety rises.

Chapter 18

I wake early the next morning and phone Green Lake Painters. I arrange for a crew to come to the bookstore. Eager for work, they arrive later that morning, and because their bid is reasonable, I get them started on prepping the bookstore for its new look. The trim and windows are taped, and within an hour, the place looks like a construction zone, with ladders everywhere, men in overalls carrying paint buckets. The first editions are on the far wall, so I'm not too worried about getting paint on them, but I had the crew cover the shelf with a tarp as a precaution.

Gavin shows up at noon with a paper bag wafting delicious aromas. He's kept his promise, but the sight of him makes my stomach twist in knots.

"Hi," he says from the doorway.

"Hey," I say. I decide not to ask him about his absence from the restaurant last night. Not yet.

"I brought lunch," he says.

"Let's eat upstairs," I suggest. "They're about to start the first coat." The foreman seems like a decent person, so I don't worry about theft of the more valuable books in the store. Besides, most people wouldn't know of their worth.

In the apartment, I set Ruby's kitchen table for two. Gavin opens a few takeout boxes and smiles. "I'm starved. Eat up," he says.

I nibble on a breadstick as he scoops a large helping of spaghetti onto my plate. "I have news," I say between bites.

"What?" he asks with wide eyes.

"I think I may have found Ruby's son, J.P."

"Really? That's amazing!"

"I'm meeting him downtown tomorrow," I say. "Get this—he's a *librarian*."

"Talk about fate," Gavin says.

I grin. "And you thought he'd be a degenerate."

"No," he says, quickly swallowing the bite in his mouth. "I said there's the *possibility* of him being a degenerate."

"Well, he sounds like a great guy," I say. "I mean, have you ever met a librarian you didn't like?"

Gavin looks thoughtful for a moment. "Yes," he says finally. "Mrs. Thorndike. The librarian at my elementary school. She scared the you-know-what out of me."

"Oh, stop," I say. "She was probably just rattled by ten-year-old boy antics."

"You're right," he agrees, nodding conspiratorially. "I suppose it didn't help that my best friend and I set a lizard loose during story time."

I roll my eyes. "Males. Anyway, I have high hopes for J.P. If Ruby's son is a librarian, imagine the partnership we could forge. Bluebird Books could sell the titles at library events, and we could sponsor summer reading programs, that sort of thing."

"The match does sound heaven sent," Gavin says. "But don't get your hopes up, OK? I mean, at least until you're really sure he is the guy."

"I know," I say. "But I have a good feeling about finally solving this family mystery." I finish my salad, and I can't help but think of the empty kitchen last night when I stopped by Antonio's. The old feelings of betrayal rush back. He said he'd be working on the marinara, but he wasn't. I bite my lip.

"Gavin," I say a bit tentatively. "I stopped by the restaurant last night around ten. I thought you'd be there working on the marinara. I was surprised to find the lights out."

"Oh," he says, pausing an extra moment. "I was exhausted last night. I decided to come in early today instead."

I nod, trying to rid myself of the pain of the past, the insecurities I've carried with me for so many years. I tell myself that Gavin is different. He wouldn't hurt me. He certainly wouldn't lie to me.

His cell buzzes in his pocket, and he pulls it out quickly, then looks at me apologetically. "I have to take this one," he says. "You finish lunch. I'll stop by a little later, OK?"

"OK," I say, trying not to broadcast my disappointment. I pick at the pasta on my plate, and wonder who's so important on the phone, and why Gavin's suddenly acting secretive.

"Sorry," I hear him say as he heads down the back staircase. "I can talk now."

An hour later, I stare at the Italian food spread out on the table, and I shake my head. Gavin's keeping something from me. I know it. Is it Adrianna? Does he still have feelings for her? Is she having some sort of crisis that he's trying to help her with? If so, why can't he tell me about it? Why can't we deal with it *together*?

I shake my head, collecting the plates and silverware and piling them in the old ceramic sink with the dripping faucet. What would Ruby have done?

I think of a time Amy and I quarreled. She'd taken one of my favorite books, Laura Ingalls Wilder's *Little House in the Big Woods*, and scribbled on each page with permanent markers. I'd always been on Amy's side, always, but when she violated something so precious to me, I began to see her in a new light. I sigh, then think of what Ruby told me that day. She set the ruined book aside, reached up to a nearby shelf, and pulled down a fresh, new copy of *Little House in the Big Woods*. "No matter how dire it seems, no situation is hopeless," she said. "Nothing is beyond fixing, my dear. Remember that, June, all right?" At the time I couldn't even look at Amy, let alone forgive her. But Ruby addressed that, too. "Some of us have to make a lot of mistakes before we become the people we are meant to be. Amy's making her mistakes. Let's be patient with her."

I close my eyes tight. "Ruby," I whisper into the air, "what do I do? I'm afraid." I think of Gavin. "I'm afraid to trust." And then I think of Amy. I see her in her pigtails on the day she ruined my book. Her hands are stained with red and black ink. "I'm afraid to forgive."

Ruby's words come to me again. "Nothing is beyond fixing, my dear." This comforts me, and I tuck her wisdom away in a place deep down, where I can find it again when I need it.

❦

Later that evening I get a text from Gavin. "Slammed at the restaurant. Miss you."

His words are vague and I try not to read too much into them, especially now that Adrianna is out of the picture. And yet, I know I'm fragile in matters of love. Instead, I pick up the phone and call Peter.

"Hi," I say.

"Hi, sweetie," he says. "How's Seattle?"

"I don't know anymore."

"What happened?"

"Nothing, really," I say. "But you know when you get that feeling that something's wrong, but you can't put your finger on it?"

"Yeah," he replies. "You have to trust that feeling."

"Well, I'm getting the feeling about Gavin. I think he's keeping something from me."

"Like what?"

"I don't know, exactly," I say. "I can't help but think that it may have something to do with his ex."

"The business partner at the restaurant?"

"Yeah."

"Here's what I think, June. I think that after all you went through, you're afraid to be made a fool again."

"Right about that," I say.

"But I think by protecting yourself, you're also putting up walls and being too paranoid."

"Maybe," I say honestly.

"If you want this to work, you can't do that. You have to proceed with total trust. If he tells you that he's going to be one place, you believe him until you have solid reason not to. Did I ever tell you about when Nate and I first started dating, how I thought he was cheating on me?"

"No," I say.

"Well, he was working late a lot, and then he skipped out on a dinner we had planned. I was beside myself, totally paranoid that he was seeing someone else."

"Was he?"

"No," Peter replies. "He was actually planning my thirty-fifth birthday party."

"I remember that party. Those flowers, that cake."

"I know, it took a lot of work," he continues.

"I really don't think Gavin's planning a party for me."

"That's not what I'm saying, silly. The point is, things aren't always what they seem."

"You're right," I say. "Thanks for listening to me ramble."

"I love listening to you ramble. If I was straight, I'd marry you."

"And live happily ever after," I say.

"No," Peter continues. "You're going to do that with Gavin. Just wait and see."

"Your confidence gives me hope," I say.

"Any offers on the apartment?"

"Yeah," I say. "One lowball offer, but we took it. Sharon thought it would be our best."

"So where does this leave things with the bookstore?"

"Not good, I'm afraid," I reply. "If I save the store, it will be by a thread. I have a lead that may pan out. Ruby had a son long ago. She gave him up for adoption under difficult circumstances. Anyway, I kept thinking that if I found him, maybe he'd want to know about the bookstore. Maybe he'd want to help."

"Smart," he says.

"Well, we'll see. I did get a bite on an adoption website from a man in Seattle who fits the profile of Ruby's son. Turns out he's a librarian, which is pretty amazing. But, it's yet to be determined if he's *the* J.P. I'm meeting him tomorrow. Gavin and I had another idea, though. We're going to host a fund-raiser. Remember how I told you that my aunt kept in touch with Margaret Wise Brown, the author of *Goodnight Moon*?"

"Yeah," he says. "How could I forget? That's amazing."

"Well, I think we're going to use that as the hook," I add. "We think people might be interested in helping to save a bookstore with such rich literary history behind it."

"When's the date?"

"We haven't gotten the invitations printed yet, but we're thinking soon, as in next month or so. That will give us just enough time to get the store cleaned up, send out invitations, press releases, that sort of thing."

"Tell me the date as soon as you have it confirmed. Nate and I will be there."

"Really?" I say with a squeal. "That would mean so much to me."

"Don't mention it," he says. "But I also have ulterior motives. Nate's favorite book as a child was *Goodnight Moon*. He's going to flip out."

"Love you, Petey," I say.

"Love you too, Junebug."

The movers arrive two days later, first thing in the morning. I see the truck pull up in front of Bluebird Books, so I set my coffee down and rush outside to the curb. There isn't much in the truck—a dozen boxes, most of them clothes—but I'm happy to reunite with my belongings. It will feel like I'm moving in, officially now.

The driver hands me a clipboard, and I sign my name on the page in front of me. "If you could just take them through the shop, then upstairs to the apartment, that would be great. The staircase is in the back."

The man looks up to the awning nostalgically.

"Bluebird Books," he says. "I remember coming to this place as a kid. My mom used to take me to story time."

"My Aunt Ruby owned the store," I say. "She passed away recently, and I'm going to try to keep it alive."

"Wow," the man says. "Sure brings back memories." There's grease under his fingernails, tattoos up and down his arms. He has the look of someone who'd rather be at the local tavern than home with his nose in a book. But that's when I remember that books do not discriminate. Ruby always said that.

"I wish I read more now," he says. "Somehow I lost interest over the years."

He and his goateed assistant reach for boxes and proceed inside the store, where they stop suddenly near a shelf by the window. I set up a Roald Dahl display last week, remembering how much I loved *James and the Giant Peach* as a girl. The tattooed man picks up a copy. "I used to love this book," he says. "Man, just seeing the cover takes me back. My fourth-grade teacher read it to us. Every day after that, I wanted a peach tree in my backyard."

"Keep it," I say.

The man looks surprised. "Really?"

"Yeah," I reply. I know that giving away books isn't exactly the point of a bookstore, nor is it a decision my former self, the financier, would approve of, but somehow it feels like the right thing to do in the moment.

"Thank you," he says with a smile, tucking the paperback into his back pocket. "That's really kind of you."

I think of what he said a moment ago, about wishing he could love reading again, and I remember something Ruby said to parents who claimed their children wouldn't read, and to bored-looking teenagers sulking through the door with their younger siblings: "All it takes is one book."

As the movers unload the truck, I glance over at Antonio's and see smoke coming out of the chimney above. Gavin must be there already, getting the ovens warmed for lunch. And then I notice Adrianna's car parked out front, and I feel a shiver creep down my back.

❦

A half hour later, the movers have emptied the truck, and it's time for me to think about heading downtown for my meeting at the library with J.P. I change into a sweater dress and leggings. I feel nervous—for Ruby, for the future of Bluebird Books. What will he be like? Will he look like her? Will he laugh the same way? Will he eat sandwiches for breakfast the way she used to?

The cab stops on the street in front of the old library, and I peer out the window at the columns that line the facade, then pay the fare and step out to the sidewalk and follow the path to the front entrance. I remember that J.P. said he'd be on the third floor, so I take the elevator up. My heart beats loudly as the doors open. I follow the pathway to the reception desk, where a young woman wearing dark-rimmed glasses is perched behind a computer screen. "Can I help you?" she asks cheerfully.

"Yes," I say, "I'm here to see J.P."

She nods. "I'll go find him."

I bite my lip nervously and stare at the doorway the woman disappeared through. J.P., presumably Ruby's son, is behind that wall. I hear footsteps approaching and I take a deep breath. The woman appears again, and she's with a man. He's tall and broad shouldered in a pin-striped white and blue oxford with a solid navy tie. Handsome. And—my heart sinks—African American. He can't be the biological son of Ruby and Anthony Magnuson.

"Hi," he says to me. "You must be June."

"Yes," I say, smiling, trying to conceal my disappointment.

"So I take it we're not related," he says with a grin.

He looks like a young Denzel Washington.

We stand there awkwardly, and I feel a lump in my throat. I wonder if he does too.

"Listen," he says. "You came all the way down here. Let me buy you a cup of coffee. I'll show you around."

I nod. "I'd like that."

We finish our coffee in the lobby area, then walk together up and down ramps, down long corridors, through winding shelves of books. "There's just something about books that makes you feel better," I say.

He smiles. "It's why I work here."

I remember the cab driver's advice. "Can we go up to the top floor?"

"Yes," he says. "You can't leave without seeing my favorite part of the library."

We walk up a set of stairs to the top floor. It's a gray day in Seattle, but light pours into the leaded glass windows all around. J.P. points to a couch in the corner of the room, where there are fewer people. "Let's sit for a while."

I nod and follow him to the squarish brown leather sofa with a chrome frame.

He sets his coffee cup down on a table in front of us. "I suppose you're as disappointed as I am."

"It's too bad," I say. "I really thought you'd be him."

"What was she like, your aunt?"

"She was, well, *wonderful*. One of a kind. She founded Bluebird Books near Green Lake."

"The children's bookstore?"

"Yes," I say. "You know it?"

He smiles. "This is too weird. Just a few months ago I sent a letter to the owner, asking if she'd like to be the bookseller at a children's event on the calendar. But I never heard back. I realize now that it's because she . . ."

I nod soberly. "Because she passed away."

"I'm sorry," he says. "I think I read a bit about the history of the store. Hasn't it been in business since the 1940s?"

"Yes," I say. "My aunt left it to me, and I'm going to try to keep it going. It will be an uphill battle, though, with all the challenges bookstores are facing these days, and the debt I'll need to cover to keep the lights on." I look down at my hands in my lap. "It sounds so silly to say this now, but I thought you would be the one. The long-lost son of Ruby who would help me save the store."

"I'm sorry," he says. "I guess you'll keep looking for him?"

"I'll try," I say. "And how about you? Will you keep looking for your birth family?"

"I suppose I'll always be searching," he replies. "It's funny, because I've had a great life, a wonderful childhood. And yet I can't help but look into the eyes of every stranger who fits the profile of my birth mother and think, 'Could it be her?'"

"I hope you find her," I say.

"Thanks," he replies. "So what next? For the bookstore?"

I tell him about the fund-raiser and Margaret Wise Brown, and his eyes instantly light up. "This is unbelievable," he says. "A literary find of that magnitude doesn't happen every day in Seattle. Have you told anyone? Does anyone from the press know?"

"Not yet," I say. "I've kept it pretty quiet until I can get the store ready for the event."

"Well," J.P. continues, "I'll lend any support I can from the library side. Just say the word."

"Thank you so much. That means a lot."

He walks me to the front entrance, where I hail a cab.

"Keep in touch, OK?" he says.

"I will," I reply, and I mean it. "You know, I think we can still think of ourselves as family."

"Sure we can," he says. "We were almost cousins, after all."

I smile and slip into the cab. "Bluebird Books on Sunnyside Avenue in Green Lake," I say to the driver. The morning didn't go as I'd expected, and yet, in some ways, I feel like it went even better.

Chapter 19

The curb in front of the bookstore is crammed with cars and a produce delivery truck that's double-parked—I also see that Adrianna's car hasn't moved since this morning—so the cab pulls up on the opposite side of the street, in front of Geppetto's, the toy store. I notice the OPEN sign in the window, and remember how Amy and I used to love going into the stationery store for a sticker, then over to the toy store with Ruby. She was always friendly with the owners, a kind middle-aged couple. And yet, the woman didn't give me a particularly warm welcome when I arrived at the store. I recall her scowl one morning as I set out for my jog, and how it sent me into a tailspin of rapid heartbeats and guilt over the future of Bluebird Books.

I pay the cab fare and decide to poke my head into the store, reintroduce myself. The door creaks loudly as I open it. I walk a few steps inside, and smile at an old jack-in-the-box toy on a nearby shelf. I've always found them irresistible, so I reach for it and begin cranking the handle. Without fail, the springy clown inside pops out of the tin box unannounced, and I feel my heart lurch. I hate that something so insignificant can make me jump like that. And I wonder: If I'm able to save Bluebird Books, if I'm able to preserve Ruby's legacy and keep it going in the future, will I finally get control of my health? Will my anxiety evaporate?

"They get you every time," a gray-haired man says from behind me.

"Yes," I say, a little embarrassed as I set the toy back on the shelf. "I'm June Andersen," I continue, turning to the man, "Ruby's niece. I just thought I'd stop in to reintroduce myself. Ruby left me the store, and I—"

"Of course I remember you, June," the man says. "I'm Bill." His brown eyes sparkle a little under the store lights. "You and your sister used to come in here."

"Yes," I say. "I was the older one."

"The better behaved one," he adds with a smile.

I look away, eager to avoid the subject of Amy.

"So you're getting the place ready to sell?"

"Sell?" I say. "Where did you hear that?"

The door to the back room opens and a woman appears. "Lillian, it's June Andersen—you remember, Ruby's niece."

She walks closer, and eyes me suspiciously. "The banker?"

I shake my head. "I used to be in banking, but I resigned. I wanted you to know that I plan to stay, live above the shop, keep the store running just as Ruby did."

Lillian looks at Bill, astonished, as if trying to determine whether to trust me, and then her frozen face melts into a big smile. "Bless your heart," she says. "And here, all this time, we thought you were going to sell to a developer."

"Over my dead body," I say, grinning.

"You're just like her, you know? That's something Ruby would have said."

"Were you close to her, in her final years?"

Lillian nods. "I checked in on her as often as I could. Some-times when I'm walking up the sidewalk, I have to resist the urge to turn in to the bookstore. I still can't believe she's gone."

"Me either," I say. "Listen, you may not know it, but in recent years, the store has faced some financial challenges. I'm going to be throwing a party, a fund-raiser, to see if I can raise some commu-nity support for the store. I'd be honored to have you two attend."

"We'd love nothing more," Lillian says.

"Let us know if we can help with anything," Bill adds.

"I will, thank you," I reply, turning to the door. "Actually, there is something. I don't know exactly how to say this, and you may not know the whole story, but I recently learned that my aunt had a child years ago." I pause, and see the startled look on Lillian's face. "A little boy who she gave up for adoption."

Bill looks at Lillian, then back at me.

"Ruby had her reasons for making it a closed adoption," I con-tinue. "But I thought if I could find him, if I could tell him about Bluebird Books, he might join forces with me and try to help save the bookstore. His name is J.P."

"J.P.?" Lillian says.

"Yes. Do you remember anything from that time? Ruby's son was born in 1970. Geppetto's was here then, right?"

"Yes," Bill says. He looks at Lillian and waits for her to speak.

"It was so long ago," she says. "I do remember Ruby's baby. . . ." Her voice trails off then, as if she's remembering dropping by the bookstore for tea and seeing Ruby with little J.P. on her hip. "I know it was very hard for her to say good-bye to her child." She's silent for a moment, then finally says, "I'm sorry. I wish I could be of more help to you."

"I understand," I say, a little disappointed. "Well, I'll keep searching on my own. He has to be out there."

Lillian nods to herself. Her eyes search my face, and then she smiles warmly. "When you're looking for something, you usually find that it's right in front of you."

"Wait," I say. "Margaret Wise Brown said something like that, I think. I read a quote from her online. I think it was something like, 'Everything that anyone would ever look for is usually where they find it.'"

"Such truth," Lillian says with a smile.

"Well," I say, nodding, "let's hope. Good-bye, you two. It was so nice to see you again."

"You as well, June," Bill says.

The door creaks open and shut, and I walk back to the bookstore. As I slip my key into the door, an appetizing aroma drifts over from Antonio's, and Lillian's words echo in my ear: *When you're looking for something, you usually find that it's right in front of you.*

Chapter 20

The next day, the seamstress arrives to measure for the new curtains. I removed the tattered drapes the night before, and now the windows are bare. "Wow," she says, stepping back to admire the large street-facing windows. "They're going to look great in here."

I show her the old curtains, lying in a heap on the floor. "They're a bit sun-bleached, I'm afraid. I was hoping you could find a similar green and yellow print, just like these."

She looks at the tattered fabric, then back at me again. "What does that remind me of?" she asks. "Wait, don't tell me." She walks to a bookshelf where a new copy of *Goodnight Moon* sits facing out. "It's this book! The great green room!"

"Yes," I say. "It's the look we're going for."

"Why hasn't any bookseller thought of that before? Everyone knows this story; everyone loves it. It's brilliant."

"If you come to our fund-raiser next month," I say, "you'll get to hear the whole history of the shop. I can't give much away now, but if not for Bluebird Books, that book you're holding in your hands may never have been published."

"Really?" she asks, astounded. "So you're having a fund-raiser? Why?"

"To keep the store in business," I reply. "I inherited it from my great-aunt, and we're going to need a cash infusion to keep it open."

The woman sighs with a smile. "Well, you can count my services as your first donation," she says. "I'll make the curtains up free of charge."

"Wow, that would be amazing. How can I thank you?"

"Don't," she says. "It's my pleasure. I have two little kids, and they love bookstores. I don't know what I'd do if I couldn't take them to a reading on a rainy day. I want to fight to save them just like you. And if these curtains can help, I will donate them." She holds *Goodnight Moon* out to me. "Mind if I take this with me to look at while I make them?"

"It's yours," I say.

She nods. "Somehow we lost our copy. My girls are going to love it. I'll have the curtains to you in a week."

A few hours later, I look up when I hear Ruby's jingle bells. Gavin pokes his head through the door. "Hi," he says a little cautiously.

"Hi."

"How did it go with J.P.?"

My eyes brighten. "You remembered?"

"Of course I remembered. I've been a little overworked at the restaurant. I'm sorry about that."

I smile as he walks toward me. "As it turns out J.P. was not *the* J.P. But meeting him wasn't a total loss. He runs events and programs at the main branch of the library, and he wants to get involved in the fund-raiser for the store."

"That's great," Gavin says. "I'm sorry that he didn't turn out to be Ruby's son. I know you really hoped he'd be."

"A minor setback," I say with a shrug. "Our J.P. is out there, I know. I'll find him. I'm not giving up that easily."

I sit in one of the wingback chairs, and Gavin follows my lead.

"Adrianna was over yesterday morning," he says.

My heart races in anticipation of his next words. "I know. I saw her car."

"She brought over the paperwork for me to sign."

"What paperwork?"

"You know, to sell her half of the restaurant to me."

"Really? So it's done?"

"Yeah," he says. "I took a big hit to my bank account, but I'm now the sole owner."

"How do you feel about it?"

"It was the right decision," he says, "for each of us. But it was also a sad day. Antonio's was hers as much as it is mine, and I know it's hard for her to say good-bye."

I nod. "You know, I never did ask you how you came to name the place Antonio's. I guess I always assumed it was someone in Adrianna's Italian family."

Gavin shakes his head and smiles. "You mean, I never told you?"

"No."

"Ruby helped us name it."

"Ruby?"

"Yes," he says. "We were just a few weeks from opening and Adrianna and I couldn't come up with a name. We fought endlessly about it, which should have been our first clue that our relationship was doomed." He laughs to himself. "I'll never forget how your aunt came by to welcome us. 'What will you call the place?' she asked. We were embarrassed to admit that our restaurant was nameless. She immediately suggested Antonio's. Adrianna and I just looked at each other and finally agreed."

"Antonio's, *of course*," I say. "She wanted the business next door to be named after Anthony, the man she had loved all those years."

"Wow," Gavin says. "I would have never put that together."

"My aunt had a lot of secrets."

"Just like her niece," he says with a wink.

"What do you mean, secrets?"

He shrugs playfully. "Just that there's so much more to discover about you. I feel like I learn something new every day." His brow furrows a little then, and his eyes show a flash of concern. He looks at his watch and shifts in his seat a little nervously. "June, I do need to speak to you about something. Something serious."

"What?" I ask, caught a little off guard.

Before he can answer, Mom's standing in the doorway. She's wearing yoga pants and a T-shirt. Her hair is in a ponytail. She looks so young. When I was in high school, everyone always thought she was my big sister. Mom smiled at that, while I barely contained my annoyance. She was a young twenty when I was born. Even now, she's barely aged, despite years of hard partying. She'd tell you that it's her daily green juice regimen, now that she's a self-proclaimed health nut after her stint in rehab fifteen years ago, but even with the promise of aging as beautifully as my mother has, I still don't think I could manage to choke down a spinach-kale smoothie each morning.

"Sorry I'm late," Mom says to Gavin. "I missed my bus. Didn't we say three?"

I flash Gavin a confused look, then turn to Mom. "You already know each other?"

Gavin stands up, leaving room for Mom to sit beside me. I bite my lip, and look from one to the other. I have no idea what to expect. He won't make eye contact with me.

I can see that something's troubling Mom. She looks nervous, and her eyebrows scrunch together to form a deep crease. "What is it? Is something wrong?"

Her eyes finally meet mine. "It's your sister, June."

I look away. How many times do I have to tell her? How many times must I insist that Amy and I will never reconcile?

But then Gavin opens his mouth and utters the words that prove me wrong: "Your sister's sick. She tried reaching out to you. She tried to tell you, but you wouldn't talk to her. So she called me."

"How did she—"

"She figured out who I was," he says. "One day she came to see you, but you were out. She stopped by the restaurant."

"What do you mean, she's sick?" *She has a cold*, I tell myself. *The flu. That's all.* I remember taking care of her when Mom was gone on one of her benders. Amy had a fever, and I remembered how, in a picture book, the mama bear had brought her baby bear popsicles. So I tucked Amy under a blanket on the couch, cleaned out my piggy bank, then walked to the corner market and returned with a box of cherry popsicles. She liked that.

"She has metastatic breast cancer, June," Mom says, looking me in the eye. "I only recently found out myself. She didn't want to worry us. But she needs us to know now, before it's too late."

My knees feel weak then, and I feel a wave of nausea as I sink into my chair. "No," I say. "No, this can't be."

"June, there's something else," Mom says. "Amy's pregnant. She had the option to terminate early on, when they caught it, but she refused. She decided to carry her baby to term, even though it meant no chance of her survival. Now the cancer's in her bones."

"No," I say, shaking my head. "I don't understand. Can't they save her? I mean, don't they have chemo and surgery and radiation for things like this? What about the baby?"

"She's having a little girl," Mom says through tears. "The baby will be fine. But Amy won't be. Her oncologists have scheduled a C-section for next week. After that, she won't have much time."

I bury my head in my hands and sob.

"She tried to tell you, June," Mom says.

Gavin places his hand on my shoulder. "I went to see her in the hospital the other night," he says. "The night I wasn't at the restaurant. I thought if I could see her, I could relay the message back to you. June, she wants to see you so badly. She begged to see you."

I stare straight ahead. "I didn't read her letters. I was so angry. I still am. But now . . . now, I . . ."

"Maybe it's time to forgive her, June," Gavin whispers to me. They are his words, yes, but I hear Ruby's voice. I hear Ruby pleading with me to forgive my sister when I still have the chance. "I mean, I don't know what you two have faced, but you're sisters."

"I know," I cry. "I know. I want to." I wipe my eyes with my sleeve.

"Come to the hospital with me today, then," Mom says. "And tell her yourself. Before it's too late."

Gavin pulls his keys from the pocket of his jeans. "My car's out back. We can go right now."

"Yes," I say, squeezing his hand.

I lock up the store, and Mom and I follow Gavin to the back door. His Subaru Outback is parked in the alley behind the restaurant, and Mom and I climb into the car. On the drive to the hospital, I think back to the day my relationship with Amy changed forever.

Five years prior

"You're leaving early today," Arthur says, leaning into the doorway of my office.

"Yeah, sorry," I say. "It's my sister's birthday. I'm surprising her with her favorite dinner, a cake, the whole shebang."

"Save me a slice of cake," he says. He's in a good mood. I count my blessings.

"I will."

It's four p.m., and if I'm fast, I can pick up the cake from the bakery—coconut, her favorite—and run to the store to get the ingredients for lasagna before she comes home at six. She's always on the 5:40 train, which puts her at our apartment at roughly 6:15, give or take ten minutes.

I rush through the grocery aisles, filling my cart with mozzarella, Parmesan, tomato sauce, and noodles. I grab a pack of romaine lettuce because I know how much she loves Caesar salad. On a whim, I reach for two Mylar balloons at the checkout counter. One features Scooby Doo with a speech bubble that says, "Happy Birthday to Roo!"

As the checker scans the groceries, I think about Ryan, twisting the engagement ring around my finger. He's been acting strange lately, which I attribute to wedding-planning stress. His parents want us to get married in New York, at the Plaza, and because there are no available dates until next summer, we'll have to extend our engagement another year. I'd just as well tie the knot down at city hall and jump on a plane to Mexico for a week. I get that he wants to please his parents, but if he really wanted to marry me . . . I shake my head, and remind myself how much he loves me. When he proposed last year, he said, "You complete me." OK, so it was a line from *Jerry Maguire*. I still found it romantic and meaningful. Ryan has commitment issues, always has. But he is committing to *me*. Forever.

I gather the paper bags in my arms, and decide to stop stressing. We're getting married, eventually, and everything's going to be fine. I race down Bleecker Street and stop in at Magnolia Bakery, where a clerk boxes up the prepaid coconut cake I ordered. I balance the box precariously in my arms with the grocery bags and balloons, and walk six more blocks to our apartment. On days like today, I'm grateful for an elevator. My last place involved lots and lots of stairs.

"Can I help you with those bags?" Glen, the doorman, asks.

"No, I'm fine, thanks," I say, squeezing beside Mrs. Hornsby, the old woman who lives in the apartment next door.

"Throwing a party, are you?" she asks, eyeing me skeptically, the way the older generation regards the antics of the young.

"Yes," I say. "It's my sister's twenty-sixth birthday. I'm surprising her with a dinner."

She huffs. "I do hope you're not having a hundred people over."

"Don't worry," I say. "Just my fiancé and a few of her work friends. We'll be quiet."

She smiles, relieved. When I was traveling for work last weekend, Amy hosted a dinner party, and evidently things got a bit loud. Mrs. Hornsby took it upon herself to tell me about it in the lobby on Sunday when I returned. "I'm not judging," she said. "You girls lead different lifestyles than I ever did. But if she's going to entertain gentlemen friends, will you please ask her to keep it down a bit, if you know what I mean?"

Initially I laughed off Mrs. Hornsby's comments. After all, her prudish ways once got a doorman fired for flipping through a Victoria's Secret catalog on the job. But Amy didn't have any "gentlemen friends," at least that I knew of. But maybe she'd been dating some-one and hadn't told me. It would be strange, since we tell each other everything.

I asked Amy about Mrs. Hornsby's comments that evening, and she acted embarrassed, and then said something about watching a movie and having the volume turned up too high, which I thought was strange, but I let it go.

I glance at my watch. I have a half hour to get the apartment decorated and the lasagna in the oven before Amy gets home. I insert my key in the door, with the balloons bobbing over my head, and walk inside. I set the bags down in the entryway and the cake on the side table, and when I go to slip off my heels, I notice a pair of men's shoes lined up on the hardwood floor. They sort of look like Ryan's shoes, the ones he bought in Italy. I peer around the corner. *Is he here? How did he get in?*

Still holding the balloons, I walk into the living room. Amy's blue pencil skirt (the one she never lets me borrow) is wadded up on the floor not far from a pair of men's pants. I hear voices, and laughter.

My heart beats faster. Amy runs out, wearing nothing but a tie around her neck. It's striped, navy blue and periwinkle. I bought it for Ryan the day he passed his LSATs five years prior. Her breasts, so much larger than mine, dangle like two perfect melons on either side of the silk tie. She gasps in horror when her eyes meet mine. "June! I thought you weren't going to be home until . . . later!"

Ryan appears in a similar state of undress, wearing socks and nothing else. "June," he says. "I can explain. I, I . . . June, please forgive us. We got carried away. We—"

Amy is crying, and Ryan is frantically getting dressed. I hear the door to the apartment close a moment later. I can't move. I'm frozen. The Scooby Doo balloon hovers overhead, beside another featuring the words "You're the BEST."

"June, I don't know what I was thinking," Amy cries. "It just happened! I feel horrible. Will you ever forgive me? Please tell me you will. Please, it meant nothing to either of us."

And that's when I let go of the balloons.

🙢

"She's in the oncology ward," Mom says when we arrive at the hospital. "Fifth floor."

I nod and walk ahead, even though my legs feel leaden. I don't know if I'm ready to face Amy, but there isn't time for more deliberation. In all likelihood, it's now or never.

Gavin and I follow Mom into the elevator and then into the fifth-floor reception area. "We're here to see Amy Andersen," Mom says to a desk nurse.

"Oh good," she says. "She could use some cheering up. It's been a hard day."

I wonder what that means. I wonder if she's in pain, or if her baby's in distress. My protective instincts kick in and I want to run to the nearest doctor and drag him by his coat to her room shouting, "That's my baby sister in there. And she's sick. Fix her! Please, make her better!" But I clutch's Gavin's arm as we walk down the long hall to Amy's room. Somehow the pain of the past has been washed away, revealing the love for my sister that was always there. I keep thinking, *She's just a few steps away. My Amy.*

The truth is, Ryan was—how do I put this nicely?—a douche bag. It wasn't the first time he'd cheated, I learned later. Though Amy was also to blame, I blamed him more. Part of me actually feels grateful for that scene I walked into on Amy's birthday, as awful as it was, because it changed the course of my life. I might not be here had it not happened. I look up at Gavin's sure, strong face, the tenderness in his eyes as he glances my way.

Mom stops in front of room 523 and places her hand on the doorway. "Ready?"

I nod, and we follow her into the room. "Amy, it's Mom," she says. The curtain's drawn around her bed, so I can't see her yet. "I've brought a guest."

"Mom, no," she says. "I look terrible. I—"

Mom pulls back the curtain, and my eyes meet Amy's.

Aside from the large swell of her belly, she's very thin, thinner than I've ever seen her. Her face is extremely pale. I realize that when I saw her at the ferry terminal that day, any sign of her pregnancy was hidden away beneath her sweater. She looked a bit gaunt then, but now? It appears that the cancer's vigorous growth has aged her ten years in a matter of weeks.

"June," Amy says through tears. She holds her arms out to me, and right before me the sick woman disappears and there is my sister, the little four-year-old with pigtails and chubby cheeks, a doll clutched in her hand.

"Oh, Amy," I say, bursting into tears. I lay my head on her chest and lean into her, weeping from a place deep down, a place where I never stopped loving Amy, where I've already forgiven her. No, my love for her never died, never withered on the vine. There was always a tiny green shoot that somehow managed to survive without sun and water. And now it's found fertile ground.

"June, please forgive me, for everything I did, I—"

I place my finger to Amy's lips. "I already have. I'm afraid I'm so thickheaded, it took the thought of losing you to realize that it was time I stopped sulking. Honey, let's not waste precious time talking about things we'd both like to forget."

She nods. "June, I'm going to have a baby. A little girl."

"I know," I cry. "Mom told me."

"You're going to be an aunt," she says. "Aunt June."

"Sounds nice," I say.

Amy's smile melts away then. "You know I don't have much time left. And I have to make a plan for my baby girl."

"Amy, don't, let's not—"

"But we have to," she says. "We have to face the facts. I will die soon after her birth. There's no way around it. And I have to make plans for her. She doesn't have anyone."

"What about . . . ?"

"Her father? He checked out. June, I met him at a bar. He's not a bad guy; he just isn't ready to face this. Mom helped me draw up some legal papers. He signed away his rights to paternity. It's better that way. I needed to know that in five years, after I'm gone, he's not going to show up out of nowhere and say, 'That's my daughter,' and uproot her from her life. I won't have that."

"Then what *do* you want, Amy? Tell me, and Mom and I will make it happen."

She looks at Mom, then back at me. "June, I want *you* to raise her."

"Me?"

She smiles. "You raised me, just about."

Mom nods. "You did, and you did a wonderful job."

"But I—I don't know anything about babies."

"No one does, at first," Amy says.

"And I worry I couldn't give her the life she deserves. I don't know if Mom told you, but the bookstore's facing serious financial hardship. What if I—"

"You'll find a way, June," Amy says. "You always do." She smiles to herself. "Remember the time the refrigerator broke in the middle of August? Mom was gone, so you pulled out the phone book and called a repairman. He fixed the thing for free. What were you, like, ten years old?"

"Nine," I say, remembering the way I attempted to pay the man in pennies from my piggy bank.

"June, I want you to raise my daughter." A single tear streams down her face, a strong, sure tear. One thirty-one years in the making. It falls onto a tube attached to her arm. "Will you?"

I swallow hard. "Amy, it would be the greatest honor of my life."

She squeezes my hand. "Thank you."

I nod, and lay my head on Amy's belly. "Hello, little missy," I say. "This is your Aunt June speaking. We're in for a lot of fun in this life, you know that? I'm going to tell you all about your mommy." I feel Gavin's arm around my shoulder as I wipe away fresh tears on my cheek. "I'm going to tell you about the time she gave her doll a haircut, and the time she made me a gingerbread cake for my birthday but used garlic powder instead of ginger powder."

Amy laughs.

"And we are going to walk around Green Lake like your mom and I used to, and we're going to feed the ducks and read books and listen to music and dance. Your mommy loves to dance. She's the best dancer I know, and you will be too. And she's a great singer, too, even if she occasionally gets the lyrics wrong." I turn to Amy and smile. "Remember how you used to sing 'What a Wonderful World'?"

She grins. "Bright blessed days; dogs say good night."

"And I think to myself," I sing in a faltering voice, choking back tears, "what a wonderful world. I'll give her a wonderful life, Amy. I promise I will."

She nods. "I know you will. You'll be a better mom than I ever could."

"That's not true, honey," I say.

"It is," she insists.

"What will you name her?"

Amy takes a deep breath. She looks at Mom, then at me. "I'd like to call her Ruby."

"Yes," I say. "That's perfect." I place my hand on her belly and imagine my niece, fiery like her mama, determined like her great-great-aunt. "Yes, Little Ruby."

Chapter 21

It's a bright Tuesday morning when Little Ruby arrives, and when the nurses finally let me in the hospital room to see her, Amy jokes that we all should go out for lunch at Ruby Tuesday.

She's a beautiful child, with lots of dark hair, and blue eyes like her mom's. She has her aunt Ruby's high cheekbones. "I love her already," I say to Amy.

"I can't nurse her," Amy says through tears. "They won't let me because of the medications. It's killing me not to be able to feed her."

"Honey, don't think about it for a moment," I say.

"But I wanted everything to be perfect for her," she cries. "And she won't even—"

"There is no perfect," I say. "Better she learns that now than to cling to some false misconception that life should, and one day will, be perfect. Life is a big, beautiful mess. Chaotic and tragic and wonderful and weird. At least, that's how it seems to me, anyway."

"You should write that down," Amy says. "It sounds like a children's book."

I nod. "It does, doesn't it?" I watch Amy hold her infant, and I see she's still crying. "You know what we have to do? We have to focus on the good things, the beautiful things. We have to savor them." I point to Ruby's tiny feet. "Starting with these toes. Have you ever seen a more adorable set of toes than these?"

Amy giggles. "No, they're absolutely perfect."

"And these hands," I say, summoning the courage to steady my voice and charge ahead into unknown territory, for Amy. I can do this for Amy. "Now, she'll need a manicure in time, but look at those gorgeous long fingers. Look at the way she holds her index finger out."

Amy grins. "Like she's about to start bossing us around."

I nod. "She is a firstborn."

I remember the gift I brought for Little Ruby, and I reach inside my purse, then hand the box to Amy.

"Do you want to hold her?" Amy asks. She looks frail today, more so than yesterday. Her cheeks are colorless and hollow.

"I'd love to," I say, taking the swaddled newborn into my arms. I feel nervous, but somehow, when I hold her, it's as if I've done this before, a thousand times, perhaps. My arms fall into place naturally, and I nuzzle her cheek with my nose. Little Ruby smells sweet, like pears and fresh laundry. She sleeps soundly, but as I begin to rock in the rocker beside Amy's bed, she wakes and looks up at me with wide, alert eyes.

"Well hello, Miss Ruby," I say. "I'm your Aunt June. We're going to be spending a lot of time together, you and I." I try to be strong, for Amy, but my heart is breaking with every second that passes. For both of them.

Amy tears the wrapping paper off the gift I brought, and pulls out a copy of *Goodnight Moon*. "You remembered," she says to me.

"It was the only story that would calm you at night," I say.

"Remember how we used to look for the mouse on each page?"

"You loved that," I say, reminiscing. "I did too."

"Will you read it to her, June?" Amy asks, handing me the book. "Just like you used to read to me."

I gently turn Little Ruby around in the crook of my arm so she can see the pages, and I begin reading my precious niece her very first story.

"In the great green room . . ." I begin.

Amy is crying. And I try not to let her see that I am too.

⁂

Two weeks later, Gavin and I are heading to the hospital when Mom calls my cell phone, frantic. "She's gone," Mom cries.

I hate that I wasn't there beside her. I hate that I chose this morning to go home and shower when I might have seen her last breath, the last flutter of her eyes.

"Oh, Mom," I wail into the phone.

I hear the baby cooing in the background. "We have to be strong," Mom says. "For Little Ruby."

"Yes," I say, collecting myself. "You're right."

"It's what Amy would have wanted."

I set the phone down, and Gavin reaches for my hand. "I'm so sorry," he says.

"Me, too."

Amy is gone. My baby sister. I think of all the times I protected her from bullies on the playground at school when we were kids. And now a bully got her. Cancer. It lingered during the pregnancy, then pounced at the end. At least it had the decency to wait until Little Ruby was safe in the world.

Amy didn't want a funeral, so we save our remembrances for the burial ceremony, and instead of speaking to the handful of friends and family gathered around, I set a bouquet of pink roses on her coffin, kneel down, and speak directly to her.

"My darling sister," I say through tears. "I never thought this day would come. Don't you know that I was supposed to die first? Big sisters aren't supposed to bury their little sisters." I smile to myself, wiping a fresh tear from my cheek. "But I'll forgive you for that, just as I forgive you for stealing my stuffed animal, and scribbling in my favorite book, and taking a pair of scissors to my red corduroy dress. You know what I'm talking about. And I forgive you for the big things, too, the things that caused a silence between us for too long. But there is no hurt between us, not anymore. What happened was a part of my story, my journey. And, you know, I'm almost grateful for it. Actually, I *am* grateful for it. And I'm grateful for you. You didn't deserve to be shut out of my life. I wish I could have those years back, please know that. I will wish that every day for the rest of my life. And now I must say good-bye. Honey, don't worry about Little Ruby. Not for a moment. I will tell her all about you. I'll take her to your favorite places in Seattle, the places where we made memories. She'll grow up listening to your favorite music. I'll teach her the words to 'Billie Jean' as soon as she's old enough to talk." I laugh through my tears. "And I will love her, Amy. I will love that little girl with every ounce of my being. I will love her for the both of us. She will never know more love. You don't have to worry about that for a moment. And I'll read to her too, Amy, just like I read to you." I reach into my purse and pull out the tattered copy of *Goodnight Moon* I've kept all these years, and I open to the first page, and read to my sister her favorite book, for the last time.

"Good-bye, my darling sister," I cry, placing my hand on her coffin. I think of Ruby and Margaret. They'd be proud. *Operation Sisterhood*. I smile through my tears. "I love you, Amy, and will always love you."

I feel Gavin's hand on my waist, and I let him walk me back to the folding chairs a few feet away. I bury my face in his jacket and weep.

A moment later, I look up when I hear my mom's voice in the distance. "June," she cries. "Look at Little Ruby, come quick."

I run to her side, and I see what Mom is so excited about. Ruby's eyes are wide; her mouth is big and it forms a little O before the corners turn upward. "See that?" Mom says through tears. "I think she's just learned to smile."

I look up to heaven. "See that, Amy?" I whisper. "Your little girl just smiled for you."

Chapter 22

Mom stayed with me upstairs in the week that followed. The days and nights blurred together, the way they do when you're sleep deprived, or grieving, or both. Little Ruby kept us going, though. She gave us a purpose. Diapers and bottles and smiles. Repeat.

"I think you can handle this," Mom says as I feed Ruby her morning bottle. She leans down and tucks a pair of jeans into her duffel bag.

"Wait, you're not going, are you? Not yet!"

Mom smiles. "You don't need me anymore, sweetie. It's time you two fly solo." She pauses, and I can see the regret in her eyes. "Besides, you're already a better mother than I ever was."

Little Ruby yawns after she finishes the last drop of her bottle, and I set her in the Pack 'n Play contraption Gavin found at Babies R Us. It isn't the beautiful white crib I envisioned for her, with a ruffled bumper and matching sheets, but it works.

"But I—"

"You'll be fine," Mom says again. "I'm going out of town with Rand for a bit, but I'll be back for the fund-raiser, I promise."

At first I'm annoyed with Mom for leaving at this moment. We only sent out the press releases for the event yesterday, and we still need to get the invitations in the mail and make plans. And I'll have to do this while taking care of a baby. But none of this is Mom's fault. She has her life to live, and this is mine. If I've learned anything from Amy's tragic passing, it's to stop holding silent grudges against family members. Mom is just being Mom—often selfish, sometimes spacey, a little unpredictable. But I can love her, flaws and all. And I can forgive her for the small, annoying lapses, and the big ones too.

"OK," I say. "I guess I've got to pull the bandage off at some point, right?"

"What are you afraid of, honey?"

"Screwing up," I reply honestly, peering over at Ruby, sleeping soundly. "Look at her. She's so delicate. What if I drop her? Or forget a feeding? Or—"

"You won't," she says. "And if you make a mistake, you'll both be fine."

I nod as she picks up her bag and walks to the stairway.

"I'll call you and check in," she says. "And I'm sure Gavin will be a big help."

"Yeah," I say. "He's great with her. And she loves Antonio's. Remember when she was having a crying fit yesterday afternoon when you were leaving for yoga? Well, I brought her over to the restaurant and it totally soothed her. I think she's going to love Italian food."

Mom smiles. "You'll be great at this, honey; I know it."

I nod. "Bye, Mom."

And then she's gone, and it's just Ruby and me.

That night, Gavin brings over dinner, and instead of eating at the table, we lay a blanket on the floor and eat beside Ruby, who's having her daily allotment of "tummy time." (I read about it online this morning, and freaked out when I realized she's missed nearly three weeks of valuable neck strengthening; Gavin assured me that she won't be a hunchback.)

"I brought lasagna," he says, dishing up a sizable helping on my plate.

I smile. "And lasagna aids in what temperament issue?"

"Nervousness," he replies with a grin.

"I'm not nervous!" I say. "OK, maybe a little."

"Eat up."

I take a bite. "Wow," I say, covering my mouth. "So good."

Gavin smiles. "Any bites from the press release yet?"

"Actually, yes!" I say. "I was so busy with Ruby this afternoon, I almost forgot to tell you that the *Seattle Times* loves the idea, and they want to do a piece on the store and our fund-raiser in Friday's paper!"

"Wow," he says. "That's in . . . two days."

"Yeah, they're coming over tomorrow afternoon to do an interview. Fortunately, the walls are painted. And the shelves look good, thanks to a certain someone."

Gavin grins. "Did you see how I organized the newer books in those rows?" While the store is adequately stocked, there's a shortage of newer inventory, so Gavin displayed the new books for greater visual appeal.

"Yes," I say. "It's perfect. And don't the curtains look fantastic?" I run my hand along the edge of the new drapes.

"They do," Gavin says, scooping a helping of roasted vegetables onto my plate.

We eat in silence for a few moments. Ruby coos on her tummy, and I feel the familiar twinge of anxiety creep in. "What if no one comes?" I say. "What if the event is a failure? Then what?"

"Then we'll think of Plan B," Gavin says, lying down beside Ruby. He coos and babbles along with her.

"You'd make a great dad, you know," I say, swelling with pride.

The next morning, I strap Ruby into a baby carrier that Mom bought me, and take her on a walk around the lake before the reporter arrives at two. His name is Greg, and he's about my age.

"Your daughter?" he asks, smiling at Ruby.

"Yes," I say. "Well, my sister's. But Amy passed away shortly after this little one was born. I'm raising her now. Her name is Ruby."

"I'm so sorry for your loss," he says. "She's a beautiful baby. I have three of my own, all girls."

"Oh, wow," I say. "So, you got any tricks for me?"

"An armload," he says. "For starters, at some point around three months, she's going to think she forgot how to sleep. But don't let her fool you. Give her time to work it out in her crib. She will."

"I hate it when she cries," I say, looking down at Ruby in the carrier. I rock back and forth gently, hoping to lull her to sleep. "It kills me."

"My wife says the same thing." He smiles, looking around the shop. "Daddies are better at not falling to pieces every time they hear a squawk." I think of Gavin and how good he is with Ruby.

"This really is a lovely bookstore," Greg continues. "You know, I came here as a child."

"You did?"

"Yes," he says. "Your aunt was quite a woman. I still remember the way she'd do the voices in books. It taught me to read to my children with more flair."

"Wow," I say, touched by his sentiments about my aunt. "I wish Ruby were here to hear that. It would have made her smile."

He opens up his notebook and begins asking me questions about the history of the store, Ruby's friendship with Margaret Wise Brown, the business's uncertain financial future. I tell him everything I can think of and then he nods and closes his notebook. "Thank you," he says. "I think I have everything I need. It will be a great story. I hope you get a lot of responses from it."

"Me, too," I say.

After her evening bottle, Ruby dozes off. I know I have about three hours before her next feeding, so I decide to assemble the guest list for the invitations to the fund-raiser. Gavin's designer friend did a lovely job, and they're now printed and sitting in boxes in the apartment, waiting to be addressed.

I think of all the people I know from my past and present: former school librarians, friends, teachers, Peter and Nate in New York, J.P. from the Seattle Public Library, the other shopkeepers on the street. I add in notable Seattleites like the mayor, the CEOs of Safeco and Boeing, both of whom I met at a bank party in New York several years ago, though I'm not counting on their remembering me. When I have a decent list compiled, I look up addresses online and finish my spreadsheet.

Ruby sleeps soundly as I press a stamp on each, then stack them into a box, which I'll take to the post office tomorrow.

"There," I say to myself with a sigh. "Let this bluebird fly. Please let it fly."

I finish washing the dishes, then sit by the window and stare out at the half-moon in the clear sky. The city rests, and Green Lake sparkles in the moonlight. The street below is quiet, but just before

Ruby wakes up for her ten o'clock feeding, a dark SUV drives by, slowing down in front of the bookstore. I clutch my phone, then open the window and lean out, making my presence known. The vehicle revs its engine and speeds off before I can get a license plate number.

Chapter 23

The next day, I strap Ruby into the carrier and we walk to the nearby post office, where we mail out the invitations. "There goes our future, Ruby," I say to her as I drop the stack into the mailbox. "Let's hope for the best."

We walk to Joe's and I eagerly order a triple espresso, hoping the caffeine will jump-start my energy level but not my blood pressure. Joe comes out from behind the counter with a big smile on his face.

"How is Miss Ruby this morning?" he asks, all grins.

"Great," I say. "But I think she's starting to mix up her nights with her days, which means I'm not getting a ton of sleep."

"Well, I have something to perk you up."

"I already ordered a triple Americano," I say. "That should help."

He shakes his head, and holds a copy of today's *Seattle Times*. "I mean this." He points to the front page, and there I am, standing in front of the store with Little Ruby in my arms. The photographer came out to snap our photo after the reporter's visit. Ruby was fussy, and I felt nervous in front of the camera. I didn't expect the photo to turn out, but I'm amazed at how vivid it looks, and Ruby actually looks like she's smiling. I take a closer look and see the awning of Bluebird Books is front and center beneath the headline: LOCAL WOMAN AIMS TO SAVE HISTORIC CHILDREN'S BOOKSTORE, REPORTED INSPIRATION FOR GOODNIGHT MOON.

I gasp. "Wow. Ruby, look, we're in the newspaper!"

"You sure are," Joe says. "And you'd better go back to the store and hire an assistant, because your phone is going to be ringing off the hook today."

I give him a confused look.

"For the fund-raiser," he says. "You're selling tickets, right?"

"Yes."

"Can I buy one?"

"Of course you can," I say. "I'd be so honored."

"Good, my wife and I will be there."

I smile and thank him, then head to the door, beaming. Maybe this will work out. Just maybe.

※

The phone in the bookstore begins to ring shortly after I put Ruby down for her nap. It startles me at first. In the time I've been at the store, it's rung twice. Once, it was Mom; the second time, a telemarketer.

But now it rings nonstop. The first call comes from a man at a big architectural firm downtown who tells me his mother took him to Bluebird Books as a child; he wants to purchase four tickets to the fund-raiser. The next call is from a local author, who buys two. And on, and on, and on.

In an hour's time, I've sold fifty-two tickets. More local media call. A reporter from Seattle's NBC affiliate wants to know if I have any photos of Margaret Wise Brown in the bookstore (I tell her I'll check and get back to her), and then someone from CNN calls saying they read the *Seattle Times* piece and wonder if I'll be available for an interview tomorrow. Of course, I say yes.

Gavin walks in just as I hear Little Ruby begin to squawk on the monitor, which is when the phone rings again. "It's ringing nonstop," I say. "Do you mind getting her?"

"No problem," he replies with a smile, heading to the stairs.

I pick up the phone again. "Bluebird Books," I answer.

"Is this June Andersen?" the female caller asks. Her voice is clipped and professional.

"Yes," I say. "How can I help you?"

"I'm Joan Cooper, assistant to Bill Gates. Mr. Gates read about the plight of your bookstore in the newspaper this morning and he asked me to get in touch with you."

"Bill Gates?" I say, stunned. "*The* Bill Gates, as in, founder of Microsoft?"

"Yes," the woman says. "You see, Mr. Gates grew up here in Seattle, and his mother took him and his siblings to your aunt's bookstore often. He was especially fond of it."

"He was?"

"Yes," she replies. "And he believes you're doing the community quite a service by stepping up to save the store. He and his wife would like to attend the fund-raising event. Is it possible to purchase two tickets? I'm sure he'd also be interested in sponsoring a portion of the event, as a way to bolster your fund-raising efforts. Of course, his security guards will also be traveling with him. There are four in total."

"Really?" I say, still stunned. "I, I—yes! Yes, we'd love to have him. All of them. Please tell him how grateful I am for his support."

"I will," she says.

When I hang up the phone, Gavin is walking down the stairs with Ruby in one arm and a bottle in the other. "I thought she might be hungry." He notices the smile on my face. "You look happy. Who was that on the phone?"

"Bill Gates's assistant," I say, still reeling.

"You're kidding."

"Not kidding. He and his wife are coming to our event!"

Gavin shakes his head in amazement.

"And so are fifty-some other people," I add. The phone rings again. "There's another."

⚜

By the time the sun has set, I've sold 120 tickets, which, at 250 dollars apiece, equals thirty thousand dollars in funds raised for Bluebird Books. It won't be enough to keep the debt collectors away, but Gavin and I have planned further donation opportunities for attendees during the event.

Once Little Ruby is changed and fed and sleeping soundly in her Pack 'n Play by my bed, I wander down to the bookstore with the monitor, and Gavin and I have a glass of wine before he heads back to the restaurant.

"What a day," he says, grinning.

I nod. "I'm amazed that so many people feel so strongly about saving the store. I'm supposed to speak to CNN in the morning. Can you believe this?"

"I can," he says. "What you're doing is very worthy, and people immediately recognize that."

"Boy," I continue, "it's amazing how life changes. Just a couple of months ago, I was a banker. A banker! And now, here I am, the owner of a bookstore, with a baby."

Gavin smiles. "She's about the most perfect little girl anyone could ever hope for." A moment passes. "Are you going to let her call you Mom?"

I shake my head. "No. I may be her guardian, but her mother is in heaven, and she'll always know that. I'm fine just being her aunt." I gaze around at Aunt Ruby's bookstore with its fresh coat of paint, tidy shelves, and whimsical curtains. "And aunts are pretty awesome people."

After Gavin returns to the restaurant, I decide to go hunting for the next set of letters between Margaret and Ruby. I've been so consumed with Little Ruby and the fund-raiser, I haven't thought much about the letters, but now I turn to the bookshelf in anticipation. I feel I'm nearing the end of the scavenger hunt, and while I can't be certain, it seems there's a revelation ahead, something important Ruby wanted me to see. I search the shelves until I find a section of Pippi Longstocking books, then identify the first edition and find the letters. I read the first of them.

September 28, 1946

Dear Margaret,

All is well here. Anthony and I are happily looking ahead to fall, a lovely season in Seattle. I do wish you could come back and see it.

Every day the bookstore is filled with children and their parents. It is becoming a haven for young readers, and I am so delighted to see it. Remember the little writer's workshop you taught at the store the day before you left? Well, a little boy named Billy brought back a book he wrote, inspired by his time working with you. And, Brownie, it's quite good! Just think of how you inspired him by being here. That moment will live on, and maybe one day he'll be a writer like you.

Anthony is well. He's been busy with work of late, which means I'm spending more time alone than I like. I hate to sound paranoid, but sometimes I get the feeling that I'm being followed. I realize it's probably only my imagination, but sometimes when I'm taking the rubbish out to the alley, or locking up the shop at night, I feel like someone's there watching me. The other night, a car sped up to the block outside and slowed down and stayed there. The driver was looking into the bookstore for quite some time. When I went to the window, the car sped off. I may tell Anthony about it when he returns from his trip.

I'm afraid I have bad news about Lucille. Encouraged by the card she sent announcing her pregnancy, I picked out a baby gift (a little yellow pajama set with a hat) and brought it to her home yesterday. Well, little did I know that she was hosting a luncheon with all of her girlfriends. You should have seen the way she stepped out to the porch as if she dreaded letting them see me. As if I was an embarrassment to her. She told me it wasn't a good time, and asked me to leave. Just like that. Brownie, I fear it's too late for us. She will never accept me for who I am. To her, I will always be someone whose lifestyle she rejects.

Well, I miss you and hope you are well! Send copies of the moon book as soon as they're off press. I simply cannot wait to see them!

Yours,
Ruby

P.S. Oh, and I know it may be too late to make such a suggestion (as it is, you may be at the printing stage now), but I had a little idea for the moon book: Instead of using the word "porridge," which sounds a little stiff, why don't you use "mush"? My sister and I used to call it that, and it sounds more playful, somehow. Also, it rhymes with "hush," which would work well in a bedtime story. What do you think? Take it or leave it!

October 4, 1946

Dear Ruby,

I not only loved your suggestion for "hush" and "mush," but I immediately took it to my editor and she did too! So, we've altered the manuscript accordingly. I ought to give you a byline on this book, my dear.

And, I have a title. We're calling the book <u>Goodnight Moon</u>! What do you think? I feel that it has a nice ring to it, and so does Clem. Have I mentioned him? He's the illustrator, and a dear friend. He and his wife, Posey, are coming to stay with me at Vinalhaven soon. Wish you could join us. We'd be quite a foursome!

Have I told you, my dear friend, just how meaningful your letters are to me? I hope that in a hundred years, when someone takes it upon herself to write a biography of either of us (what fun to think about, though I daresay I'd probably read mine shrieking and squealing through parted fingers), they'll stumble upon these letters and see how truly wonderful you are. After all, what is life without good friends?

We may have great loves in our lives—and I say this not to diminish romantic love—but the wonderful thing about lasting friendship is that we will always belong to each other. I hate to think about just how lonely life would be without a confidant such as you.

It's funny, the other day I was thinking about a new story about a dog who lives alone. A dog who "belongs to himself." Yes, we must belong to ourselves, but life is infinitely richer when we can belong to each other, don't you think?

Ah, it is already almost five. I'm attending a publisher party this evening, and I must go dress. My editor will be there; maybe I'll share the dog book idea with her. For now, I'll call it <u>Mister Dog</u>. It has a certain ring to it, don't you think? All right, I'll drop this letter in the mailbox before I leave so the postman will send it on its way first thing tomorrow morning.

> With love from Cobble Court,
> always,
> Margaret

P.S. I'm sorry about Lucille. But remember, it is her loss. Truly.

I rise early the next morning thinking about what Margaret wrote about belonging to ourselves. I've belonged to myself for too long. I want to belong to someone else now. I want to share my life in the way that Margaret wrote about. Did Ruby feel that way too?

Little Ruby's making cooing sounds in her Pack 'n Play, and I reach down to pick her up, then glance at the clock: 7:13. Seattle's NBC affiliate will be here at nine, and the footage they take will be part of the evening news. Then, I'll stay put and do a taped interview with CNN's Soledad O'Brien.

Gavin appears at the stairs. "Morning! I thought you might want a little help with Ruby while you get ready for your close-up."

"Thanks," I say, depositing the baby into his arms. I eye my makeup bag, which has gotten little use in Seattle, and after check-ing my reflection in the mirror I decide that foundation is probably a good idea. "I'm nervous."

"You'll be great," he assures me. "Just smile and be yourself."

I nod, and turn back to the mirror, where I dab concealer under my eyes, then finish the look with mascara and eyeliner. "What do you think? Too much?"

"Just right," he says.

"OK," I say as I spray my hair, then give myself a once-over in the full-length mirror. I peer out the window and see a white van with a satellite tower on top. "They're here."

"Break a leg," Gavin says.

Two men dressed in jeans and fleece vests stand outside the bookstore carrying bags of camera equipment. "Hi," I say, opening the door. "I'm June."

They set up their equipment and attach a mic to my shirt. I sit in the wingback chair by the fireplace and after they get footage of the bookstore, they turn the camera to me.

"Here, put this earpiece in your ear," one of the cameramen says. "You'll hear the anchor's voice that way and you can talk to her as if you're having a conversation. Just look right into the camera."

"OK," I say nervously.

The first interview, with the NBC affiliate, is quick and pain-less. I answer four or five questions, and it's over. Just like that. In a few minutes, I hear another woman's voice in my ear.

"Hi, June?"

"Yes," I say.

"Good morning, this is Soledad O'Brien. How are you?"

"Good, thanks," I say. "I have to tell you, I've never done a TV interview before."

"You want to know a secret? It's really easy."

"OK, if you say so."

Somewhere in the distance a producer counts back from five, and then Soledad begins. "And we're back with June Andersen of Seattle, who, in the age of booming Internet book sales, is making it her mission to save a beloved Seattle brick-and-mortar bookstore, but not just any bookstore. Bluebird Books in Seattle's Green Lake neighborhood is believed to be the birthplace of the legendary children's book *Goodnight Moon*. Now, June, can you tell us why you've decided to work so hard to save the store?"

"Thank you, Soledad. Yes, my aunt Ruby was a wonderful woman who believed in the power of literature. I grew up right here in the bookstore, where I got to see, firsthand, just how transformative books can be. When Aunt Ruby passed away a few months ago, she left the store to me in hopes that I'd find a way to save it."

"I understand that the bookstore is in financial distress and that you're hosting a fund-raiser to keep the doors open," Soledad says.

I pause before answering. "Yes, that's right. We'll need quite an infusion of funds to keep the lights on and to keep Chase and Hanson Bank from proceeding with its foreclosure process."

"Even the business element of your story is personal," Soledad continues. "As I understand it, you used to be a vice president at Chase and Hanson. Is that right?"

"Yes," I say honestly. "I was the very person in charge of shutting down small businesses like Bluebird Books. I used to see things from a black-and-white perspective, but now that I'm on the other side, I realize that sometimes people just need a little more time, or maybe a second chance." I think about Arthur then. And I wonder if he's watching, and what he's thinking.

"Well said from a former financier," Soledad says. "Now, can you tell us a little about the *Goodnight Moon* connection? Is it true that the book was somehow inspired by the bookstore?"

"Yes," I say. "My aunt Ruby and Margaret Wise Brown, the author of *Goodnight Moon* and at least one hundred other children's books, were very good friends. They corresponded for many years." I hold up the letters I recently found in the Pippi Longstocking book. "In their letters, each woman encouraged the other in significant ways. And my aunt Ruby was instrumental in encouraging Margaret to continue writing when she was facing her own demons and insecurities. And, in 1946, Margaret came to Seattle and visited Bluebird Books. The experience served as the inspiration for perhaps her greatest work to date, *Goodnight Moon*."

"That is truly remarkable," Soledad says. "So many of us, including myself, have read this book to our children over the years and thought, 'Wow, this is really special. But where did the idea come from? What compelled this author to write it?' And yet, until now, there is no explanation. Truly fascinating. And for anyone who'd like to attend the fund-raiser or make a donation to help save Bluebird Books, we'll put a link up on our website with information on how you can get involved. Thank you, June. We wish you all the best."

"Thank you so much, Soledad."

And just like that, the lights shut off, and the cameraman smiles. "You did great," he says.

"I hope so. Honestly, it was such a blur. I don't know what I said."

"Everyone says that," he reassures me. "I promise, you'll watch yourself on TV and you'll think, 'I did pretty great!'"

"Do you know when the piece will air?"

"Probably in a day or two," he says. "They usually shoot for the next day, or the day after."

"Great," I say, just as the phone begins to ring.

"Feel free to grab that," the cameraman says. "We've got everything we need. We'll just pack up now."

"Thanks again," I say, running to the phone. "Hello, Bluebird Books."

"Yes, is this June Andersen?"

"Speaking."

"Ms. Andersen, this is Edward Newton from HarperCollins Publishers in New York City. Our corporate communications office ran across the *Seattle Times* article, and, well, I wanted to be in touch, since we are the publisher of *Goodnight Moon*."

"Oh, yes, hello," I say.

"Ms. Andersen," he continues, "we see that your event is in three weeks, and we'd like to create special copies of *Goodnight Moon* that we'll rush to the store for your event. Each book's cover will be affixed with a sticker that reads "In honor of Bluebird Books, the birthplace of *Goodnight Moon*."

"Wow. That is . . . wonderful."

"I have to tell you," he says, "I was quite shocked to read that a bookstore in Seattle could be the birthplace of this legendary title, and I admit, I didn't altogether believe it. But our historian did some digging and we found some journal entries from the Brown estate that support what you say you've found in the letters between your aunt and Margaret. All this to say, it's a rare literary discovery, and we'd like to celebrate it with you."

"I'd be delighted," I say. "We have at least one hundred coming to the event, and probably more. The invitations just went out."

"We'll make sure you have enough," he says. "How about five

hundred, and several more boxes for the shop? I assume they'll be hot sellers at Bluebird Books."

"That would be amazing," I reply. "If we can meet our fundraising goal, we plan to reopen the store next month."

"Well," Edward says, "all of us at HarperCollins wish you the very best of luck."

"How did the interview go?" Gavin asks, nestling Little Ruby into my arms.

"Great," I say, indicating the phone. "That was someone from HarperCollins, the publisher of *Goodnight Moon*. They want to donate several boxes of special edition books for the event."

"Wow, that's amazing," Gavin says. "Things are looking good for Bluebird Books."

"Let's hope. I don't want to get too excited until we have the money we need to pay off the bank."

He kisses my forehead, then walks to the door. "Come by at lunch. I'm making tortellini."

"And tortellini solves what problem?"

"Worrying," he says. "It helps you stop worrying."

Chapter 24

While Ruby has a morning nap, I decide to get started re-arranging the bookshelves. If we're going to have more than one hundred people in the store, we're going to need room for them. Carefully, after removing and stacking the books from the waist-high shelves that occupy the center of the store, I line them along the exterior walls. After a half hour, I'm amazed at how much space the shift has made.

I pause and wipe the sweat off my brow as the phone rings at Ruby's desk. I suppose I might be here another twenty-five years and still call it Ruby's desk. It will always be hers and no one else's. "Hello, Bluebird Books," I say, a little out of breath.

"June, this is J.P., the guy who was almost your cousin—from the library."

"Oh hi!" I say, happy to hear from him. "Did you get my invitation?"

"Not yet," he says. "But I heard about it, and I wanted to say that I'm coming, and that the library is totally behind your efforts. We want Bluebird Books to be the official bookseller for all of our children's events this year."

"That's amazing, thank you," I say.

"Also, I spoke to my friend who's the director of Friends of the King County Library, and he says each year they give a grant to a bookseller who has shown extraordinary community service. These grants are meant to help booksellers thrive in increasingly challenging times. Anyway, I pitched Bluebird Books to him, and he says it sounds like a shoo-in."

"We would have made great cousins, you know?"

"I know," he says.

In the rush to get the store ready for the party, I realize that I miss Ruby more than ever. I long to hear her voice. I need her to know that I'm trying to save Bluebird Books, and I need her to tell me, like she did when I was a child, that everything's going to be all right.

Mister Dog. The dog who belonged to himself. I remember Margaret writing about the title in the previous letter. Of course. I find the first edition, and inside is a single yellowed envelope. It's addressed to my aunt, but I don't recognize the handwriting on the envelope. It's certainly not Margaret's. I quickly open the letter. It's dated December 12, 1952, years after the last pair of letters Ruby left for me. What happened in between? I eye the letter and read the typewritten words:

Dear Ruby,

I am Margaret Wise Brown's sister, Roberta. I regret to inform you that Margaret passed away last month in France, where she was recovering from surgery. I hate to be the bearer of this news, but since you and Margaret were very close she'd want you to know. I hope it is a comfort that Margaret's death was quick and painless. The physician told me that after surgery, she had a terrible time staying in bed. Wanting to go out to the gardens to examine the birds in the lemon trees outside her window, she tried to convince a nurse that she was well enough to walk by kicking her leg up can-can style. Sadly, the action released a fatal blood clot. She died seconds later.

I found a stack of letters from you to Margaret in her Cobble Court home. She kept them in a box on her desk, and it is obvious that you were a beloved friend of hers. I am returning these letters to you. I thought you might like to have them. Perhaps they will bring you some peace.

In looking through them (I hope you don't mind), I grew to admire the friendship the two of you shared. I also had no idea of the pain I caused my sister. I hope you understand it was unknowingly. Of course, I wish I could turn back the clock now and make her see that I loved her every ounce as much as she loved me. I wish I could tell her that I accepted her just as she was. I believe in my heart that she knew that when she died. It took time, but our relationship strengthened over the years. It brought a tear to my eye reading about Operation Sisterhood. If only everyone had a sister like Margaret who refused to let go. I pray that you and your sister, Lucille, have found your own common ground, though it is not my business to ask about those details.

Well, I do hope these letters are a comfort to you. I know you know, as I do, that as long as this world spins, there will never be another Margaret.

> All my best wishes,
> Roberta Brown Rauch

I set the letter down, feeling the grief that Ruby must have felt so many decades before. And then I notice a key on the floor. It must have fallen out of the book when I opened it. I pick it up and examine it closely, with a sense of familiarity. The treasure chest. Yes. Aunt Ruby used to keep a treasure chest in the store. After story time, she'd let one child insert the key into the lock, and then everyone could reach in and pull out a candy or a sticker, or a small toy. I used to love that treasure chest. It was magical.

And now, Ruby's given me the key.

"June?" Mom's standing in the doorway when I turn around, with Gavin right behind her. "Look who brought lunch."

Gavin holds up a paper bag that I can smell all the way from inside the bookstore.

"What are you doing?" Mom asks, walking toward me.

I wipe away a tear and hold up the key. "Ruby left me this. Remember the treasure chest?"

Mom nods. "You girls used to love that."

"Are you going to open it?" Gavin asks.

I eye the screen of the baby monitor and see that Little Ruby's still fast asleep, then walk to Ruby's desk, and pull out the chest beneath. I insert the key into the old lock, remembering watching Ruby do the same a hundred times before.

I lift the lid and peer into the chest, which is lined with red velvet. And there, waiting for me, is a copy of *Goodnight Moon*. I open the cover and see the copyright. It's dated 1947. A first edition. In perfect condition.

Mom is crying as I lift open the cover of the book. The dust jacket is brittle and it almost feels as if the edges might disintegrate beneath my fingers. "I wish Amy were here," I whisper to Mom.

"She's with us," she says, smiling.

Inside the book is a single letter, from Ruby. It doesn't look old like the previous letters I've found. It's addressed to me, and it looks as though Ruby took a paper and pen just a few months ago and wrote it out, perhaps the last thing she did in the bookstore before she departed.

Gavin places his hand on the small of my back.

"Read it," Mom says tenderly. "It's time you knew, honey."

"Knew?" I search her face. There are tears in her eyes. Tears of guilt, regret. And tears of love. She hasn't been a perfect mother, and for long stretches of time she wasn't even a good mother, but I forgave her a long time ago, and I love her in spite of it all.

I turn to the letter, open the envelope, and with a shaky voice, I read aloud:

> My dearest girl,
>
> And now you come to the end. You've read the letters, and I'm proud of you for finding them all. I knew you would. I wanted you to have them so you could know me, really know me. I never kept a diary, and if I had, I might have been too shy to share it with you. All I have are these letters, and I wanted you to read them.
>
> After Margaret passed away, her sister, Roberta, was kind enough to return the letters to me. I was so heartbroken about my friend's sudden passing that I couldn't bear to read them again. I tucked them away in a shoe box and put Margaret out of my mind, for it was too painful. She died much too young, at the prime of her life. But her memory always remained in my heart. You see, she left a part of herself here. And she took a part of Bluebird Books with her too.
>
> June, what I'm trying to tell you is this bookstore is the birthplace of *Goodnight Moon*. Of course, you've pieced that together from the letters, haven't you? Indeed, this is where it all began. I've kept this to myself all these years. It didn't feel right to broadcast it. And when I wanted to, it always felt like the wrong moment. But I knew someday I'd leave it all here for you to find. A

treasure to be discovered. I'm hoping that you can use it to save the store. I'm hoping that people will want to come to the place where Margaret took inspiration for her iconic children's book, a book that has touched so many children, and adult children.

June, do with it what you will. I should add that the signed copy of *Goodnight Moon* you are holding now is worth a small fortune. Margaret stood at the printing press hovering over the line the day the book was printed (she was wonderfully bossy like that, and I loved her for it, even if it did drive the printers mad!), and she plucked the first finished copy off the conveyer belt. It had a mistake in the back. Flip to the last page, and you'll see it. The plate slipped, and instead of one mouse on the windowsill, there are two. She said that it was fate, that the two mice were representative of the two of us. Two friends, looking out into the moonlight together on a peaceful night, looking out into a world of possibilities. That's the Margaret I loved so. The world was her oyster. She never stopped dreaming.

Well, the book is yours now, to sell, to keep, to do with what you please. There are a great deal more valuable first editions in the shop, and please, sell them if you must to keep a roof over your head. I bought them all for you. June, everything I did was for you. Always.

These sentiments might sound silly to you, perhaps even unexpected. But now comes the moment when I will tell you my deepest, longest held secret. In 1970, I was forty-six years old when I gave birth to my first and only child, a baby girl, with cherub cheeks and blue eyes that were so kind. No, not a boy, even though I wanted onlookers to think she was a boy (I dressed her in blue as a disguise, and left her birth certificate vague: J.P.).

As much as I loved her, with all my heart, I had to say good-bye to my child, for her own protection. Her father was a Magnuson, a wealthy and powerful Seattle family, and though he was a good man, and I loved him dearly, he was already married to someone else. He passed away five months before my little girl was born, and when his wife learned of my baby, she was furious. I feared she'd use her influence, her attorneys, to find a way to make me pay. And she tried. When my baby was seven months old, I set her out on a blanket in the store. I turned my back for a moment, and a man in a suit and dark glasses nearly had her in his arms. I screamed and it scared the man off. He drove away in a black Cadillac, but he was back the next day, peering into the window before the shop opened.

I couldn't live like that, knowing that my baby might be abducted at any moment—night or day. She wasn't safe. I went to the police, but they didn't seem at all concerned. Besides, a Magnuson was the chief of police at that time.

So I made the heart-wrenching decision to give my baby away, for adoption. It was an open adoption, so I could still see her whenever I'd like. But I didn't let the Magnuson family know that. In fact, I sent word through their attorney that I'd given the baby (boy) away to a wealthy family in New York, and that I hoped Victoria Magnuson would be happy now. It threw her off. The Cadillac stopped coming by. But I still needed to find my baby girl a new home, and I knew just the place. Somewhere close. With the only family I had in Seattle.

June, what I'm trying to tell you is that my baby is you. My niece, the only mother you know, raised you. She did her best, and so did I.

Of course, I questioned the arrangement a thousand times, especially when things got bad at home for you. Fortunately, I was close and able to intervene when I realized the difficulties of the situation, and while your mother worked to improve things at home. And she did. I knew she would. She loved you like her daughter, June. And for that, I shall always be grateful.

None of us is perfect, and perhaps my decision for you wasn't the best one. But it was the only one I could make at the time. I had to know you were safe.

Could you tell? Could you see my love for you? It was the love of a mother. My dearest daughter, this isn't the life I imagined, but life never quite goes as we imagine, does it? I didn't get the house with the picket fence. I didn't get the doting husband. I didn't even get to hear you call me Mommy. But I still got you. And that was the best of all.

Your father never got to meet you, but he would have loved you at first sight, just as I did. You are the culmination of our love, a gift to each of us at the moment we least expected. A gift that came at the end of our love story. As fate would have it, Anthony and I would never have a happily ever after, but you gave me a happy ending.

And through it all, there was this bookstore, this marvelous bookstore. It always kept me going when I felt I couldn't anymore. It was, and is, my rock, my peace. I hope it will be that for you too. You've been gone too long, honey. Come home, and this time, stay.

There is one more thing. A final plea, if I may. As you've read the letters between Margaret and me, I trust that you've picked up on the theme of sisterhood throughout. Margaret was like a sister to me during the time she walked this earth. She helped ease the pain of my estrangement from my own sister, Lucille. Sadly, Lucille died before we were able to reconcile. It wasn't the ending I'd hoped for us, and it has haunted me every day since. I pray that you and your sister, Amy, won't have that same end. In fact, even more than I fear the loss of Bluebird Books, I fear for you and Amy. Sisters are part of one another, no matter what. They belong to each other. Going

about life without your sister is like going without a limb. You
feel it every day. I want a happier life for you, and for Amy.
Promise me that you both will try?

I look up and my eyes meet Mom's. "She'd be so happy," Mom
says through tears. I nod and turn back to the letter.

Oh, and the locket. How many times did you ask me to
show you what I kept inside? I lost count. Is it around your neck
now? Of course it is. Open it, dear. Inside is one final surprise.
With all my love, from this lifetime and the next,

Your loving mother,
Ruby

I'm so choked up, I can't speak. Mom's arms are draped around
me. Gavin watches with tears in his eyes.

Nobody says anything. It's a comforting silence. A silence
thirty-five years in the making. All I can think of is Ruby. My
mother. My *mother*. I feel so many emotions, but mostly love. Such
love. I reach to my neck, where her locket rests, and follow the chain
to its edge, where I unclasp it and let it fall into my palm.

"Sit down," Gavin says gently.

I nod, and take a seat on the bench by the fireplace, then fiddle
with the hook on the locket. It sticks, but I try again. This time it
clicks open, and I see a tiny lock of blond hair.

"It was yours," Mom says, "when you were a baby." She points
to an inscription. "Look, there's your name." I squint and see
"June Patricia" engraved at the center of the locket. Of course, Patricia was Ruby's middle name. I always thought Mom named me
that as a way to honor Ruby.

"J.P.," I say through tears.

"She never took it off," Mom says. "She always said it kept you close to her heart." She wipes a tear from her eyes.

"The scholarship I received," I murmur. "It was Ruby, wasn't it?"

Mom nods. "She took out an additional mortgage on the shop to send you."

"Oh, Mom," I cry, burying my head in her shoulder. "I didn't know."

"Yes, you did," she says. "Your heart knew."

I nod. Yes. *Everything that anyone would ever look for is usually where they find it.*

Resting at the bottom of the chest is a thick stack of old envelopes, tied with twine. I know they're the remaining letters exchanged between Ruby and Margaret in the years before Margaret's death, and I can hardly wait to read them.

I look up when I hear the shuffling of footsteps behind me. May stands in the doorway. "I can tell by the way you smile," she says. None of us heard her come in, and at first it startles me. *How long has she been here?* Her normally perfect hair looks a little disheveled. She's been crying, but she's smiling. "You look just like her."

"May, I . . . I don't know what to say," I begin. "I realize this must be as life altering to you as it is to me."

"This makes us sisters, I guess," she says, taking a step toward me. "All this time, I thought I had a brother." She wipes away a tear from her cheek. "I guess I just assumed that my father would have loved him more than me." She looks around the bookstore. "This was where his heart was, here with Ruby. He'd come home late every night. I'd wait up for him, though, just so I could see him for a few moments before my eyes got heavy. You see, he chose Ruby over me. It sounds awful when you lay it out like that, but it's the truth."

"Oh, May," I say, touching her shoulder. "Your father was in a very difficult position."

"*Our* father," she says.

My eyes sting. I'm still struggling to make sense of it all. Amy is gone, yes. But now, as May stands before me, I feel that I've been given an unexpected gift. A sister.

"He once gave me a copy of *Goodnight Moon*," she continues. "It was a first edition. I didn't know it at the time, but he must have gotten it from Ruby. All I knew is that he brought it home on my tenth birthday, and I thought it was the most glorious thing I'd ever laid eyes on. On the inside cover, he wrote a poem. A love letter to his daughter. These were the only words he'd written to me. And I treasured the book that held them. But when I came home for my father's funeral and learned that Ruby was pregnant, I was so angry. It was the ultimate betrayal to Mom and me. So I boxed up the book, and the only photos I had of him, and left it at the bookstore with Ruby's name on it. I wanted to sever that last tie, to his memory." She lets out a deep sigh, tinged with pain. "And even in spite of my anger, there was a part of me that wished I had forgiven him, accepted his love of Ruby." She shakes her head. "But it was too late."

I blink hard. "Why didn't you just come talk to Ruby?"

"I couldn't," May says. "I just couldn't. I came into the shop a few times after Father died, hoping I'd see the book on a shelf somewhere. I even wrote a letter to Ruby years ago, inquiring anonymously about the book. I wrote that I'd pay a small fortune for it. I was too prideful to face her, to face the fact that I'd heartlessly returned such a precious gift of my own accord."

"But she would have given it to you," I say, "if she only knew."

"I just couldn't face her. I was too angry."

"You were hurt," I say. "People act out of character when they're in pain."

"Even all grown up," she continues through tears, "I still didn't feel that I deserved my father's love."

"But you did, May. And I'm sure he regretted that you were trapped between two worlds the way you were."

May takes the copy of *Goodnight Moon* in her hands and flips to the inside cover, where the note from her father might have been. "Well, it's gone now," she says.

"Wait," I say, remembering the final few boxes under Ruby's bed that I still need to sort through. "Come with me."

Mom follows May and me up the creaky staircase to the apartment and picks up Little Ruby from her Pack 'n Play. She winks at me before returning downstairs to Gavin, leaving me alone with May.

"I always wondered what it was like up here," May says. "Their little love nest." Her words aren't harsh and cold like they were on the first day we met. The edges are softer now.

We walk through the doorway, and May takes in the sight. "It's lovely," she says. "I can see why my father liked being here. The place is so simple, but that's what makes it special. Mom couldn't do simple. Everything had to be gilded and ornate."

I kneel down beside Ruby's bed, and May takes a seat beside me. "I'm sorry," she says to me.

"For what?"

"For breaking in to the bookstore, for spying on you the way I did. I only wanted to—"

"I forgive you," I say quickly.

"You really do?"

"I really do."

I pull out a box, and then another. Each contains books and notebooks, old bills and paperwork bound together with string. Then I reach for the third box and lift the edges. I can tell by the look on May's face that she recognizes something inside. "That's it!" she cries, leaning closer. "That's the box."

I watch as she pulls out a framed photo of our father with May as a child. She looks angelic with her dark hair and velvet coat. They're holding hands, and May looks up at him as if he's the greatest person in the world.

Beneath a few other framed photographs is the book. I recognize the cover immediately. May takes it into her hands and the spine creaks as she opens it.

"My darling daughter," she begins, reading the words her father wrote on her birthday in 1947, "when you're sad and lonely, and when you doubt the good in this world, I wish I could always be there to make it right for you, to cheer you up. But when I'm not, I hope you'll look at the moon and feel my love. Love always and forever, Daddy."

She leans down and kisses the words on the page, then begins to cry. Her chest shakes as she weeps, and I set my hand on her shoulder. "We were named after the most beautiful months in Seattle," I say. "May comes before June." I pause. "You came first. Don't forget that." May nods, and we cry together, unself-consciously, like only two sisters can.

Chapter 25

Gavin's standing in the doorway of the bookstore on the night of the fund-raiser. He looks handsome in his gray suit. "What do you think?" he asks, grinning. "It's a book party, so I thought I'd go for the F. Scott Fitzgerald look."

"You look crazy handsome," I say, planting a kiss on his lips. I feel fidgety and nervous. "I just hope the night goes well. It has to."

"Where's Little Ruby?" he asks.

"Mom's upstairs with her for the night," I say. "I figured I wouldn't be a very good event host with a baby strapped to me." I see that Gavin's holding something behind his back. "What do you have in your hands?"

He smiles mischievously, then reveals a tiny calico kitten purring in his arms. "Every proper bookstore needs a kitten," he says proudly.

"Aww, that's sweet," I say. "What should we call her?"

"How about Margaret?"

"Too formal. But Ruby used to call her Brownie. How about that?"

The kitten purrs at my feet, and Gavin smiles. "You know, she actually *looks* like a Brownie." He reaches into his back pocket. "Oh, I have something to show you."

He hands me an eleven-by-seventeen sheet of paper that's been rolled up and smashed a bit from its time in his pocket. "You remember how we were talking about making this Bluebird Books and Café?"

I nod.

"Well, I had an architect take a look at how we might do that," he says as I unfurl the paper. "These are just preliminary sketches." He leans in over my shoulder. "See, the bookstore would remain just as it is. We'd take this wall down, here, and join the two together."

I study the drawings carefully. The architect has done a wonderful job, and I can almost feel the sense of community through the drawings—children stocking up on new storybooks, then having lunch or hot chocolate and a cookie with their parents next door.

"I love it," I say. "I really do."

Gavin exhales. "I was hoping you would." He folds the drawings back up and tucks them into Ruby's old desk drawer.

"The place looks great," he says.

"Did you see the impatiens out front? A local nursery donated them. It's funny, I kept looking at the front of the shop and thinking, 'What's missing?' And then I remembered the impatiens."

"Why do they call them impatiens?"

I smile the way Ruby might have. "They're a reminder for us to be patient."

Gavin nods in agreement. "And we will be. We've done our work, and now we see if the community can come through with the rest."

Peter and Nate arrive first. Gavin hands them each one of the special edition copies of *Goodnight Moon*, with a list of further donation options tucked inside, and they marvel at the bookstore. "It's gorgeous," Peter says, embracing me. "I can see why Margaret Wise Brown was inspired by this place."

"Thank you so much for coming," I say. "You scored some serious friend points, you know?"

He grins. "Where's the munchkin?"

"Upstairs with my mom. Come by tomorrow and I'll introduce you two. She's going to love her godfather."

Peter and Nate help themselves to hors d'oeuvres and wine as more guests filter in—the owners of Geppetto's, Joe and his wife, J.P. and three of his coworkers from the library, and dozens of other people I don't recognize. Gavin and I greet them all and extend our heartfelt thanks. And then, just as the jazz band from Antonio's begins to play, Bill Gates and his wife, Melinda, appear. A man in a black suit with an earpiece stands in the distance, and I assume it must be a bodyguard. Bill (Bill!) extends his hand to me with a warm smile. "You must be June," he says.

"Yes, hello, Mr. Gates," I say, smiling.

He introduces me to Melinda, then marvels at the bookstore. "It's just as I remember it as a boy," he says, walking to the spot where Ruby used to hold court at story time. "I'd sit right here and listen to your aunt read, and I swear it was one of my fondest memories of early childhood."

"Ruby would be touched if she knew that Bluebird Books meant so much to you," I say.

"I'm sorry to hear of her passing," he says.

Gavin hands Melinda a copy of *Goodnight Moon*, and she and Bill smile and each grab a glass of white wine. Just then, I feel a tap on my shoulder.

"Excuse me, June?" A thin man who looks to be in his seventies, with gray hair, stands beside me.

"Yes," I say.

"My name is Clive," he continues. "I wanted to come tonight because, well, when I was fifteen years old, I was on vacation here in Seattle. Thing is, I hated the trip. I hated the rain. I hated the annoying cousins I had to bunk with. Then, one day, my mom took me to this bookstore. I was completely against the idea at first, but then I sat down at a little table right over there, and an author, a real author, talked to me and some other children about writing. She wrote books for children, and she talked about writing stories inspired by our lives. Her enthusiasm was absolutely infectious. I went home and wrote my first story. I suppose it's why I went on to write as many novels as I have."

"Wait," I say, astounded. "You said your name is Clive. Are you Clive—?"

"Clive Cussler, yes," he says with a disarming smile. "It all started here, here in this bookstore. It's why I think I keep coming back to the Pacific Northwest as a setting."

Gavin sidles up beside me. "Is that who I think it is?" he whispers into my ear.

"Yes," I say. "Clive Cussler. I'm kind of freaking out right now."

"I think everyone's here, just about," he says. "Want to go up and say a few words?"

I nod, taking a deep breath.

Gavin squeezes my hand. "You can do this. For Ruby. For Little Ruby. For us."

I smile, and walk up and stand in front of Ruby's desk. I tap a knife to my wineglass and smile out at the crowd, which quickly quiets.

"Hello, everyone, and thank you so much for coming to the Blue-bird Books fund-raiser this evening! I'm June Andersen, Ruby Crain's . . . *daughter*. I know that many of you were touched by my mother over the years. Tonight I've talked to world-famous authors and technology entrepreneurs—you know who you are—who came this evening to pay respect to this store and to my mother's lifelong work of introducing literature to children. And I am so amazed by the stories I've heard about the many ways this bookstore has inspired so many people." I take a deep breath. "As you know, Ruby shared a friendship with one of the greatest children's book authors of all time, Margaret Wise Brown, the author of *Goodnight Moon*. Rather than boast about her friendship with such a luminous woman in literary history, Ruby kept quiet about it, leaving the discovery for me to find when I inherited the store a few months ago. And a discovery it was, indeed. In letters between Ruby and Margaret, I saw how each of them, in her own particular style, confided in and encouraged the other. And perhaps most notable was the way Ruby encouraged Margaret to keep writing when she felt she'd lost her way."

I pause to look around the room, filled with warm, smiling faces. I see Adrianna and her new boyfriend standing together, and I feel a burst of contentment then, for her, for myself. I clear my throat, and begin speaking again. "You may be excited to learn that this bookstore, the very place we all are standing, was actually the birthplace of *Goodnight Moon*. HarperCollins has graciously sent a special edition copy for each of you. And as you thumb through the pages of the book, I hope you'll see it with fresh eyes. For on each page is a piece of Bluebird Books, and a piece of Ruby."

The crowd cheers and claps, while I smile, take a deep breath, and reach beneath the desk, where the mockup and first edition wait. "And I am delighted to show you two items Ruby treasured, which have never before been seen in public. First, the only known existing mockup of the book, as given to Ruby in 1946, shortly before *Goodnight Moon* was published. And, also, the very first printed copy, which Margaret plucked for Ruby from the printing press the day the first batch was printed."

Gavin appears by my side, and I hand him both the mockup and first edition, which he'll later take up to the apartment for safekeeping. "As you know, Bluebird Books is facing significant financial hardship, not an unfamiliar plight for children's bookstores in this age. But we are determined to continue Ruby's legacy and fight an uphill battle if we must. But we can only do that with your help. Inside your very own special edition of *Goodnight Moon* is a pledge sheet, which lists the various ways you can lend your support to this bookstore. If you will, please take a moment and fill out the form and leave it with Peter, the man by the door, who will see that the funds are collected this evening." Peter waves to the crowd. "Please enjoy the music and the wonderful appetizers from Antonio's restaurant, and thank you all, again, so much for your wonderful support."

There's a round of applause, and then Bill Gates raises his hand. "May I say something?"

"Yes," I say quickly. "Please."

"Hello, everyone," he says. He doesn't have to introduce himself; everyone knows who he is. "I grew up here in Seattle and spent many happy hours of my childhood at this bookstore. Places like this are important because they ignite the love of literature in our children. They ignite their imagination. Ruby Crain of Bluebird Books did just that—for me, and for so many other Seattle children over the years. And now the store is on the verge of closing. Stores like this, all over the country, in fact, share a similar fate. If we don't stand up for children's literature, and support businesses like this, they will disappear right before our eyes. I ask you to join me in supporting Bluebird Books so it will continue to be a place of curiosity and discovery for children, for years to come."

After the applause quiets, I weave my way through the crowd to Peter.

"I think you've hit it out of the park tonight," he whispers.

"Thanks," I say.

"Now, go have a glass of wine," Peter adds, shooing me off. "Let me collect the money. That's my job."

I say a prayer then. *Please, please let it be enough to keep Bluebird Books open.*

Gavin slices a cake that a baker friend decorated to look like the "great green room," and after everyone's had a slice, the party begins to wind down.

I nervously eye the desk, where Peter is collecting a final contribution form. When the last guest leaves, Nate and I lock the door and rush to Peter.

"How'd we do?" I ask.

Peter scratches his head. "I've crunched the numbers eight ways," he says, shaking his head. "I'm sorry, June, it's not going to be enough."

My eyes widen. "Even with the ticket sales? Even with the extra donations?"

He nods.

"Did you count my IRA and my savings?"

"All of it," he says. "We're still short. By a lot."

I collapse in a defeated heap on the floor, and sink my head into my hands.

"Listen," Peter says suddenly, "Nate and I have some savings. Not a lot. We were going to use it for our kitchen remodel this winter, but we really don't need a Viking range, right, Nate?"

"Right," Nate says cheerfully.

"No," I say, shaking my head. "I couldn't. I couldn't ask you to do that."

Peter nods soberly. "And I'm afraid even if we gave you every penny of that pot of remodel money, it still wouldn't be enough." He thinks for a moment. "You could sell the first editions—maybe to a collector?"

"And sell the soul of the bookstore? It wouldn't be right."

He nods, and I stand up and let out a deep sigh. "I guess this is it," I say. "We tried and we failed."

I look around at Bluebird Books, at Ruby's life's work. "But it was worth trying for," Peter says. "You'll never regret it."

I look up and see Gavin standing at the door out on the sidewalk. He began shuttling back dirty dishes to Antonio's after the last guest left. We must have locked him out.

I walk to the door dejectedly, and see that he's holding an enormous bouquet of flowers, lavender roses.

"Someone knows my favorite flower," I say flatly as I open the door for him.

"I wish I could take credit, but they're not from me," he says, handing me the bouquet.

I shrug and set the flowers down on a nearby shelf.

"Aren't you going to open the card and see who they're from?"

"Flowers aren't going to save the bookstore," I say.

Gavin frowns. "You mean we didn't raise enough?"

I nod.

"Oh, June," he says. "I'm so sorry."

My eyes sting with fresh tears, and I hardly notice that Gavin has picked up the card in the vase and has torn open the flap. A moment later, he smiles. "June, you're going to want to read this."

I already know what it is. More well-wishes from a community member who loved Bluebird Books as a child. I'll just have to write them, all of them, to tell them I failed, and that the store will be closing.

Gavin hands the card to me. His eyes are blazing with excitement. "Read it!"

I look down at the typewritten card and read:

June,

I saw you on CNN. You killed it, kid. I've closed down thousands of businesses. I figured I could help save this one. Foreclosure papers destroyed. I'll cover the balance personally. Here's the thing: A long time ago, I was a little boy who loved books. You reminded me of that.

Yours, Arthur (a.k.a. the nicest asshole you've ever met)

"Peter, Nate," I cry, "come here!"

I read the note to them. Each of us reads it over and over again. We cry. We cheer. We open another bottle of wine and toast the future of Bluebird Books.

I shake my head. "I never would have guessed that Arthur would come through. I guess I should thank you, Peter. You made me e-mail him."

Peter nods. "See? You knew he had a heart."

"Guess so," I say. "I just didn't know it was a big heart."

Chapter 26

After Peter and Nate head to their hotel, Mom comes downstairs and I tell her the good news before we say good night to her. Ruby is asleep upstairs in her new crib, a gift shipped to the store from Gavin's sister, and after Mom leaves, it's just Gavin and me standing on a carpet of confetti, surrounded by half-eaten plates of cake and hors d'oeuvres. I reach for a plate atop a bookshelf and begin cleaning up, but I feel Gavin's arm on my waist.

"It's too nice a night to clean," he whispers into my ear. "We'll get the rest in the morning. Come sit with me."

"But what if the food attracts mice?" I say. "You know these old buildings."

"Let them have a few extra crumbs tonight."

We move two chairs by the big windows in the store and stare up into the sky. I lean my head against Gavin's shoulder.

"You did a good job tonight," he says.

"Do you think Ruby would have been proud?"

"Yes," he says. "So proud." He grins. "Did you see the way Bill Gates was hovering over the dessert tray? It's not every day that the richest man in the world walks in and eats three of your cannoli."

"I can't believe Arthur came through for me."

Gavin nods. "Funny to think that he of all people ended up being the hero."

"I know. But what did Ruby always say?" I pause to recall her words. "Yes, 'When you're looking for something, it's right where you find it.'" I smile to myself. My feet ache and I feel a sense of peaceful exhaustion. I turn to Gavin and smile at him. "I think I'm cured."

He turns to me, confused. "What do you mean?"

"My anxiety," I say, shaking my head, a bit in disbelief. "I don't know how to explain it other than to say it's just . . . gone."

Gavin squeezes my hand.

"I mean, I know that life's not perfect or anything. It'll never be. But I feel peace." I look at him again, cautiously. "Do you?"

"Yes," he says, nuzzling his cheek against mine.

I nod. "I guess I just can't help but wonder."

"Wonder what?"

"I wonder what's next?"

Gavin grins. "For us, you mean?"

I nod shyly.

He stands up and turns my chair to face him. His smile is big and warm. "Well, first I'm going to kiss you, and then I'm going to marry you. After that we're going to have a baby so Little Ruby can have a sister. Or maybe two. Three, if you'll agree to it."

I smile, unable to stop laughing.

He lifts me into his arms then. "And we're going to run the bookstore-café together. We're going to make it the best children's bookstore-café in the country. And we're going to keep it afloat with blood, sweat, and tears, and lots of love."

He turns to the back stairs that lead to the apartment and kisses my forehead lightly before carrying me up. "And all along the way we're going to write our own story. And it will be a beautiful one, filled with all the things we love."

"Books," I say.

He smiles and nods. "And good food."

"Naturally."

At the top of the stairs, he pushes open the door to the apartment with his elbow. "In the great green room, there was a shelf of first-edition books—"

"And a dripping sink," I add.

"And stacks of old newspapers."

I put my finger to his lips and say, "And a very handsome man who cooks."

"And there were lots of generous Seattleites sitting in chairs."

"And one little kitten who looked at you and became smitten."

"And pasta and cannoli and a guy wearing fleece."

"And a quiet old lady who is finally at peace." I wipe a tear away. "Do you think she is, Gavin? Do you think we made her proud?"

"Yes," he says, lying beside me on the bed. He kisses my lips with such tenderness, such love.

"Goodnight, Gavin," I say. My eyelids are heavy, and he peels off my shoes, then nestles beside me.

"Goodnight, June," he whispers softly in my ear. And when I close my eyes, I dream of the bookstore. Amy is holding her baby downstairs by the window, showering her with love. Ruby sits in a rocking chair in the corner of the little apartment with her knitting needles and a ball of yarn. It's where she's always been, of course, and it's where she'll always be, watching me as I sleep under the light of the moon.

And if I listen closely, I can almost hear her whispering, "Hush."

Acknowledgments

E very novel has its own special journey, with special people who shepherd it (and its author) along. For this novel, I owe my biggest thanks to Elisabeth Weed, my dear literary agent and friend. Aside from my husband, the first person I share fledgling novel ideas with is Elisabeth. I remember the moment I told her the concept for this book. I nervously e-mailed her a brief synopsis, and her immediate enthusiasm told me that I *needed* to write this novel. But not only that, she encouraged me to make it a bigger, more heartfelt story than I'd ever imagined. As an author I've learned to do two things over the years: trust my heart, and trust Elisabeth.

Heartfelt gratitude also goes to my wonderful editor at Penguin, Denise Roy, who edits my books with such super-skill. Thank you for your amazingness, Denise, and for the dozens and dozens of brilliant suggestions that made this book stronger, deeper, better.

A team of fabulous people must be thanked, heartily, for their help, encouragement, and expertise: the amazing Jenny Meyer and Shane King; Dana Murphy; Dana Borowitz; Elizabeth Keenan, Ashley McClay, Phil Budnick, Kate Napolitano, and everyone else at Penguin who has worked so hard to share my books with readers.

Also, a special thanks to the legendary and very kind children's book author and illustrator Thacher Hurd (who happens to be the son of Clement Hurd, the illustrator of *Goodnight Moon*) for chatting with me on the phone and telling me a sweet story about his time as a toddler at Margaret Wise Brown's house in Maine that I will never forget.

To my family, who constantly encourages and inspires me— Terry and Karen Mitchell, Jessica Campbell, Josh Mitchell, Josiah Mitchell—thank you. A special note to you, Jessica, my dear sister: This book is for you because you have taught me more about life, friendship, and wisdom than any other friend. (And thanks for never running off with one of my boyfriends!) And to you, Katherine Estacio Mitchell, my beautiful sister-in-law: Read between the lines, and you will find yourself in this novel—your strength, resilience, and courage.

I suppose this book wouldn't be here without me being a mom first. And so I thank my three boys, Carson, Russell, and Colby, who begged me to read the "moon book" over and over again when they were tiny (and even now). It was in those moments that this novel began to grow.

And Jason, thanks for handling all those muddy T-ball practices solo while I wrote this book in my cozy office. xo

If you loved *Goodnight June* and are looking for more from *New York Times* bestselling author Sarah Jio, please enjoy the first chapter of Sarah's first novel, *The Violets of March*, which was a *Library Journal* Best Book of 2011.

Chapter 1

"I guess this is it," Joel said, leaning into the doorway of our apartment. His eyes darted as if he was trying to memorize every detail of the turn-of-the-century New York two-story, the one we'd bought together five years ago and renovated—in happier times. It was a sight: the entryway with its delicate arch, the old mantel we'd found at an antique store in Connecticut and carted home like treasure, and the richness of the dining room walls. We'd agonized about the paint color but finally settled on Morocco Red, a shade that was both wistful and jarring, a little like our marriage. Once it was on the walls, he thought it was too orange. I thought it was just right.

Our eyes met for a second, but I quickly looked down at the dispenser in my hands and robotically pried off the last piece of packing tape, hastily plastering it on the final box of Joel's belongings that he'd come over that morning to retrieve. "Wait," I said, recalling a fleck of a blue leather-bound hardback I'd seen in the now-sealed box. I looked up at him accusatorily. "Did you take my copy of *Years of Grace*?"

I had read the novel on our honeymoon in Tahiti six years

prior, though it wasn't the memory of our trip I wanted to eulogize with its tattered pages. Looking back, I'll never know how the 1931 Pulitzer Prize winner by the late Margaret Ayer Barnes ended up in a dusty stack of complimentary books in the resort's lobby, but as I pulled it out of the bin and cracked open its brittle spine, I felt my heart contract with a deep familiarity that I could not explain. The moving story told in its pages, of love and loss and acceptance, of secret passions and the weight of private thoughts, forever changed the way I viewed my own writing. It may have even been the reason why I *stopped* writing. Joel had never read the book, and I was glad of it. It was too intimate to share. It read to me like the pages of my unwritten diary.

Joel watched as I peeled the tape back and opened the box, digging around until I found the old novel. When I did I let out a sigh of emotional exhaustion.

"Sorry," he said awkwardly. "I didn't realize you—"

He didn't realize a lot of things about me. I grasped the book tightly, then nodded and retaped the box. "I guess that's everything," I said, standing up.

He glanced cautiously toward me, and I returned his gaze this time. For another few hours, at least until I signed the divorce papers later that afternoon, he would still be my husband. Yet it was difficult to look into those dark brown eyes knowing that the man I had married was leaving me, for someone else. *How did we get here?*

The scene of our demise played out in my mind like a tragic movie, the way it had a million times since we'd been separated. It opened on a rainy Monday morning in November. I was making scrambled eggs smothered in Tabasco, his favorite, when he told me about Stephanie. The way she made him laugh. The way she understood him. The way they *connected.* I pictured the image of two Lego pieces fusing together, and I shuddered. It's funny; when I think back to that morning, I can actually smell burned eggs and Tabasco. Had I known that this is what the end of my marriage would smell like, I would have made pancakes.

I looked once again into Joel's face. His eyes were sad and unsure. I knew that if I rose to my feet and threw myself into his arms, he might embrace me with the love of an apologetic husband who wouldn't leave, wouldn't end our marriage. But, no, I told myself. The damage had been done. Our fate had been decided. "Good-bye, Joel," I said. My heart may have wanted to linger, but my brain knew better. He needed to go.

Joel looked wounded. "Emily, I—"

Was he looking for forgiveness? A second chance? I didn't know. I extended my hand as if to stop him from going on. "Good-bye," I said, mustering all my strength.

He nodded solemnly, then turned to the door. I closed my eyes and listened as he shut it quietly behind him. He locked it from the outside, a gesture that made my heart seize. *He still cares.* . . . About my safety, at least. I shook my head and reminded myself to get the locks changed, then listened as his footsteps became quieter, until they were completely swallowed up by the street noise.

My phone rang sometime later, and when I stood up to get it, I realized that I'd been sitting on the floor engrossed in *Years of Grace* ever since Joel left. Had a minute passed? An hour?

"Are you coming?" It was Annabelle, my best friend. "You promised me you wouldn't sign your divorce papers alone."

Disoriented, I looked at the clock. "Sorry, Annie," I said, fumbling for my keys and the dreaded manila envelope in my bag. I was supposed to meet her at the restaurant forty-five minutes ago. "I'm on my way."

"Good," she said. "I'll order you a drink."

The Calumet, our favorite lunch spot, was four blocks from my apartment, and when I arrived ten minutes later, Annabelle greeted me with a hug.

"Are you hungry?" she asked after we sat down.

I sighed. "No."

Annabelle frowned. "Carbs," she said, passing me the bread basket. "You need carbs. Now, where are those papers? Let's get this over with."

I pulled the envelope out of my bag and set it on the table, staring at it with the sort of caution one might reserve for dynamite.

"You realize this is all your fault," Annabelle said, half-smiling.

I gave her a dirty look. "What do you mean, my fault?"

"You don't *marry* men named Joel," she continued with that *tsk-tsk* sound in her voice. "Nobody marries Joels. You date Joels, you let them buy you drinks and pretty little things from Tiffany, but you don't marry them."

Annabelle was working on her PhD in social anthropology. In her two years of research, she had analyzed marriage and divorce data in an unconventional way. According to her findings, a marriage's success rate can be accurately predicted by the man's name.

Marry an Eli and you're likely to enjoy wedded bliss for about 12.3 years. Brad? 6.4. Steves peter out after just four. And as far as Annabelle is concerned, don't ever—*ever*—marry a Preston.

"So what does the data say about Joel again?"

"Seven point two years," she said in a matter-of-fact tone.

I nodded. We had been married for six years and two weeks.

"You need to find yourself a Trent," she continued.

I made a displeased face. "I hate the name Trent."

"OK, then an Edward or a Bill, or—no, a Bruce," she said. "These are names with marital longevity."

"Right," I said sarcastically. "Maybe you should take me husband-shopping at a retirement home."

Annabelle is tall and thin and beautiful—Julia Roberts beautiful, with her long, wavy dark hair, porcelain skin, and intense dark eyes. At thirty-three she had never been married. The reason, she'd tell you, was jazz. She couldn't find a man who liked Miles Davis and Herbie Hancock as much as she did.

She waved for the waiter. "We'll take two more, please." He whisked away my martini glass, leaving a water ring on the envelope.

"It's time," she said softly.

My hand trembled a little as I reached into the envelope and pulled out a stack of papers about a half-inch thick. My lawyer's assistant had flagged three pages with hot pink "sign here" sticky notes.

I reached into my bag for a pen and felt a lump in my throat as I signed my name on the first page, and then the next, and then the next. Emily Wilson, with an elongated *y* and a pronounced *n*. It was the exact way I'd signed my name since the fifth grade. Then I scrawled out the date, February 28, 2005, the day our marriage was laid to rest.

"Good girl," Annabelle said, inching a fresh martini closer to me. "So are you going to write about Joel?" Because I am a writer, Annabelle, like everyone else I knew, believed that writing about my relationship with Joel as a thinly veiled novel would be the best revenge.

"You could build a whole story around him, except change his name slightly," she continued. "Maybe call him Joe, and make him look like a total jerk." She took a bite and nearly choked on her food, laughing, before saying, "No, a jerk with *erectile dysfunction*."

The only problem is that even if I had wanted to write a revenge novel about Joel, which I didn't, it would have been a terrible book. Anything I got down on paper, if I could get anything down on paper, would have lacked imagination. I know this because I had woken up every day for the past eight years, sat at my desk, and stared at a blank screen. Sometimes I'd crank out a great line, or a few solid pages, but then I'd get stuck. And once I was frozen, there was no melting the ice.

My therapist, Bonnie, called it clinical (as in terminal) writer's block. My muse had taken ill, and her prognosis didn't look good.

Eight years ago I wrote a bestselling novel. Eight years ago I was on top of the world. I was skinny—not that I'm fat now (well, OK, so the thighs, yes, maybe a little)—and on the *New York Times* best-seller list. And if there were such a thing as the *New York Times* best life list, I would have been on that, too.

After my book, *Calling Ali Larson*, was published, my agent encouraged me to write a follow-up. Readers wanted a sequel, she told me. And my publisher had already offered to double my advance for a second book. But as hard as I tried, I had nothing more to write, nothing more to say. And eventually, my agent stopped calling. Publishers stopped wondering. Readers stopped caring. The only evidence that my former life wasn't just a figment was the royalty checks that came in the mail every so often and an occasional letter I received from a somewhat deranged reader by the name of Lester McCain, who believed he was in love with Ali, my book's main character.

I still remember the rush I felt when Joel walked up to me at my book release party at the Madison Park Hotel. He was at some cocktail party in an adjoining room when he saw me standing in the doorway. I was wearing a Betsey Johnson dress, which in 1997 was *the ultimate*: a black strapless number that I'd spent an embarrassing amount of money on. But, oh yes, it was worth *every penny*. It was still in my closet, but I suddenly had the urge to go home and burn it.

"You look stunning," he had said, rather boldly, before even introducing himself. I remember how I felt when I heard him utter those words. It could have been his trademark pickup line, and let's be real, it probably was. But it made me feel like a million bucks. It was so Joel.

A few months prior to that, *GQ* had done a big spread on the most eligible "regular-guy" bachelors in America—no, not the list that every two years always features George Clooney; the one that listed a surfer in San Diego, a dentist in Pennsylvania, a teacher in Detroit, and, yes, an attorney in New York, Joel. He had made the Top 10. And somehow, *I* had snagged him.

And lost him.

Annabelle was waving her hands in front of me. "Earth to Emily," she said.

"Sorry," I replied, shuddering a little. "No, I won't be writing about Joel." I shook my head and tucked the papers back into the envelope, then put it in my bag. "If I write anything again, it will be different than any story I've ever tried to write."

Annabelle shot me a confused look. "What about the follow-up to your last book? Aren't you going to finish that?"

"Not anymore," I said, folding a paper napkin in half and then in half again.

"Why not?"

I sighed. "I can't do it anymore. I can't force myself to churn out 85,000 mediocre words, even if it means a book deal. Even if it means thousands of readers with my book in their hands on beach vacations. No, if I ever write anything again—if I ever write again—it will be different."

Annabelle looked as if she wanted to stand up and applaud. "Look at you," she said, smiling. "You're having a breakthrough."

"No I'm not," I said stubbornly.

"Sure you are," she countered. "Let's analyze this some more." She clasped her hands together. "You said you want to write something *different*, but what I think you mean is that your heart wasn't in your last book."

"You could say that, yes," I said, shrugging.

Annabelle retrieved an olive from her martini glass and popped it into her mouth. "Why don't you write about something you actually *care* about?" she said a moment later. "Like a place, or a person that inspired you."

I nodded. "Isn't that what every writer tries to do?"

"Yeah," she said, shooing away the waiter with a "we're fine, and no we would not like the bill yet" look, then turning back to me with intense eyes. "But have you actually *tried* it? I mean, your book was fantastic—it really was, Em—but was there anything in it that was, well, *you*?"

She was right. It was a fine story. It was a bestseller, for crying out loud. So why couldn't I feel proud of it? Why didn't I feel *connected* to it?

"I've known you a long time," she continued, "and I know that it wasn't a story that grew out of your life, your experiences."

It wasn't. But what in my life could I draw from? I thought about my parents and grandparents, and then shook my head. "That's the problem," I said. "Other writers have plenty to mine from—bad mothers, abuse, adventurous childhoods. My life has been so vanilla. No deaths. No trauma. Not even a dead pet. Mom's cat, Oscar, is twenty-two years old. There's nothing there that warrants storytelling, believe me; I've thought about it."

"I don't think you're giving yourself enough credit," she said. "There must be something. Some spark."

This time I permitted my mind to wander, and when it did, I immediately thought of my great-aunt Bee, my mother's aunt, and her home on Bainbridge Island, in Washington State. I missed her as much as I missed the island. How had I let so many years pass since my last visit? Bee, who was eighty-five going on twenty-nine, had never had children, so my sister and I, by default, became her surrogate grandchildren. She sent us birthday cards with crisp fifty-dollar bills inside, Christmas gifts that were actually cool, and Valentine's Day candy, and when we'd visit in the summers from our home in Portland, Oregon, she'd sneak chocolate under our pillows before our mother could scream, "No, they just brushed their teeth!"

Bee was unconventional, indeed. But there was also something a little *off* about her. The way she talked too much. Or talked too little. The way she was simultaneously welcoming and petulant, giving and selfish. And then there were her secrets. I loved her for having them.

My mother always said that when people live alone for the better part of their lives they become immune to their own quirks. I wasn't sure if I bought into the theory or not, partly because I was worried about a lifetime of spinsterhood myself. I contented myself with watching for signs.

Bee. I could picture her immediately at her Bainbridge Island kitchen table. For every day I have known her, she has eaten the same breakfast: sourdough toast with butter and whipped honey. She slices the golden brown toasted bread into four small squares and places them on a paper towel she has folded in half. A generous smear of softened butter goes on each piece, as thick as frosting on a cupcake, and each is then topped by a good-size dollop of whipped honey. As a child, I watched her do this hundreds of times, and now, when I'm sick, sourdough toast with butter and honey is like medicine.

Bee isn't a beautiful woman. She towers above most men, with a face that is somehow too wide, shoulders too large, teeth too big. Yet the black-and-white photos of her youth reveal a spark of something, a certain prettiness that all women have in their twenties.

I used to love a particular photo of her at just that age, which hung in a seashell-covered frame high on the wall in the hallway of my childhood home, hardly in a place of honor, as one had to stand on a step stool to see it clearly. The old, scalloped-edge photo depicted a Bee I'd never known. Seated with a group of friends on a beach blanket, she appeared carefree and was smiling seductively. Another woman leaned in close to her, whispering in her ear. *A secret.* Bee clutched a string of pearls dangling from her neck and gazed at the camera in a way I'd never witnessed her look at Uncle Bill. I wondered who stood behind the lens that day so many years ago.

"What did she say?" I asked my mother one day as a child, peering up at the photograph.

Mom didn't look up from the laundry she was wrestling with in the hallway. "What did *who* say?"

I pointed to the woman next to Bee. "The pretty lady whispering in Aunt Bee's ear."

Mom immediately stood up and walked to my side. She reached up and wiped away the dust on the glass frame with the edge of her sweater. "We'll never know," she said, her regret palpable as she regarded the photo.

My mother's late uncle, Bill, was a handsome World War II hero. Everybody said he had married Bee for her money, but it's a theory that didn't hold weight with me. I had seen the way he kissed her, the way he wrapped his arms around her waist during those summers of my childhood. He had loved her; there was no doubt of that.

Even so, I knew by the way my mother talked that she disapproved of their relationship, that she believed Bill could have done better for himself. Bee, in her mind, was too unconventional, too unladylike, too brash, too *everything*.

Yet we kept coming to visit Bee, summer after summer. Even after Uncle Bill died when I was nine. The place was kind of ethereal, with the seagulls flying overhead, the sprawling gardens, the smell of Puget Sound, the big kitchen with its windows facing out onto the gray water, the haunting hum of the waves crashing on the shore. My sister and I loved it, and despite my mother's feelings about Bee, I know she loved the place too. It had a tranquilizing effect on all of us.

Annabelle gave me a knowing look. "You *do* have a story in there, don't you?"

I sighed. "Maybe," I said noncommittally.

"Why don't you take a trip?" she suggested. "You need to get away, to clear your head for a while."

I scrunched up my nose at the idea. "Where would I go?"

"Somewhere far away from here."

She was right. The Big Apple is a fair-weather friend. The city loves you when you're flying high and kicks you when you're down.

"Will you come with me?" I imagined the two of us on a tropical beach, with umbrella cocktails.

She shook her head. "No."

"Why not?" I felt like a puppy—a scared, lost puppy who just wanted someone to put her collar on and show her where to go, what to do, how to be.

"I can't go with you because you need to do this on your own." Her words jarred me. She looked me straight in the eye, as if I needed to absorb every drop of what she was about to say. "Em, your marriage has ended and, well, it's just that you haven't shed a single tear."

On the walk back to my apartment I thought about what Annabelle had said, and my thoughts, once again, turned to my aunt Bee. *How have I let so many years pass without visiting her?*

I heard a shrill, shrieking sound above my head, the unmistakable sound of metal on metal, and looked up. A copper duck weather vane, weathered to a rich gray-green patina, stood at attention on the roof of a nearby café. It twirled noisily in the wind.

My heart pounded as I took in the familiar sight. Where had I seen it before? Then it hit me. *The painting. Bee's painting.* Until that moment, I had forgotten about the five-by-seven canvas she'd given me when I was a child. She used to paint, and I remember the great sense of honor I felt when she chose me to be the caretaker of the artwork. I had called it a masterpiece, and my words made her smile.

I closed my eyes and could see the oil-painted seascape perfectly: the duck weather vane perched atop that old beach cottage, and the couple, hand in hand, on the shore.

I felt overcome with guilt. Where was the painting? I'd packed it away after Joel and I moved into the apartment—he didn't think it matched our decor. Just like I'd distanced myself from the island I'd loved as a child, I had packed away the relics of my past in boxes. *Why? For what?*

I picked up my pace until it turned into a full-fledged jog. I thought of *Years of Grace. Did the painting accidentally end up in a box of Joel's things too? Or worse, did I mistakenly pack it in a box of books and clothes for the Goodwill pickup?* I reached the door to the apartment and jammed my key into the lock, then sprinted up the stairs to the bedroom and flung open the closet door. There, on the top shelf, were two boxes. I pulled one down and rummaged through its contents: a few stuffed animals from childhood, a box of old Polaroids, and several notebooks' worth of clippings from my two-year stint writing for the college newspaper. Still, no painting.

I reached for the second box, and looked inside to find a Raggedy Ann doll, a box of notes from junior high crushes, and my beloved Strawberry Shortcake diary from elementary school. That was it.

How could I have lost it? How could I have been so careless? I stood up, giving the closet a final once-over. A plastic bag shoved far into the back corner suddenly caught my eye. My heart raced with anticipation as I pulled it out into the light.

Inside the bag, wrapped in a turquoise and pink beach towel, was the painting. Something deep inside me ached as I clutched it in my hands. The weather vane. The beach. The old cottage. They were all as I remembered them. But not the couple. No, something was different. I had always imagined the subjects to be Bee and Uncle Bill. The woman was most certainly Bee, with her long legs and trademark baby blue capri pants. Her "summer pants," she'd called them. But the man wasn't Uncle Bill. No. How could I have missed this? Bill had light hair, sandy blond. But this man had thick, wavy dark hair. *Who was he? And why did Bee paint herself with him?*

I left the mess on the floor and walked, with the painting, downstairs to my address book. I punched the familiar numbers into the phone and took a long, deep breath, listening to the chime of the first ring and then the second.

"Hello?" Her voice was the same—deep and strong, with soft edges.

"Bee, it's me, Emily," I said, my voice cracking a little. "I'm sorry it's been so long. It's just that I—"

"Nonsense, dear," she said. "No apologies necessary. Did you get my postcard?"

"Your postcard?"

"Yes, I sent it last week after I heard your news."

"You heard?" I hadn't told very many people about Joel. Not my parents in Portland—not yet, anyway. Not my sister in Los Angeles, with her perfect children, doting husband, and organic vegetable garden. Not even my therapist. Even so, I wasn't surprised that the news had made its way to Bainbridge Island.

"Yes," she said. "And I wondered if you'd come for a visit." She paused. "This island is a marvelous place to heal."

I ran my finger along the edge of the painting. I wanted to be there just then—on Bainbridge Island, in Bee's big, warm kitchen.

"When are you coming?" Bee never wastes words.

"Is tomorrow too soon?"

"Tomorrow," she said, "is the first of March, the month the sound is at its best, dear. It's absolutely *alive*."

I knew what she meant when she said it. The churning gray water. The kelp and the seaweed and barnacles. I could almost taste the salty air. Bee believed that Puget Sound was the great healer. And I knew that when I arrived, she would encourage me to take my shoes off and go wading, even if it was one o'clock in the morning— even if it was forty-three degrees, which it probably would be.

"And, Emily?"

"Yes?"

"There's something important that we need to talk about."

"What is it?"

"Not now. Not over the phone. When you get here, dear."

After I hung up, I walked downstairs to the mailbox to find a credit card bill, a Victoria's Secret catalog—addressed to Joel—and a large square envelope. I recognized the return address, and it only took me a moment to remember where I'd seen it: on the divorce papers. There was also the fact that I'd Googled it the week before. It was Joel's new town house on Fifty-seventh—the one he was sharing with Stephanie.

The adrenaline started pumping when I considered the fact that Joel could have been reaching out to me. Maybe he was sending me a letter, a card—no, a romantic beginning to a scavenger hunt: an invitation to meet him somewhere in the city, where there'd be another clue, and then after four more, there he'd be, standing in front of the hotel where we met so many years ago. And he'd be holding a rose—no, a sign, and it would read, I'M SORRY. I LOVE YOU. FORGIVE ME. Exactly like that. It could be the perfect ending to a tragic romance. *Give us a happy ending, Joel,* I found myself whispering as I ran my finger along the envelope. *He still loves me. He still feels something.*

But when I lifted the edge of the envelope and carefully pulled out the gold-tinged card inside, the fantasy came to a crashing halt. All I could do was stare.

The thick card stock. The fancy calligraphy. It was a wedding invitation. *His* wedding invitation. Six p.m. Dinner. Dancing. A celebration of love. Beef or chicken. Accepts with pleasure. Declines with regret. I walked to the kitchen, calmly bypassing the recycle bin, and instead set the little stack of gold stationery right into the kitchen trash, on top of a take-out box of moldy chicken chow mein.

Fumbling with the rest of the mail, I dropped a magazine, and when I reached down to pick it up, I saw the postcard from Bee, which had been hiding in the pages of *The New Yorker*. The front featured a ferry boat, white with green trim, coming into Eagle Harbor. I flipped it over and read:

> *Emily,*
>
> The island has a way of calling one back when it's time. Come home. I have missed you, dear.
>
> All my love,
> Bee

I pressed the postcard to my chest and exhaled deeply.

From Sarah Jio

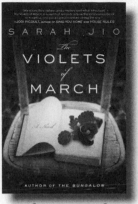

978-0-452-29703-6

978-0-452-29767-8

978-0-452-29838-5   978-0-452-29839-2   978-0-14-219699-1

"Sarah Jio's writing is exquisite and engrossing." —Elin Hilderbrand
www.sarahjio.com